Canon Solutions America
FutureAuthorsProject
A partnership with the School District of Palm Beach County

2014
From Rough Drafts
to Masterpieces

A compilation of works by Palm Beach County
middle and high school students

Canon

CANON SOLUTIONS AMERICA

Dear Canon Solutions America Future Authors Students, Parents, Teachers and Supporters::

Congratulations on being a part of the 9th year of this partnership between the School District of Palm Beach County and Canon Solutions America. Since 2006, we've had the pleasure of seeing hundreds of middle- and high-school students improve their writing skills and achieve their dreams of becoming published authors.

Each year we are even more inspired by the energy and creativity of these aspiring young writers. Watching them become published authors and light up when they see their book for the first time becomes more of a thrill at each book signing. These expressions of delight serve to confirm that we have achieved the goal we set out to accomplish – cultivating a passion for writing and reading among the next generation of writers.

Exciting new opportunities for these students and other aspiring authors are available today thanks to a new age of digital book printing and publishing. The result is a win-win for authors and book lovers alike – bringing a rich diversity of books to market for all of us to enjoy. All of us at the Canon Solutions America (CSA) offices in Boca Raton, Florida are proud to lead the way in providing a Who's Who of digital book manufacturers with innovative digital printing solutions that empower authors with new avenues for showcasing their emerging talents.

The CSA Future Authors Project is made possible by a public-private partnership supported by a team of dedicated people, in particular, the teachers and support staff of the School District of Palm Beach County. We salute the teachers, Nicole Amado, Cartheda T. Mann, and Katrina Sapp Holder for their unwavering dedication to students and for coaching them through the writing process. At the District, Director of Secondary Education Diane Fedderman, worked tirelessly to ensure every detail of the program was in place. In addition, professional authors took time out of their busy schedules to spend a few hours with the students to share tips and experiences. And, of course, the program would not be possible without the support of our generous sponsors.

As a Boca Raton corporate citizen for more than 20 years and a leader in providing digital printing solutions for the book industry, we are delighted to support this program and help transform each student's dream into a reality. We look forward to continuing our support of the Future Authors Project to help ignite a world of writing possibilities for future generations of Palm Beach County students.

writing possibilities for future generations of Palm Beach County students.

Sincerely,

Eric H

Eric Hawkinson
Director of Marketing
Production Print Solutions, a division of Canon Solutions America
Canon Solutions America
Boca Raton, Florida

Dear Fans of From Rough Drafts to Masterpieces:

Ernest Hemingway said, "We [writers] are all apprentices in a craft where no one ever becomes a master." Honing their craft is exactly what fifty-three students from various Palm Beach County schools accomplished during an eight-day workshop. They enjoyed the opportunity to improve their writing skills, be inspired by professional authors, and ultimately, become published writers themselves. *From Rough Drafts to Masterpieces* is a result of the Canon Solutions America Future Authors Project, which is collaboration between the School District of Palm Beach County and Canon Solutions America.

Together, we've shown what can be done when the public and private sectors work synergistically to bring unique educational opportunities to our students. It is critical for students to observe the collaborative efforts of the adults around them as their world of work in the future will depend on positive team work and partnerships. This program serves as an exemplar in partnering with the School District to enhance opportunities for our young authors.

The Canon Solutions America Future Authors Project stands as a role model for other companies willing to join hands with the District to bring new growth experiences to students. We at the District salute the executives at Canon Solutions America and all of the sponsors that have come forward to make this program so successful for the past nine years.

We know that we will continue to help our students hone their writing skills, grow their love of writing and, perhaps someday, become professional authors. Thank you for the role you play in making the Canon Solutions America Future Authors Project successful.

Karen Whetsell
Assistant Superintendent
Division of Teaching and Learning

Table of Contents

Marisol Almanza 2
Split *4*

Eeshani Behara 6
The Winning Ticket *8*

Rebecca Bullock 12
The Lost People *14*

Modeline Celestin 21
Bronze Heirloom *22*
The Girl Who Hid In The Dark *24*
Good Girl, Bad Habits *25*

Aliese Dashiell 27
Mired in Muck *28*

Jada Diogostine 29
A Story of My City & Life *31*
A Friend Is Someone *34*
I Am Who I Am *35*

Ja'Mya Felton 37
Mystery Bag *38*
The Feel of Music *40*
Adoring Mother *41*

Lindsay (Molly) Fulop 42
In Agony *44*
Writer's Block *44*
Blades *45*

Rachel Glismann 46

The Delving *47*

Sarah Gomez 48

Offing *50*

Mother *55*

Laura Gust 57

Unbroken Beauty *59*

Aalisha Jaisinghani 60

Caged *61*

Fruit of Tantalus *61*

Possible Strikes *62*

Apeksha Labroo 64

Found Words *65*

The Ticket Stub *68*

Enemy Lines *71*

Natasha Leonard 72

The Well *73*

Anthony Li 81

I Can't Bear This Anymore *82*

Logan Lockhart 86

The Truth *87*

Destiny Lumpkin 90

Idols and Legends *92*

You Don't Know Me *93*

The struggle...I Remember The Time *94*

Samantha Marshall 96

Bite The Bullet *98*

Distraction *104*

Isabella Martins-Simonsen 106

Music *107*

Gary Merisme 108

Insidious Influences *109*

Elysia Ngo 110

The Fangirl *112*

Real Gold *113*

Je'Cynthia Nonor 118

Nothing Was Ever the Same *119*

Remember Me *120*

Emily Pacenti 121

Musician *123*

A Cemetery Conundrum *124*

Callista Payne 131

In the Library *133*

No Strings Attached *138*

Triton Payne 139

Worth It *140*

Jake Perl 143

Please *145*

Two Men Walk Out of a Bar *149*

Al'Licia Pittman 152

A Kiss to Remember *154*

Colors To A Blind Soul *157*

When I Prayed *158*

Julian Pollifrone 159

The Fight *161*

The Enigma *165*

Juan Puerto 166

Grass-chins and Pebble-faces *168*

Garage Sale *169*

Tin Can *171*

Lillian Riso 175

Nothing Special *177*

Soldier *185*

Carlos Rivera 186

The Bottom of the Ninth *188*

Jac'Quanda Robinson 192

The Person Behind the Person *194*

Culture *195*

Diary of Naj Patel *196*

Francisca Rodriguez 197

Our Protectors *199*

The New Girl and Her New Best Friend *200*

Brittany Segura 202

24 hours *203*

Hanging Fire *204*

The Ward *206*

Rose Sintulaire 208
Bring Back Our Girls Alive *210*
Doorboxed *211*
The Wrong Way *212*

Kiara Smith 214
Excerpt from "Clash" *216*
The Artist *224*

Moyra Stewart 225
The Mountain *227*
Rotten Love *229*

Monica Tam 230
Dropping Like Flies *231*
The Sole Ascension *232*

Lauren Villanueva 236
Night of the Beast *237*
Reget *239*
Welcome Home, Spencer *240*

Noelle Wamsley 247
A Dark World *249*

About the Teachers   **259**

About the Authors   **263**

Steve Alten *264*

Zelda Benjamin *265*

Dwight Seon Stewart *266*

Jennifer Tormo *267*

About the Program   **269**

Canon Solutions America
FutureAuthorsProject

A partnership with the School District of Palm Beach County

2014
From Rough Drafts
to Masterpieces

Marisol Almanza

My name is Marisol Almanza and I was born on April 28th, 2000. For the last three years, I've been a student at Don Estridge High Tech Middle School and will now be a freshman at John I. Leonard in the fall. Since the age of 5, I've loved writing. Writing is like an outlet for me that benefits me in so many ways. Transmitting my thoughts and emotions through words has helped me more than any therapist could. The passion I feel for writing is the same passion I feel for music and films. I aspire to become a great author and to have my name known internationally. Stephen King has definitely influenced my writing since he knows so much about the craft. He has written the majority of my favorite books, like Carrie and The Shining.

The Red Hot Chili Peppers have also been a big part of my life. They do more than just change words into music. They make poetry and add a great beat to it. Although I mainly stick to doing short stories, I'd like to push myself into songwriting. If John Frusciante could become the great musician that he is while he was hooked on heroin, I can do the same without damaging myself.

I'd like to thank my editors, Mrs Adamo and Poettis as well as my other mentors. You know who you are. I'd also like to thank my family for helping me become the writer that I am and my work is dedicated to you.

Reflection

Week One

I spent the first week of the program deciding what piece I wanted to work on and juggling with ideas. I do regret not using my time wisely and now I realize that I need to work on my time management to become a better writer.

Week Two

The second week was more stressful than I thought it would be. The deadline came sooner than I expected, but I was able to complete a piece in time. I really enjoyed the past two weeks and I hope to do this again in the future.

Split

The black ball point pen sits on the splintered wooden table, waiting to end a holy union with its slick ink. The room is quiet with a single man's sob breaking the silence. He hesitantly grabs the pen and glances over at the picture frame sitting on the countertop. He thinks of the day it was taken, his wedding day, and how beautiful his soon-to-be ex-wife looked. He tears his eyes away from it and focuses on the divorce papers before him.

His nose is red as he wipes it. Dead skin clings onto the sides of his nose, flaking off with every rub. His nostrils flare as he sucks up the mucus seeping down the valley above his lip with a sharp inhalation. A dull light hangs above the man, shining down upon his face. His prominent cheek bones catch the light and cast a shadow beneath them, covering his pale cheeks in a shadow. The sides of his face look like dark and empty voids. His chapped lips are slightly parted, only letting light streams of air escape his body. Saliva slowly dribbles out of the thin crack between the sides of his mouth, lubricating his dehydrated lips.

His fingers are bent to accommodate the pen, his ring finger eclipsed by a golden band that had only recently been removed. Sweat accumulates between his fingers and the pen, the moisture causing the pen to swiftly slip out of his grasp. After a quick flinch, his trembling hand reaches out to retrieve it and envelops his fingers around the pen as he did before. His forearm sits at the edge of the table, balancing on it like a seesaw. It is coated in a thick layer of hair, all standing on end. His shoulders are sloped downwards, failing to conceal his feeling of defeat. A slight cramp caused by the man's poor posture pinches his shoulder and he brings his hand up to soothe the cramp. His neck is bent down, hanging his head above the divorce papers. A chill runs down his spine and goosebumps invade his neck as the cold shiver crawls deeper into his skin.

He shakes his leg under the table, his foot rapidly tapping on the floor. His weak calf showing the years of neglect he put his body through as ripples run through it with every tap. His cracked heel hovers above the ground while the ball of his foot kisses the floor with every tap. The movement of his foot travels through his unfit body and is expelled onto the chair, causing the wooden legs to squeak loudly with age. An impulsive itch tickles the nerve endings in the webbing of his toes. He wriggles his toes together, but fails to satisfy his body's urge to suppress the itch, just as he failed to satisfy his wife.

He slowly places the tip of the pen against the paper and sleekly signs his name above the line. His chest rises, and then deflates. He looks down upon his signature and watches as the ink permeates into the paper. He sets the pen down on the splintered wood and remains slouched in his chair. The room is quiet now, except for a single man's sob.

Eeshani Behara

Normally, I don't write about myself. I can't sum up my life story in just a paragraph or two. Anyways, let's just start simple.

My name is Eeshani Behara and on June 7th, 2002, the world welcomed a beautiful baby girl. I am going into the 7th grade at Don Estridge High Tech Middle School. I decided to join this workshop because I wanted to improve my writing and editing skills. Also, I wanted to be able to accept constructive criticism better than I was before. I love writing because it's a great way to express my feelings. Some of my favorite things other than writing are singing, playing violin, musical theater, and playing tennis. I want to make a shout out to all my friends and mentors who made my 2 weeks here memorable. Also, I want to make another shout out to Ms. Adamo and Ms. Poettis for being great editors and helping me improve my writing. It was a wonderful 2 weeks here and I will never forget it.

Reflection

Week One:

This week was my first time at the workshop. It was a warm welcome. It wasn't as productive as I wanted it to be. I didn't even get my first piece done (it was under a major editing process). I felt that I understood the way the program works, letting us explore different genres and ideas to come down to our pieces. The mentors were super nice and helpful. We also went on a field trip to Canon offices where we see how they print out books. We also learned about a Dutch company called Océ partnered up with Canon. Overall, it was a wonderful kick start to the workshop.

Week Two:

This week was pretty hectic, but more productive. The editing process of my story came to a close and was finished. I thought I could rush in a second piece in time, but I missed the deadline. It was crazy trying to get all the work done in only 4 days! Even though I never finished my second piece, I think I wrote some of my best work here. I am extremely proud of myself of what I accomplished here. This was a truly wonderful summer that I will never forget.

The Winning Ticket

Let's see... fashion...entertainment... Brenda thought as she flipped through her magazine.

Aha! Horoscopes! "Gemini: This summer, you will receive new, lasting memories and mass riches-"

Mass riches?! No way! I wonder what it could be... Ugh! Mom's not here yet!

"MOM!" Brenda hollered "You have to take me to the mall! Lindsay's going to be there!"

"Okay honey," her mom replied in her tender voice. "Just a minute."

"You said that five minutes ago! Come on, I'm going to miss the sale!" Brenda whined.

"All right. Let's go!"

As Brenda's mom turned on the ignition, she noticed the small glowing yellow gas pump icon on the dashboard.

"We need to stop by the gas station," she said.

Brenda sighed and rolled her eyes. "Whatever."

When the car pulled into the vacant gas station, Brenda's mom noticed that the mini-mart was selling lottery tickets.

"I'm feeling lucky!" stated Brenda's mom. "Let's buy a lottery ticket. Give me your lucky numbers."

"Okay, be quick."

The small slip of paper with the pink and yellow slobs of color smearing it, with the tiny black print numbers reading: 3, 7, 9, 23, and 1. The car rumbled along the dusty pavement road when Brenda and her mom were leaving the gas station.

"Okay honey, have fun!" her mom told Brenda. "Just remember to stay with your friends, don't go home with strangers, text me often so I can check on you, don't-"

"Yeah, yeah, yeah. I got it. Don't embarrass me!"

"All right then, go have fun. I'm picking you up at 7. Please come out quickly. We're having meatloaf for dinner!"

Brenda and her friends strolled around the mall, and found their favorite store: Forever 21. They immediately ran in for a mini shopping spree. They were met by bright lights and piles of clothes surrounding them. Their favorite songs blaring through the loudspeakers.

"Come on, Brenda! There are some really cute tops over here!" Lindsay's voice carried across the store.

"Coming!" Brenda shouted. She wandered to the tops section and didn't see the puddle of water on the floor. She fell with a large thud. A loud squeal from her sneakers grabbed everyone's attention. Before she knew it, Brenda had a sharp pain piercing through her arm and everything seemed to fly by in a blur. As her eyes were closing, she heard a faint "Brenda!" from Lindsay in the distance.

At the hospital, Brenda opened her eyes, squinting at the bright lights.

"Oh Brenda! Honey, are you OK? " asked Brenda's mom.

"Yeah, I'm fine. What's going on?" Brenda wondered.

"Everything is fine. You just slipped on some water and fell. Your friends called the ambulance to take you to the hospital and the doctors notified us. The doctors think you broke your arm, but we're still waiting for the X-rays. Your dad and Tommy are here" Brenda's brother, sitting in a nearby chair, legs dangling above the ground, glanced up from his game on his mom's iPhone at Brenda as she sat up in her bed.

"Oh, she's awake" said Tommy, resuming his game again.

The family changed the channel from Tommy's cartoon show to the news on the hospital TV.

"And the numbers for the mega millions lottery contest are: 3… 7… 9… 23…" the reporter began.

"Mom, this sounds a lot like our ticket that you bought at the mini-mart." Brenda froze.   "… and 1!" the reporter announced the last number.

"Mom!" shouted Brenda, "those were our numbers. We won!" Brenda's mom began to carefully pull out the ticket from her pocket, but nothing was there.

"Honey? Do you remember where we left the ticket?" her mom's voice sounded hesitant.

"I thought you had it!" Brenda was getting worried. Her parents and Tommy tried checking their pockets, but found nothing. She frantically tried digging the hand of the uninjured arm into her pockets.

"What?! We can't lose our ticket! We have to keep looking!"

"Honey, calm down," said Brenda's mom "We'll keep looking around the room."

"B-but w-we have to f-find it!" Tommy stuttered and whined, his voice choking back his tears.

After a while the doctors came back with the X-ray results.

"Okay, these pictures are showing a broken arm. We're going to put her arm in a cast and in 6 weeks, she'll be good as new."

Oh man! I have no lottery ticket and a broken arm?

The doctors took Brenda to get her cast put on. Disheartened, the family made their way to the car. The car engine started with a rumble and they drove home.

"Hmm…" "Brenda's mom was trying to retrace her steps. "After I dropped Brenda off at the mall, I dropped the ticket in the cup holder, on my way home." She rummaged through the cup holders. "It's not here either!"

"You probably dropped it behind the seats instead," Brenda stated. "Pull over."

Brenda's dad slammed the seat down to check behind it. The golden light from the car flickered on, so the family could see beneath the car compartments. Food crumbs were scattered everywhere along with other pieces of junk.

"Oh, that's where my Star Wars action figure went!" Tommy shouted.

"I don't care about your old, broken crap, Tommy. Keep looking for the ticket." Brenda retorted.

"Brenda, be nice to your brother," Brenda's mom said.

"Ugh. Fine, whatever." Brenda kept digging through the tiny opening in between the seats and found something.

"Mom, I see something!" She stretched her uninjured arm down the gap. "I can't reach it." She tried to pull her arm out. "Help! My arm's stuck!"

"I'll help you, honey!" her mom used one arm to move the seat over and reached her other arm down as the little glowing light led the way. While Brenda was pulling her arm out, her mom finally grasped a small piece of paper.

"What's this?" she wondered. After she turned it over and looked at it again, she noticed something stunning. She smiled.

Brenda's mom shouted, "Guys! It's the ticket. The WINNING lottery ticket! It's been in the seat!"

Brenda was ecstatic. "You found it?"

"No, we found it, together. We won! We're rich!" her mom cheered.

Brenda's mom pulled Brenda in for a huge hug. It was that moment when Brenda realized that her mom wasn't so bad after all.

Rebecca Bullock

"We are what we repeatedly do. Excellence, therefore, is not an act, but a habit." –Aristotle

To me, writing is an escape into another universe. I'm not sure how my life would be without it. After all, I've been writing for as long as I can remember. I can usually find composition books or journals full of little stories in them, all the way back to elementary school. Anyway, I was born and raised in West Palm Beach, Florida. Currently, I attend A.W Dreyfoos School of the Arts for Communications. I switched from the vocal program when I transitioned from Bak Middle School of the Arts to Dreyfoos and haven't regretted it since. When I'm not writing, you can usually find me with a good book, or hanging out with my family.

Reflection

Week One:

Week one was surprising. I hadn't known what to expect. It didn't seem like it during the time, but the week went by so quickly. I met more people that liked writing and was given great critiquing, so overall I thought it was a great experience.

Week Two:

Week two was very busy. Our two editors were usually crowded by people, so most of the time we had to wait for a while. However, when I finally saw the finished product, I could see the difference between my unedited story and my edited one. I'd have to say this week was the better one of the two.

The Lost People

"Watch it, the floor is-"

The warning came too late, and Abigail felt something against her foot, and she tripped. Soon, the floor where her feet were a moment ago rose up to meet her and a large splash met her ears. The stream continued to flow and seep mud over the top of her clothes. She could feel the mud touch her back very cold and unwelcoming.

"…uneven."

Footsteps echoed across the chamber.

"I tried to warn you," Fiona kneeled down next to her, "are you just going to lie there?"

Shifting her head slightly to the side, Abigail just groaned and stuck her hand out in Fiona's direction.

"Just help me up,"

Fiona put the flashlight beneath her armpit and grabbed Abigail's hand. She dragged her up, careful enough to stay on the rock that parted the muddied stream.

As she climbed up, the mud began to slide down her back like a snake, and Abigail shuddered. Snakes were definitely not a possible future pet.

"You alright?" Abigail could hear her stifle a laugh.

"Well let's see, I've been digging around these ruins with you for hours and so far we haven't found anything. Plus, I'm covered in freaking mud."

A cold silence hung in the air between them, and eventually Abigail felt her annoyance subside into guilt.

"Look Fi, I didn't mean to snap. I'm just annoyed."

"Well, at least you got a free mud bath, Abby," Fiona joked, "Now your skin will glow so much, you can be like a third flashlight. We could use one."

Taking careful steps, Abigail felt a different surface beneath her feet. It wasn't as cold as the rock, but it creaked slightly from misuse. Sticking her hand out, she felt a rough material surrounding both sides of it.

After checking the structure, Abigail began her trek across the bridge. She could hear water flowing far beneath her. It wasn't a long walk, though Fiona's humming didn't help.

Both of their flashlights snaked across the walls to land on a strange structure in front of them. If they hadn't been paying attention, they may not have seen it. It was a circular structure covered in dust and dirt, half buried underneath the cave floor. The walls that had survived seemed to layer on top of each other, and windows adorned the sunken-in walls below these layers. Some of these windows held cracks; some were intact, though most were completely broken and littered the ground like a carpet. The top of the entire structure disappeared into darkness that even the girls flashlights couldn't pierce through. A sign was crumbling further towards them, limp as a ragdoll.

As their flashlights trailed over it, Fiona's flashlight stopped. The sign was caked with grime and cobwebs. Fiona brushed her hand across it, taking only miniscule bits of dust with it. However, it was enough to reveal a symbol beneath it that had almost faded into the sign itself.

"It looks kind of like an apple," Fiona said after a few moments.

"An apple? Are you sure?" Abigail moved closer and indeed, it did resemble an apple.

"I think so."

"Not gonna lie, that's really weird." Abigail said.

"I know. What a waste of fruit. Someone only took one bite out of it."

Abigail rolled her eyes at that and walked further toward the structure. Fiona followed her, and the two girls tried to find a way in.

"I think the door to get inside was buried or something. Let's go in through one of the windows," Fiona said.

They nodded in agreement. The two girls began to hit the window with their flashlights. At first, it held firm, but with their combined efforts they began to see small cracks. Those turned into bigger cracks, and eventually with one last shove, the window shattered into pieces.

Both of them climbed inside, careful to avoid the jagged edges of glass that protruded from the broken window.

The smell of dust welcomed them. There were holes in the walls around them that gave entrance to the dirt from the outside cave. Desks and chairs were scattered around, some standing straight and some not. The paint on the walls has been long gone, faded and torn with its pattern illegible. More glass littered the floor and the desks, making both of the girls thankful that they were wearing boots. It was all in a spell of silence.

"Let's explore. There's got to be something exciting here. It looks completely untouched." Fiona said, "I'll take this part of the room."

"Of course. I get the side that has all the desks." Abigail grumbled, but complied.

Abigail began to search all of the desks, thankful they were upright and not turned over. Many of the drawers were only filled with more dust, and what looked to be broken boxes on top of them. Upon further inspection however, they just seemed to sit there and after a few attempts, she moved on.

Towards the end of the path, Abigail felt her foot brush against something solid, and she leaned down to pick up the small device. She noticed the entire screen was covered in cracks. The device was small, but seemed to fit in her hand pretty well. It was mainly black with an occasional stripe of gray line of color here and there. Brushing off the rest of the stray glass on the front of it, Abigail saw a small button on it. Curious, she pushed it.

Nothing happened.

Disappointed, Abigail turned it over. She noticed it was basically the same as the front, except it also had a faded version of the apple-like figure again. After staring at it for a little while, she thought about setting it on the desk near her, but Fiona's voice caught her attention.

"Find anything?" Fiona called over, poking up from behind a pile of rubble.

"Just a bunch of boxes and little boxes, with glass everywhere."

Fiona walked over and her flashlight reflected off of the device and she froze. It was in Fiona's hand before Abigail could count to three.

"Have you ever seen this before, Fi?" Abigail said, a little annoyed that Fiona had snatched it away from her.

"Only in books." Fiona muttered, tracing her finger across the broken screen.

"You alright?" Abigail touched Fiona's shoulder, and Fiona looked up at her, her eyes filled with excitement.

"I remember researching that The Lost People had technology similar to this."

The two girls look from each other to the device, then back at each other.

"Do you think it's them?" Abigail felt her heart pounding in her chest. Time seemed to stand still as the two stood close together and only stared. Abigail gripped Fiona's hand tightly keeping them both standing straight.

"I wasn't sure." Fiona admitted in a whisper, "I didn't want to get my hopes up until you said something."

Fiona turned the device over in her hand and traced the apple symbol.

"This is it, Abby. I just know it. This device looks really old. Possibly over 500 years old. This has to be something that belonged to them,"

"Are you sure, Fi? Maybe it's something else."

"No I'm positive Abby. I know it's them. The Lost People were said to have lived 500 years ago, and this structure fits that description. These have to be our ancestors Abby,"

This is what they had been waiting, what they had been looking for.

"So Mr. Johnson was wrong," Abigail began, breaking the spell.

Immediately, Fiona's face broke out in a smile and she jumped up in excitement.

"We did it, Abby! We found them! I knew they were real I just knew it. I deserve an 'A' on that paper. I spent so much time researching for that paper. But nooooo, Mr. Johnson said they weren't real. He said there wasn't enough 'physical evidence to prove it'. Well how's this for evidence of The Lost People?"

"It seems to fit," Abigail said, "Let's keep that."

Fiona put the device in her backpack, making sure to brush the stray glass off beforehand.

"I saw some stairs when I was looking," Fiona angled her flashlight over to the other side of the room, "They look pretty solid. Let's see if we can climb higher."

Indeed, there were some stairs behind a doorway—which was missing its door. The steps shifted slightly as they stepped up on them, but the staircase held firm. As they walked up the stairs, they came to another doorway, but this time it had a door. It groaned it protest as the girls tried to open it. Rust rained down from the hinges until the girls shoved together. It swung open, and Abigail stumbled inside, losing her balance. She dropped her flashlight and fell onto something hard. She felt it crack underneath her hand.

"Abby?" A light angled towards her, and Fiona was staring at her.

"I'm okay. I just fell on something. Probably some rocks." Abigail opened her eyes to find her own flashlight, when she froze. She hadn't fallen on rocks.

She had fallen on bones.

Both girls went as pale as the bones on the ground. This shock wasn't like before. It wasn't excited or happy, but instead it was based on horror.

"F-Fi…" Abigail gripped her friend's arm for dear life, her knuckles turning white.

"It's okay Abby. They're just skeletons. Just like the ones from those Halloween decorations." Fiona grabbed Abigail's arm and pulled her up, trying to smile reassuringly. "Let's just keep going. There's something over there." She pointed her flashlight to one of the walls.

It was easier said than done. Many of the bones didn't form full skeletons, and lay in different corners. Some of the full skeletons peeked out from a few desks, and some were in their way. It took quite a lot of coaxing for Fiona to convince Abigail to step over them, but even then their progress was at a grueling slowness.

The girls shone their flashlights over the wall, and Fiona traced her finger across the writing.

"It's really hard to read," Fiona squints her eyes, "Someone also carved something in the wall."

"I hope we can hurry up. This room creeps me out," Abigail eyes the bones; as if afraid they'll get up and start walking.

"I think the carved part is a date. I can't make out the first part, but the last part says 14."

"Maybe it's a combination?" Abigail said.

"Maybe. The words are too faded. Give me a couple seconds."

Abigail obliged and began to wander around. There were more of those devices on the ground, some in worse condition than others. She hadn't gone far when Fiona called her back.

"I think I've got it."

Abigail walked back to her.

"Okay. So most of it is completely gone. But I can make out the general story. I think." Fiona said.

"What does it say?"

"I think they were afraid Abby."

Abigail stared at her then looked around at the building walls.

"Why? You said The Lost People were said to have some of the greatest technological advances of their times."

"Yeah they did."

Fiona climbed over a desk and followed the story, speaking it to Abigail who only stood and watched.

"Here they say things were going really well. They continued to develop. They got even further then they had imagined."

"I still don't understand what went wrong."

"I'm getting there. I believe they started to drift apart." Fiona said, "The more they developed, the less they made face-to-face contact with each other."

Abigail looked between the wall and the skeletons.

"People never seemed to have time for each other. They grew and grew until finally, nobody was there to help each other out. People grew secluded from each other." Fiona pointed to the furthest part of the wall.

"So they locked themselves away. Ultimately, they closed out all the outsiders. They didn't want everybody to be like them. So they tried to fix their problem."

Her voice stopped and it was silent. The air seemed to grow thicker with this revelation, and they suddenly felt like unwelcome visitors in a tomb.

"That's really sad," Abigail said, breaking the silence. Her voice reflected the sorrow that both of the girls felt.

"Maybe we should go. We've already discovered a lot." Fiona said, gesturing toward the door.

"It's probably really late." Abigail agreed.

Abigail walked forward to grip her hand again, and the two began to walk back. Retracting their steps, they walked past the bones of The Lost People, down the stairs, and back through the broken window.

The two then began their trek back. They walked across the bridge and began to jump over the muddied stream when Fiona spoke up.

"Hey Abby?" She said as they neared the middle of the stream.

"Yeah Fi?" Abigail helped her to the next rock, noticing the tide was higher than usual.

"I think I'm going to take the 'F'," Fiona said.

Abigail didn't interrupt her.

"It's just, I feel like they didn't want to be found you know? If they're really our ancestors, than I think they saved us. If they hadn't locked themselves away, we may have never been friends or something. I think if someone found some of the stuff in there, they'd try to make something similar and the whole process would happen again, right?"

Fiona jumped to the bank next to Abigail, who remained silent for a few moments before replying.

"That sounds good," Abigail nods in agreement.

"Let's promise here, as present and future archeologists," Abigail held out her hand, with only her pinky outstretched.

"Alright," Fiona held out her hand, and they linked their hands together.

"I promise."

"I promise."

Modeline Celestin

"If we, citizens, do not support our artists, then we sacrifice our imagination on the altar of crude reality and we end up believing in nothing and having worthless dreams."
— Yann Martel, Life of Pi

I am in a world that is constantly revolving. From the busy ants constructing their home against the abandoned building, to the millions of people waking up and performing mundane tasks, the world is in continual motion. With no source of beginning and an indefinite ending, the hands of the clock pause for no one. It is as precious as it comes and whisks by. Rarely, does a person stop and immerse himself with the beauty and complexity of life. There is art, history, and mathematics all around us, but few are chosen to acknowledge the absolute simple, intricateness of life. I often find myself asking, "What do I live for?" To take cognizance of what my former biology teacher once said and live simply to "survive and reproduce?" Or perhaps, I live to "serve others through the merciful grace of God and obey his words," as my pastor often emphasized. After much solitary deliberation, I have come to a concrete conclusion that I live for the unknown. Beautiful, is it not? The mysterious ways the world functions, that is. There are millions of puzzle pieces scattered everywhere, but somehow they find a way to perfectly fit together in the end. I have to admit; not having the slightest clue of what will happen next is scary, yet exhilarating. My heart resides within nature. It can be seen in the deep soil, the vast trees that sway in the wind, the rivers that continuously flow, and the creatures that roam the Earth. Nature is embedded in my heart. It is in my birth name and it will cradle me to my grave.

Reflection

I am honored to have been selected to participate in the *Canon Solutions America Future Authors Project* this year, as a mentor. It has proven, yet again, to be an amazing experience. I've gained much knowledge over the course of eight days. Not only did I learn from my teacher, Mrs. Cartheda Mann, and the brilliant authors, but I have also learned from my peers as well. I provided the young writers with constructive criticism, and in return they filled my days with laughter. Thanks! Visiting Don Estridge High Tech Middle School and Canon Solutions America was quite the learning experience. Socializing with students who share a same passion as me was refreshing. It truly is fascinating how you can move from being complete strangers to establishing close relationships in a short amount of time. This program has helped me become a more creative and genuine individual, to which any amount of debt is incomparable.

Bronze Heirloom

Riddle:
I am the one whose name is engraved into a prison cell,
And whose casket has been furnished since birth.

The stench of burnt cigarettes and wasted dreams,
Permeate my existence, or lack thereof, suffocating others.

I feed off the prosperity like a parasite,
And drink water that's in the same condition as
myself— contaminated.

My menial labor supplies me with bread,
Eaten from broken plates with tarnished silverware.

I am indifferent to the sound of gunshots,

Yet police sirens induce the palpitations of my heart.

A threat to the greater good of society, am I.
To live in a tenement with my seven half-siblings.

My feet are bedded with rough calluses,
Yet I continue to roam the streets in search of vulnerable men.

Dark evenings are consumed with radio static,
Cries of hunger pains, and bottles of potent pills.

Grotesque scars hidden underneath stained rags,
Symbolize the atlas of my genealogy.

The misfortune of my forefathers,
Taints my presence.

My desolate home inhabits,
A wasteland filled with carcasses.

I am dead,
Yet I was never fully alive.

Who am I?

Answer:
      I am the 47%.

The Girl Who Hid In The Dark

Fear resonated in her eyes as realization set in. Her large, hazel eyes nearly bulged out of their sockets as her pupils dilated. She adjusted the large spectacles on her round face as she glanced around the room, unsure if this was all a trick. Her friends and family stood before her, holding streamers and balloons that read "Happy 17th Birthday!" The freckles on her pale face became more apparent as her face heated from excitement. Her frail hands tried to mask her contentment, but failed. Teeth hidden behind her pursed, rosy lips poked from their hiding place, revealing strips of metal and green rubber bands. Her posture suddenly became ridged, as a look of confusion surfaced on her face. Her eyebrows arched while her mouth stood slightly agape.

"How could I forget my own birthday?" she mumbled to herself.

She seemed transfixed on that matter. Her blank stare suddenly became glassy with sorrow. Tears streamed down onto her blotchy cheeks as her shoulders shook with defeat. Her mother squeezed through the crowd and approached her. Wrapping a sweater around her daughter, she escorted her daughter upstairs to her bedroom.

Whispers filled with untold truths were exchanged between the party guests.

"I hear she suffers from anxiety attacks," someone from the back eagerly gossiped.

"Bless her soul," an elderly woman said with remorse.

Silence fell abruptly as the mother returned to the lobby.

"I'm sorry everyone, this party will have to be cancelled. Valerie is just too exhausted to join us. Thank you for coming."

A look of hurt flashed across her face as she went back upstairs to console her daughter.

Good Girl, Bad Habits

I DIED.

I wailed.
I saw.
I slept.
I fed.
I defecated.

I smiled.
I crawled.
I touched.
I spoke.
I laughed.

I sang.
I danced.
I praised.
I obeyed.
I worshipped.

I imagined.
I dreamt.
I questioned.
I read.
I studied.

I applied.
I received.
I moved.
I socialized.
I learned.

I lied.
I stole.
I cursed.
I drank.
I smoked.

I overdosed.
I binged.
I purged.
I cut.
I bled.

I visited.
I confessed.
I reflected.
I cleansed.
I recovered.

I traveled.
I observed.
I discovered.
I understood.
I grew.

I adapted.
I worked.
I earned.
I met.
I gained.

I loved.
I wed.
I bore.
I lost.
I relapsed.

I suffered.
I contemplated.
I pointed.
I shot.
I felt.

I LIVED.

Dear Sponsors, Authors, and Teachers of *Canon Solutions America Future Authors Project*,

I am very grateful, once again, for your contributions and efforts in allowing us to pursue our dream of becoming published authors. First and foremost, I would like to thank the sponsors — Boca Raton Public Library, BankAtlantic Foundation, Lawrence Sanders Foundation, and Xplor International — who have financially assisted with the operation of Canon Solutions America Future Authors Project. Your funding is much appreciated. I would also like to thank the authors — Mrs. Zelda Benjamin, Mr. Dwight Stewart, and Mr. Steve Alten — who provided us with genuine advice on how to not only become excelling writers, but powerful leaders. I would like to thank the Representatives of Canon Solutions America for the insightful tour; it helped me gain an introspective outlook on the process of printing. Last but not least, I would like to thank Mrs. Cartheda Mann, along with the teachers from Don Estridge High Tech Middle School and Mrs. Diana Fedderman, for their continuous efforts in positively changing our lives.

Sincerely,
Modeline Celestin

Aliese Dashiell

Hello and good day/afternoon/ evening to you, person reading this book! My name is Aliese Dashiell and I am going into 8th grade at Jupiter Middle School. I moved here to Florida from Tennessee about a year ago, and I love it here! I'm just a girl who loves writing, reading, friends and family, swimming, making parodies, music, being random and playing video games. (Especially Pokémon, Sonic the Hedgehog and Kirby. Please stop judging me reader.) I am also one of the few people who does not hate Palm Beach Writes with a passion.

Reflection

Week 1:
The first week was a lot of fun; I saw some old friends of mine and made a lot of new friends. The mentors were right when they said the days flew by! I had a few ideas, but none of them turned out the way I had intended so I decided to work over the weekend on story ideas.

Week 2:
I ended up with a couple nanofiction ideas and a short story idea after a weekend of brainstorming. My story never got very far, but, thankfully, one of my nanofictions was approved on the last day. This was a great learning experience for me, as I learned a lot from the mentors, editors, and guest speakers. Although it was a lot more work than I expected, I still had a good time.

Mired in Muck

Casey stifled a shriek as the viscous sludge engulfed her face and covered her nostrils. The intense stench of the chunky matter dulled her senses and she struggled to breathe as the slime crept towards her eyes. She squirmed around, unsure of what to do.

"Please, sit still!" said the facialist applying her mud mask.

Jada Diogostine

"In order to succeed, your desire for success should be greater than your fear of failure."
— Bill Cosby

Hello, fellow readers, authors, family members, and friends. My name is Jada Diogostine. I am 14 years of age, and I live in Belle Glade, Florida. I love writing. Writing is my passion. I love to write poetry and short stories. When I am bored, I just sit and let all my thoughts flow onto paper. I remember when I was in the 4th grade and was preparing to take the FCAT writing test. The prompt was to convince the principal to consider things you could change about the school. I can honestly say writing to that prompt was hard for me, because I had only 90 minutes to write a five paragraph essay. We had Palm Beach Writes for practice, and I had done pretty well, but this was different; it was the FCAT. So imagine how well I did on my FCAT Writes. Well, when summer came and I got the results and found out I had scored a 4.0. I was so excited. That influenced me to excel in my writing. Over the years I was in advanced writing classes, and I tried my best. In my 8th grade year, I didn't have long to learn the basics of writing because I entered school a month before the FCAT Writes. I went to Saturday tutorial, and did everything in my power to learn what was needed to pass the test. In the end, I passed the test with 4.0 and continued to write. Later on, my teacher introduced me to this wonderful program.

Reflection

Over the past eight days I have accomplished more than I had expected to. I thought that we would just sit and write, and write, and write. But, I thought wrong. My peers and I were too shy to talk to each other at first, but as we got use to each other, we began to form close friendships. We all got along great, which made a nice working environment. We were able to critique each other's writing easily. I can honestly say it is better to write with a group of people who have a passion just like you.

It has been an honor to be a part of the Canon Solutions America Future Authors Program. I have learned many different writing techniques. At times it has been challenging to think and write immediately. Editing many drafts was also a challenge. I really like that this program was located at my new school, Glades Central Community High School, where I will be entering my freshman year in the fall. I have had many interesting and memorable experiences, a great beginning for my summer.

A Story of My City & Life

Most people have a story to tell about their life or the city they are from. It can be about anything; like their culture, ethnicity, parents, siblings, friends, or even school. Well, here is a little background of my life in my city. My name is Jada Diogostine. I was born on December 6, 1999 at St. Mary's Hospital in West Palm Beach, Florida. I have been raised in Belle Glade, Florida. I am the child of Mike Diogostine and Jodi Webb-Diogostine. My only sister, Miranda Diogostine, graduated from Glades Central Community High School, in 2010. I was a student at Gove Elementary School K-6th grade, a student at Lake Shore Middle School, and will be a freshman at Glades Central Community High School this coming school year (2014-2015).

Pursuing this further, my life has had many obstacles, not just any typical obstacles. When I was younger, my mother and father separated. From that day forward, it has been very hard for both of my parents. I live with my mother, while on the weekends I go to my father's house. My parents are friends, not just for me, but for them, too. They are very proud of me in many ways; they don't just tell me this every day, they show it. For example, I am an Explorer with Palm Beach County Sheriff's Office. I have been in the program for six years. I was a lieutenant for two years and was a backup for captain when the captain was not there for nearly a year and half. I was a Junior Explorer Major (the highest ranking official) in the program for a year, until I moved up to the Explorer program recently. The greatest effect this has had on me is that I became a role model to younger children, who look up to me not only in the program, but in my community. I also excelled in school, as **Student of the Year** out of 135 students in the "Character Counts!" program during my 6th grade year (2011-2012). "The Character Counts!" program honors students who best exemplify the Palm Beach County School District's six character pillars: trustworthiness, respect, responsibility, caring, fairness and citizenship. My parents were proud. Being a published author of a couple of poems, an essay, and even a few stories is another good reason why my parents can be proud.

On the other hand, my city is known for both positive and negative things. Many people look at Pahokee, South Bay, and Belle Glade very differently. So many people share a perception that these cities are all about gangs and violence, for example. To be honest, young people think of leaving our area to pursue professions, just like everywhere else. Our options may be a bit different; like, most boys want to play football, basketball, or baseball. We're a sports town and have excelled in this area over many decades! Some others may desire to become a doctor, lawyer, and mechanic. On the other hand, growing up in a violent community can have an effect on many people's lives. Riots, shootouts, gangs, and robberies are the type of things that many people lose family members or even close friends to. I think to myself when people say negative things about the Glades' cities, "It is not only where I live, it's all around the world." Where are the states, cities, and communities, that don't have a few bumps in the road?

One positive thing that most people agree on is, the "Muck" is known for having one of the best high school football programs in the nation; with more football players making it to the NFL than other high schools, nationally. In fact, the New York Times reported that the small, rural Glades Central High School has produced more current National Football League players than any other high school in the country. The Raiders have won six Florida High School football titles, tying for the second most in state history with Lakeland and University Christian. Their historic rival is the Pahokee High School "Blue Devils". The most commonly known meet that the two are known for is called the Muck Bowl, one of the most famous high school rivalry games in the nation. It draws up to 25,000 spectators each year – both in the stadium and broadcast nationally on ESPN, some years. Glades Central has won 17 out of the 25 games since 1984. Many people know my dad as "Mike D", who is a local celebrity on Friday nights in the "Muck" and around Palm Beach County to call these games. He uses "MOVE THEM STICKS" to motivate the football players on the field.

Lastly, you may have heard of Anquan Boldin Stadium and Dr. Effie C. Grear Stadium. The Anquan Boldin Stadium is located in Pahokee, and named after the pro football player, who played football and basketball for Pahokee High School. His quarterbacking prowess led him to be named Florida's Mr. Football in 1998. He was drafted by the Arizona Cardinals in the 2003 NFL Draft, began playing for the Baltimore Ravens in 2010, and is currently with San Francisco 49ers. In Belle Glade, The Dr. Effie C. Grear Stadium is the "Home of the Raiders", named for the school's long-term principal, Dr. Effie C. Grear. One of our most recent celebrations occurred during the 2014 BCS National Championship game, when Glades Central graduate Kelvin Benjamin, a wide-receiver for the Florida State University team, made the winning touchdown, sealing the National Championship for FSU. Kelvin Benjamin was selected in the first round of the 2014 NFL Draft as a wide receiver for the Carolina Panthers. I could identify many others, historic and contemporary, who young people look up to as excellent sportsmen, who have left a path that someone in the future can follow.

My city, my area, just like others, has a mix of experiences, some negative, some positive.

A Friend Is Someone

"Friendships in childhood are usually a matter of chance, where as in adolescence they are most often a matter of choice."
— David Elkind

A friend is someone
You turn to.
A friend is someone
You can confide in.
A friend is someone
Who stands by your side.

A friend is someone
Who lifts your spirit.
A friend is someone
Who encourages you.
A friend is someone
You treasure always.

A friend is someone
Who makes you smile.
A friend is someone
Who brightens up your day.
A friend is someone
Who is hard to find.

A friend is someone
Who you can call.
A friend is someone
Who has your back
A friend is someone
Who knows the song in your heart.

A friend is someone
Who believes in you.
A friend is someone
Just like you.

I Am Who I Am

"I feel like when people judge me they're not judging me, because they don't know who I am."
—Gisele Bundchen

I am who I am.
I'm not perfect;
I'm far from it.
Sometimes I feel
Judged for who I am.
For what I look like.
For how I feel.
I remember when I was a kid;
I didn't have to worry about this.
Now looking in the mirror,
I see who I am.
I see a difference from when I was younger.
I am now becoming a teen,
Just trying to survive long enough to discover.
Who I am.
Sometimes I ask myself,
"Who are you to judge?"
"Are you perfect?"
These thoughts run through my mind
When people judge others for being who they are.
Just turn around and say to them,
"I am who I am."

To the Sponsors, Authors, and Teachers of Canon Solutions America Future Authors Project,

I would like to first say "Thank You" to sponsors, the Boca Raton Public Library, the Bank Atlantic Foundation, the Lawrence Sanders Foundation and Explore International for their support of the program. Their contributions have assisted the program with fulfilling needs. Your generosity is greatly appreciated. To the authors, Mrs. Zelda Benjamin, Mr. Dwight Stewart, and Mr. Steve Alten, who dedicated their time to come out and speak about their published books, how they started writing, and what made them start to write, I am grateful. To the representatives of Canon Solutions America, thanks for showing us the amazing publishing technology and for explaining how the machines work. Last but not least, I would like to thank our teacher, Mrs. Mann, and teachers at Don Estridge High Tech Middle School for supporting and assisting us with our development in writing.

Ja'Mya Felton

Hiya! I'm Ja'Mya L. Felton, but everyone calls me Mya. I was brought into this world March 10, 1999, born and raised in Belle Glade, Florida. I am an incoming sophomore attending Glades Central Community High School. I am a junior varsity cheerleader, an "Elite Dancer", and an outstanding writer. My goals in life are to become an orthopedic surgeon, to continue to write, so one day I can read my creations to my grandchildren, and, most importantly, to become successful and to show life that I am a competitor, who can make a significant contribution to society.

Reflection

These past two weeks have been an amazing journey for me. Throughout this experience I've gained so much knowledge. Week one was a week of outside shyness but inside pure excitement. We traveled to Don Estridge High Tech Middle School, were I met my first published author; also, I got to meet many other former writers. Week two was a little stressful for me. Not only was I maintaining my work with the Future Author's program, but I was attending a Driver's Ed class at school also. I was able to keep my word to my loving teacher Mrs. Mann, who extended her hours to accommodate two of us, and who I had promised to finish out the Future Author's program with great success, which I honestly did do.

Mystery Bag

I awoke to a cloudy sky, looking out my window as birds flew by. Sitting up in bed, I could smell the aroma of food down ahead. I rushed down stairs to fine my mother, wearing her self-knitted apron, standing over the stove. "How about we take a ride after breakfast?" she said in her sweet loving voice. I accepted her invitation and begin to devour my breakfast. After demolishing our breakfast, we grabbed our things and began our trip.

Not many people were on the road. A wispy rain fell gently, so softly in fact, everything was damp and kind of eerie feeling. Sadly, along our journey the rain increased "big time" – repeated gusts of wind, raindrops sounding like hurled skittles on the top and windows of the car. Cows and horses on the countryside were running for cover from the rain. Riding along the road, we noticed a little girl and her mother, who happened to be standing near an open field. Being the generous woman my mother is, she pulled over, stopped the car, and offered a ride. The little girl and her mother were ecstatic. Hastily putting their things in the trunk, they hopped into the backseat. Ounces of rain were attacking the backseat, in the short elapse of time it took them to get settled and close the car door. I reached into the glove compartment, grabbed a few napkins, and handed them to the little girl and her mother so that they could dry off the backseat.

"Hi, I'm Pateshia and this is my daughter Ja'Mya," my mother said, briefly turning around with a smile.

I turned my head towards the backseat and waved hello.

"Hello. I'm Joanne, and this is my daughter Jada. Thanks so much for the ride."

Chatter occupied our space for several minutes. Joanne laughed so hard at the most inappropriate joke I had ever heard a daughter repeat in her mother's presence; so vulgar that mommy and me hushed. It was like a wind suddenly cleansed the atmosphere. Clearing her throat, mom, turning around again with a polite smile, and noticed Joanne hadn't put her tattered, fully zipped Jansport backpack in the trunk. Joanne repeatedly looked into the bag, unzipping and zipping, waiting a few minutes or so; then, unzipping and zipping again. This went on for several minutes. My mother got curious, and somewhat suspicious.

"So, watcha got in the bag?" asked my mother.

"None of your business!" replied Joanne.

My mother was quiet, tried to ignore Joanne's tactless response, and, pursed lips, white knuckled-hands on the steering wheel, she continued to drive. Joanne also continued looking into her bag. My mom got more and more suspicious as to what was in Joanne's bag, so she made another attempt to ask her.

"When are you going to tell me what's in that bag of yours?" she asked.

"None of your damn business!" Joanne deliberately replied.

Having enough, finally my mother pulled over and demanded to know what was in the bag. Or, she said she was going to put the little girl and her mother out of the car. Joanne rushed out of the car, grabbed her daughter's hand, slid her across the wet seat to the car door, took her out, and slammed the door. The tires screeched and dust from the sandy roadside engulfed the car as my mother swiftly drove off and started our journey back home.

An hour or so later, as we pulled into our driveway, I looked into the back seat and noticed the mystery bag was still there. Guess what was in the bag? Unfortunately, it's none of your business.

The Feel of Music

Sitting in your house,
Quieter than a mouse,
Sick with boredom,
Sitting, thinking, what can you do?

Blasting mixtures of music,
Inside, you start to tingle,
With an idea bolder than lightning,
Turning on your radio, there it is.

The sound of music,
Sound that gets everyone moving,
The key that gets a family together,
There's nothing like music.

Sound of music hits your soul,
Feelings in your heart start to boil
You dance nonstop,
Music feeds your soul!

Adoring Mother

You were there
As I turned around
With every stare

Every life lesson
Turned out to be
A unique blessing

With every tear shed
I remained with
Constant fear

Always by my side
Was the mentor
With such pride

So grateful to be
The person seated
And given belief

Never would there
Be another person
Who treated me

As greatly as you do
Whose love was
Pure and true

Lindsay (Molly) Fulop

"Words are our most inexhaustible source of magic, capable of both inflicting injury and remedying it." – Albus Dumbledore

Despite what the name next to my picture says, everyone knows me as Molly and I'd like to keep it that way. I've lived in Florida my whole life with my parents and Rosie, my Labrador-Doberman-Rottweiler—well, we're not exactly sure what she is—mix of a dog. As for my education, I'm a rising Digital Media sophomore at Dreyfoos School of the Arts and I wouldn't ever consider being anywhere else. When I'm not doing homework (Not doing homework? Ha! That's funny.), I'm playing piano, fencing, sometimes swimming, and most importantly—and most commonly—of all, reading anything I can get my hands on. In my future I will, hopefully, be a professional photographer, a successful writer, or both. I'm shooting for both, myself, but that's irrelevant. Well, that brings us to the present, and from there comes the end of this autobiography, so I hope you read on and enjoy my writing!

Reflection

Week 1:
The first week was, honestly, a little stressful. There were a lot of thousand mile stares and scrapped ideas the first two days. As it went on, though, I got used to this type of work and I found that I was enjoying myself quite a bit. The mentors and the editors definitely helped raise my spirits. It got to the point where I was excited about re-writing. Getting my first piece approved left me feeling like I was the queen of the world and it gave me what felt like a ton of creative energy. By the end of the week, I went home excited to come back.

Week 2:
The second week was a breeze after the first. I got my second piece approved after six or seven re-writes and I was relieved beyond words. I had met my goal and that meant that the rest of the week could now be spent working on whatever I wanted to. I managed to work out a third piece on the very last day, and I practically danced around the room I was so happy. Thursday rolled around much faster than I would have thought and I was sad to go. I hope I get to come back next year!

In Agony

Pain burned its way through Morgan's veins like a corrosive wildfire, slaughtering any coherent thought. Tears streaked down her face and she gasped for air. She fell to the ground, crying out as she collided with the cold linoleum. Morgan's mother ran frantically to her side. "What did you do?!"

"I stubbed my toe......again."

Writer's Block

The writer sets his cheap mechanical pencil to the blank notepad and starts to write. In that moment, his hunched shoulders tense and the immense weight of his characters' newly-formed world appears. With the slap of the notepad onto the desk, the weight increases and his shoulders roll and crack beneath it. The weight slowly bows the writer down until he is stooped over his pad, crushing his ribs into the unforgiving edge of the desk. A groan of frustration bursts from him and the notepad is flung aside. His characters call out to him, their voices like a siren's song. Their hands guide his exhausted body back towards his notepad, and for a moment he is sorely tempted to begin again.

An idea is right at the edge of his mind, tickling his consciousness. He reaches out towards it, but even his lean outstretched arm can't grasp it. He extends his arm forward until the tendons burn from over extension and the veins stand at attention on his thin pale wrist. The idea is almost in his grasp, but, when he is centimeters away, it vanishes. With a sigh that is one part disgust and three parts dejection, he throws himself into the back of his tattered office chair.

The writer buries his face into hands that are dusted with graphite and splattered with spots of drying red ink leftover from a previous editing session. His writing hand is a twisted knot of cramps that throbs every second. His other hand attempts to massage the pain away, but it soon gives up and withdraws to the writer's side.

His hands rake through his mass of tangled black hair, his fingers creating greasy spikes that stick out in every direction before aggressively ruffling it back into a helmet of curls. He pulls at the unwashed strands as if the small pain will spark new thoughts. He meets no success. Violently, he shakes his head back and forth, trying to thrust inspiration out like a swimmer trying to force water out of his ears. His efforts result in a silver cloud of graphite dust and eraser shavings that settle on the up-turned collar of his day-old button up shirt.

He brings his head to a full stop, his gangly body following suit. His eyes, however, still move. They scan, catalogue, analyze, and see things only he can, taking in every detail of his faraway world and committing it to memory. The writer's blue eyes are clouded, dominated by a hazy faraway look. His pupils are dilated with fatigue and a myriad of other emotions flicker through his eyes as his story unfolds. With a snap, his eyes flash back to reality. Inspiration has struck, and it will not be ignored.

A new vigor possesses the writer, and his movements become jerky and eager. His pale arm clumsily gropes for the notepad, missing twice in his excitement before finally catching a hold of it. He pulls the notepad back towards him and continues writing.

Blades

Jane watched the figure in the mirror. She felt the blades closing in, causing her heart to pound wildly. They were a hairs breadth away, the blades' sharp edges glinting. Let it be quick, she prayed and closed her eyes. A harsh snick sliced the air.

"It's just hair. It'll grow back," her hairdresser comforted.

Rachel Glismann

My name is Rae- sometimes Rachel, but most often Rae. I was born in Southern California 16 years ago and raised in Southern Florida. Ironically, I hate the sun.

I began writing before I could even read. I would make up stories and poems in my head and recite them aloud for my mother to write down for me. When I could finally write for myself, I never stopped. Many years have passed and I'm lucky enough to be able to attend Dreyfoos School of the Arts for Communications, spending every day doing what I love.

Reflection

Week 1:
This week has been both exciting and nerve wracking. This is my first year here, so my time this week has mostly been spent adjusting. I completed a nanofiction however, which is something I've wanted to try since day one.

Week 2:
Time has flown by. As the week comes to an end, I wish I would have brought some writing pre-prepared to the workshop. Between my indecisive nature and my creative process being regrettably much slower than most, I am left with only one piece from this program that is completely polished and green lighted to publish. I may have fallen short, but this has been an incredibly valuable experience that's helped me grow as a writer and has helped me gain insight into the professional world of writing.

The Delving

The man browses his selection of blades, pinpointing the ideal tool. He turns to the woman lying on the table. She's dead silent as he pierces her skin, gouging her abdomen. He rummages through her insides, meticulously removing her intestines, laying her organs beside her. He reaches for his prize. "Congratulations! It's a baby boy!"

no photo available

Sarah Gomez

"Unlike a drop of water which loses its identity when it joins the ocean, man does not lose his being in the society in which he lives. Man's life is independent. He is born not for the development of the society alone, but for the development of his self."
— B. R. Ambedkar

I was born on June 4th, 14 years ago. My name doesn't mean anything terribly interesting, there isn't some dramatic story to my life, I will be attending FAU High for 9th grade, and I'm a rather ordinary person. I was raised by hardworking Colombian parents who give me everything I ever need and love me to the end of the world and back. I consider myself a jack of all trades, I've been writing since I was a little girl, I love to draw/ doodle on every paper I get my hands on, I'm an amateur ailurophile, I got a 6 on my FCAT Writes in both fourth and eighth grade, I swim, volunteer, occasionally practice guitar, and several other things. Growing up (and still today), I was never a "cool" person, friends were never my area of expertise and I didn't care much for things most people my age care about. So for the longest time, it was just me, my cats, and my growing intellect. This lead to me having a lot of time to read, so I read about everything, Greek mythology, medicine, history, art, and subjects like these helped me develop my skills and interests. I try to think of myself as an individual, I don't like having to depend too much on others for everything. I also believe that to succeed in life, everyone should know themselves better than anyone else. I know myself well, I know what I like (ex. psychology, cats, indie music) and what drives me up a wall. My dual nature leads me to want several things in life, I want to be successful and travel around the world, but I also want to study medicine, law, psychology, journalism, or maybe one day all of them. Sometimes occurrences in life may seem random, but I believe that I am in full control of my life and whatever I decide to make of it.

Reflection

Week 1:

I mainly threw around ideas for the first couple of days before deciding on my short story. I ended up writing around seven pages and then when it was edited, I had to cut out around two pages. I was upset that I wasted so much time writing things I eventually cut out, but I realized that I preached way too much. By the end of the week, my story was changed entirely, and I learned a lot about time management. Also, delicious pizza.

Week 2:

This week went by way too quickly. By Tuesday, my short story was all done, but the ending was still a bit off. I began working on the bio sketch, which I wrote the week before. As I write this, there's about 3 hours left and I'm making last minute edits to my works, as well as coming up with names. Over these two weeks, I've become MUCH better at fixing my own work, and I also got to explore a genre I've been interested in for a while. Also, delicious Panera Bread.

Offing

In the mail, I get a copy of a magazine with a glossy cover and individual waxy pages. The numerous photographs are showcased safely, forgotten worlds of a never ending green and deserts with carmine skies seem stored behind museum glass. My brother and I flip through them gingerly, him for the pictures and I for the wonder, lands now abandoned riddle my mind, wanting to be explored. The world is a palette full of colors and lands to explore, yet out of all the places on the Earth, my family lives in the plainest corner of the world. My brother and I are called for dinner, we hastily get up and listen to the dark wooden floors of our metal house creak under his small feet and the tall, never ending bookshelves shake ever so slightly. The smell of wood burning reaches my nose, the slight bitter scent beckons me to open the door to the dining hall. The hall is desolate, save for my parents and the dark, lean figures hovering over every object.

"Helen you know how it is up there."

"Are you going to arrest me for speculating?"

"No, but you need to realize that everywhere on the surface is an absolute hellhole, what if the kids start getting ideas?"

I didn't know which was more odd, the fact that my parents were arguing or that they were speaking about the surface.

"Where are we going? Are we gonna visit grandma? Are we going on a vacation?" My brother fired questions at my mother.

"No, no, it's nothing. Eat your fish," My mother cooed.

I stared down at whatever fish was served with slight disgust. I despise fish, we eat it all the time. If I dare make a comment about it, my father remarks about how I should swim to the surface and eat a whole damn cow if I hate fish so much. I crane my neck to look out the window in the hall, where I am greeted by the same sight as always. Lonely roads and metal houses, a never ending abyss. The more I look, the more the spiral brings me down, it's a huge cycle. I look outside, get upset, get frustrated, and then repeat. Perhaps it's just a passing phase that stirs and pokes at the longing and wanderlust in my mind. Any hope of excitement fades down here, just like everything else. Only the manmade devices that clench the ground stay put.

I turn my attention back to dinner. In that instant, the house rumbles, as if it was waiting for my attention. We all grip the table to prevent it shaking too much. My mother's face loses color and all our heads swivel to face the window. In the midst of the houses outside, the abyss spits out masses of multi-colored garbage, traveling along the street in a tight pack. Every eye in the house is focused on the mass as it glides past the window. The lights within our house highlight the plastic wrappers and decomposing fish stuck in the trash.

"Don't worry sweetheart, it's normal, just like the usual pollution. Let's go upstairs, I think it's your bedtime." My mother says to my brother as she tears her eyes away from the window to lead him upstairs. At some point in time, children reach an age where they stop doing or believing what mother and father tell them, the age where they start wondering. I started wondering at twelve, and three years later, I'm still going strong.

"Why are they getting bigger? Are they from, y'know…up there?" I ask my dad as soon as my brother is gone.

"Honey if I knew, I would tell you. I need you to not touch the subject for a while, your mother and brother are worried. For now, we just need to stay safe." He sees the slight frown on my face. "Go to sleep, it'll be better in the morning" He undoes the large window drapes, enveloping the room in darkness, and leads me upstairs.

After what feels like an eternity rolling around under my sheets trying to sleep, I look over at my clock and see it's only two in the morning. I eventually crash down on the bed and resort to just thinking. My life is just a bunch of routines sewn together to make a timeline that just repeats itself. I am destined to rot here like a worthless fish. The bittersweet feeling of despair sets in when I realize that I'll become one of the souls walking in circles in the small town, and my parents tell me everywhere else is like this. My eyelids are heavy and my back is tired. I stare down my washed out walls in an attempt to stay awake. Of course, I doze off.

Frantic shaking wakes me up. The first thing I see is my panicked brother's eyes glanced from me then the window. I open my mouth to ask what's wrong, but my eyes meet the window and I understand. I can actually see the neighboring houses shaking, and the masses of pollution colliding with the metal giants. It's not long before my parents burst into my room. My mother's hair for once, is not perfect and my father's face gives into panic. Everything is out of place, the whole scenario feels so otherworldly, and I can't help but feel excited.

"Pack lightly, we're going to the evacuation center." My mother tries to speak calmly.

I'm surprised the evacuation center is still in use, it hasn't been used since I was a little girl. I think it was a threat like this, but not nearly as big. I throw whatever clothes I can fit into my suitcase, along with the magazines from the mail and I run downstairs. My parents open the door to the corridor that connects all the houses together to the community buildings. The glass looks like an elongated bubble protecting the corridors, which were swarming with panicked faces trying to get to the evacuation center.

It's chaos. The hallways are enveloped in shrieks and yells, frenzied bodies pushing against me are all I feel, but I can only think of my newest magazine, which I left in the living room. In one rush of adrenaline, I pushed through the crowd of people to get to my house. I run swiftly and retrieved the goods, before realizing that I had lost my family. I would never reach them in time through the hallways, so quick thinking revealed that the car could be the only way there. I wasn't old enough to have my permit, but I hopped into the submarine-like machine we called the AutoSub through the conning tower, cone shaped opening, and flipped on functions I could remember, the various switches and meters displaying levels were scattered about. The AutoSub sputtered to life slowly, lighting up the leather seats with side windows, protected by the tough silver outside. Somehow I got out of the garage with minimal damage. My driving was irregular, either halting roughly, hand always on the emergency break, or swerving without stopping with my foot glued to the gas pedal. I was less than a block away from the center, when the AutoSub shook like my house did, and the world did a 360. Nausea filled my system and worried thoughts of crashing the car filled my head. I turned slowly to look out the car window and the hallways filled with people started to look filled with ants, and my foot wasn't on the gas pedal. I looked out the window on the parallel side of the sub, and saw to my horror, that my parent's AutoSub was stuck on a particularly large wad of trash. Oh god help me I'm going to die if this car keeps going, Jesus I know it's been a long time but – wait, does garbage float? I couldn't fathom if it could make it all the way to the surface, but the AutoSub showed no signs of stopping.

The bleak navy water outside the window swayed around, as if beckoning me to come back. I notice the change in pressure already as the car kept elevating. This was it, I realized, if the car reached the surface I would find out. Of course, getting down would be a problem, but that could be solved later. My eyes were glued to the window for the next fifteen minutes, the dark sea opening up to a world of new shades, this cerulean world seems so different from the dark depths of the sea where I used to reside. In one violent movement, the car stopped moving, and the window showed not blue, but white foam and green water. My mind spun, catching up with me, realizing how dangerous it would be if I dared open the hatch at the top of the AutoSub. Nobody had seen sunlight or blue sky in years, nor has anyone felt wind or breathed the polluted surface air in several years. The surface had been void of contact, human life reserved to the bottom of the ocean, and pollution ruled the Earth. For a moment, the realization of how alone I am right now reaches me. Panic rises up in me and i feel like a grain of sand in the ocean. Guilt for selfishly for ditching my family to see this wonder alone only adds on to my worries. Yet, even if I face disappointment or worse punishment, I was the one made the journey up here. Never on my way up here did I stop, so the glory was mine to take. I escaped my mundane life independently. My wonder would be quenched, all the what-ifs answered, but I doubt it would stop here. My arms turn to jelly and sweat begins to gather at my neck, but my hands are steady and ready to open the hatch. It twists open, filling the car with the sound of waves crashing against the car, and the faint smell of sea breeze. I pop my head out the hatch and witness the hazy blue sea contrasting against the mellow sun in the sky, accented with heavy pink and blue clouds, the waves moving against the horizon with a mighty breeze. The glory before me is inhabited, nobody up here to share with me, so for this mere moment in time, the world is simply me and my wonder.

Mother

She walks in with her sewing kit in hand, head up and back straight, her sun-kissed arms radiate warmth as they pull me close for a hug. I tried to assure her that all was fine, but she would never settle for anything short of perfection.

Her eyes scan me up and down, absorbing my dress' details, deciding on where to begin. Her eyes are dark, not even a faint chocolate glow as she tells me to stand still. They're like her mother's, like mine, perception passed down through generations. Needle and thread are out, an eye for detail makes the oversized dress more form-fitting.

Her fingers recite their memorized movements, pulling the sides of the dress' bust, measuring in her mind how loose it should appear. Elegantly long fingers slip the belt through the holes of the dress, pushing the needle through the dress and the hard belt to sew them together. Her thin fingers bend and loop around the thread, chasing the needle. Her head swoops down, her neck cranes, and her teeth cut off the thread. Her coarse fingers pull out the chiffon under the dress to give it a full look. Rough hands, with calloused skin laced over popped out veins, gingerly flatten my dress and softly transition to my face. Delicate, steady fingers move across my face, applying various make up products. Her artistic history shows. Like a painter, she blotches imperfections. She selects her paint carefully, plucking them out of her box, various powders that matches the golden skin she passed on to me. The treasured tools that belong to her are the ones she shares with me without a thought.

My mother won't be still until her raven eyes meet perfection. Arms stretch to open cabinets, drizzling hair creams into the palm of her weathered hands. Each finger caresses each curl on my head, enveloping it in cream for a perfect twist, the opposite of her dark, flat hair. Her slender neck stretches and is misted by a puff of sweet mango perfume. High cheekbones and her slender face curve as her determined brow relaxes and her lips break their usual line for a smile. She takes a moment for herself, twisting her hair into a bun in a fluid motion, revealing a petite jaw and an array of beauty marks. She looks at us in the mirror, bathroom lights shining on her black hair, cheekbones and bags under her eyes emphasized. The tired look will never fade, but will be overcome by her proud smile. Her narrow lips release a huff of satisfaction. Her sensitive feet slip into heels, she sprays one more round of perfume on me, her lips open once more to slowly exhale, and we smile together in the mirror.

Laura Gust

Hi, I'm Laura Gust, happily entering sophomore year at Royal Palm Beach Community High. I was always that quiet girl in the back of the room. I was raised as an only child since the only sibling I have is 14 years apart from me. I've always loved being alone though. It gives me room to do anything I like to do. I'm very nice if you start talking to me, but I will not talk to anyone first unless I have to. I tried writing out when I was younger, but I loved to read. I would end up comparing myself to authors so I gave up writing for awhile. I never gave writing up truly I would always write here and there and I learned to truly love it. Though I'm still not book writing author kind of material. I've been through a lot of rough experiences, so I write things like death or sickness because I know the feeling pretty well. But someone doesn't like me writing that, cough cough, Adamo. My aunt was the one who raised me for the most part, but I do have two parents that work very hard. When I was little I seldom saw them, only in the morning and at night. I've always been an English teacher's pet because I loved English classes for the most part; grammar was always a huge issue for me though, especially when I was younger. I'm so glad I got a chance to do this though; it was a hell of a ride.

Reflection

Week 1:

My first week was kinda suckish. I didn't really know what I was getting myself. I didn't really make any friends at all in this program. Though I was kinda in awe about some very gorgeous people, I'm not a stalker I swear. My editors declined my short stories at all points in time, I don't have emotion in the short stories I write. I was persistent, but it didn't go anywhere. We had an author come in that sure loved chocolate, and she is really sweet. I always was in my little chair alone with a laptop or pen and paper so I was set. But I really didn't get any work accomplished.

Week 2:

My second week was pretty much the same. We had three authors come in all different types of writers, there was a poet, a magazine editor, and a book editor. They all helped me out in my own little different ways. I figured out that I sucked at short stories and one of my editors said why don't you try poetry , now I'm writing poetry. I'm going insane about how many times I have to edit it though. I swear I've written the same poem 5,000 times. Well, maybe not that many times, but still it was a lot. I'm currently about to rip the person's who made sonnets head off. I'm learning to love this program though and I'm hoping that I can come back next year.

Unbroken Beauty

Scars criss-cross her once flawless and fair skin.
Many casts wrapped around frail limbs aching.
Luscious locks now become short and thin.
Seizure-like fear leaves her body shaking.

Enters hospital grim reaper waiting.
Old, brittle, broken bones are never healed.
Treatment terminated, blood pressure high.
Ran out of cures, her fate has been now sealed.

Eyes tie her to her mortal family.
Hands once delicate, now long and bony.
Skeletal frame flails 'round lamely.
All her former beauty, inner trophy.

Her health fades, her body withers away.
Unbroken beauty in warm heart will stay.

Aalisha Jaisinghani

Aspiring musician. Lover of heavy metal and rock music. Indian emigrant. Overachieving perfectionist. MMA trainee. You basically know me personally now.

Reflection

Week 1:
Not so productive.

Week 2:
Sort of productive.

Caged

It was only a matter of seconds before the beast attacked. Alana was unarmed and vulnerable. Hastily, she glanced around, hoping to devise an avoidance strategy, but there was no hope. Perspiration trickled down her face and neck as the monster menacingly approached. It would only end fatally.

"You failed? Grounded indefinitely!" her mother said.

Fruit of Tantalus

He's looking for someone who won't be there,
But his hopeful eyes cannot be restrained.
A weighted mind dragged down by his despair
Anchored to heartache, he's forever pained.

The tempting apple a mere inch away
He's left broken- it taunts his desire
He reaches for the fruit; to his dismay,
As he gets closer, it ascends higher.

His heart is vacant, filled with empty air
A hopeless longing is all that's contained
He can't escape the emotional snare,
Freedom from longing can't be ascertained.

Possible Strikes

The room is vacant. She strides in, a bare hand grasping the strap of her gear bag. It's empty except for the numerous punching bags that are scattered around the room. She plops her bag in the corner.

She pushes her enclosed fist through the opening of her gloves, slipping into her shin guards with haste. She clenches her fists as she positions herself in front of a bag, an innocent target. Her right foot is firmly planted a foot behind to the right of her left. With one swift movement, she drives her left fist into the bag, but it only moves about a millimeter. She steps back.

Moving to the left, she performs the perfect right roundhouse kick, feeling the edge of the shin guard chafe her skin. Her leg extends outwards perfectly straight, her calf muscles bulging out as her shin collides with the rough exterior of the bag. The impact causes the bag to shake, pushing it back inches away from its original location. She almost smiles.

She takes a deep breath. It only takes her five seconds to throw at least ten different blows, her legs and arms alternating strikes with an incredible momentum. The gloves seem tighter though there's no difference; a layer of perspiration begins to form across her body. She continues to kick, switching between roundhouse and front kicks, her calf muscles popping out on her legs under the straps of her shin guards.

The bag is her father. The bag is her ex-boyfriend. The bag is her backstabbing best friend. She's relentless. Twenty minutes slip away. The shorter part of her dark hair escapes her hair-tie, and a couple strands of hair thinly cover her eyes. She ignores it, continuing to throw punches until she throws one slightly-off punch. Pain shoots up through her wrist.

She stops, out of breath, taking a step back again. Drenched in her sweat, she clutches her right wrist with her left hand, her breathing heavy. She grabs a water bottle from her bag, drinking half of it immediately. Looking up at the clock, she realizes it's only been half an hour. Dropping the bottle back into her gear bag, she approaches the same target, disregarding the other punching bags in the room.

Her arms and legs start to feel like they're burning, and her wrist throbs, as if someone had slammed a hammer down on it, but she doesn't care. Her pain threshold is her greatest pride. Every following attack causes an aching, but it's more satisfying than painful.

She takes one more step back, taking a deep breath. Her leg extends faster than ever and pushes into the bag, so hard that it falls over with a thud. A full smile extends out on her face.

The gloves and shin guards left marks on her skin where the edges pressed in. She slips them off, packing up her gear bag.

Before walking out, she takes another look at the fallen bag, content.

Apeksha Labroo

It's Apeksha. I'm 16 years old, going to be a junior, and of course, I love to write. I have an awesome brother and parents who constantly support me.

Through the years, this writer's workshop has grown to become a home to me. I absolutely adore writing but tennis, math, and annoying Aalisha are close seconds.

I can't thank Ms. Poettis and Ms. Adamo for all their help and guidance. They've taught me that to be a true writer, you must be willing to change.

Reflection

Week 1:

This week was very productive. I was able to write a short story in strictly dialogue. At first, it was pretty difficult. It took me a while to be able to describe a situation in just dialogue. Nonetheless, I was able to push through it and get it done. The editors liked it and for that, I was really happy. I saw old friends again and it felt good to be able to reconnect. I can't wait for the next week..

Week 2:

This week went well. I wrote a descriptive essay and I had fun writing it. Unfortunately, I injured myself and missed a day, but other than that, it was good. Aalisha told me my nano-fictions weren't substantial so I didn't use them. I had a great time and hope to come back.

Found Words

It was past midnight but that moment was the only time when the pandemonium around the woman was tamed. With the grandchildren sleeping silently in the extra room and the house looking somewhat decent , there was finally time to sit down and relax. As the woman lay on her bed, her eyes focused on the antiquated column of shelves in front of her. The old carvings etched on the edges created elegant yet irregular lines around the mass piles of English textbooks, workbooks, and guidebooks.

Almost immediately, the woman's eyes fixated at the single wooden shelf that held the entirety of her book collection. The antique was frail with its chipped paint and endangered screws. The amount of books that were shoved into the small area made it more hazardous. With the weight of all that combined, it was evident that the crowded ledge was soon going to meet its awaited end.

She got up and walked to her treasured compilation. Her finger glided against the colorful bindings of the numerous novels. As she scoured the assortment, her eyes caught the sight of a bright red edging at the end of the shelf. Instantly interested, her hands found the edges of the crimson hardcover. As her hands felt the smooth material of the vegan leather, she knew exactly what it was: her ancient worn-down journal. It had been years since she had even glanced at the chaotic piece of her past. The cherry faux leather cover felt rough in her delicate hands and the small doodles that she had drawn at the center were faded now. Her small signature curved extravagantly on the bottom right corner of the front page in dark blue ink. The smell of the musty papers along with the dust tickled her nostrils. Turning the pages, the woman relived her youth. Each punctual error extracted a grimace. Each snarky remark made her chuckle. Twisting the ends of her unkempt gray hair, she closed her eyes, remembering the days when she cried over grades and boys, when utter turmoil could be fixed with a large tub of Double Chocolate ice cream. The farther she ventured on within the withered pages, the more the woman witnessed her life as if it was one of her novels.

As the recollections of her life flashed before her, she found herself longing to do what she had once loved. She yearned to feel the way she once did, when her scrawls would fly across page after page until her hands tired. When she would spend hours in front of a typewriter clicking away new thoughts and ideas. It wasn't just a hobby, it couldn't be. A hobby would not feel like a highly addictive drug. It was a passion, a vital organ in her body that could not be extracted without causing major damage. The more the woman thought about it, the more the craving grew. She couldn't take it anymore. She was through being an adult and leaving her desires behind. Right now, she could be a child, be herself.

With that, she ran to the study, taking the journal with her. When the occupied rooms came into view, she tip-toed so the children wouldn't stir. As she passed by, a glimpse of the snoring angels made her smile. Not wasting another second, she dashed. The long curls on her head bounced as she hurried to reach her destination. After such a long time, the possibility of falling and hurting her hip or waking up the children that were very reluctant to go to bed wasn't so significant. Right now, she was the kid on a secret mission.

As the woman rounded the corner, she could see the white double doors leading to the study. The newly painted doors still smelled fresh like chemicals, however, her olfactory senses didn't mind it as much as they usually did. She walked inside and took in the view. The first thing she set eyes on was the old rickety desk that stood at the center of the room, the one that her father had sworn up and down was where his best ideas were made. Grinning to herself, she moved towards it. Letting her fingers roam the old wood finish, she could practically feel the thoughts in her head zipping past each other to form perfectly straight lines. Even now, the small indentation from when she used pencils to inscribe hearts and smiley faces were visible. Tracing the drawings, she moved to sit down in the incommodious seat. The squeaky chair that had bugged her beyond anything didn't seem so bothersome now however. Instead, the infuriating noises were tolerable, welcoming even. She rotated in several circles, her wild hair swooshing around her. Again, the child within her wandered free. After she had her fun, she got to business. The woman scooted closer until there was no room between her and the edge of the desk. She positioned herself further off the chair until her short legs could touch the ground. Within one of the many pencil holders, she found her grandmother's old fountain pen, the one her grandmother gave her when she was five. The memories of watching her grandmother teach her how to write filled her brain. She remembered being enchanted by the stunning purple ink as it scribbled across the parchment and listening to her grandmother's grand stories about princesses and fairytales. Waking from her reverie, she gently laid the beaten journal on the desk. The routine that she had inhabited as a kid became present again. Her shoulders rolled back, she pulled her hair into a messy ponytail with her legs crossed on the uncomfortable chair.

As she sat there, the woman let her mind wander. The possibilities were endless; every scenario played through her head like a reel. The reason she had loved doing what she used to do suddenly became apparent. All the jumbled thoughts, unfinished phrases and nonsensical language bounced from empty space to empty space in the confines of her brain. Every pause she ever made in her life could become a comma, every end a period. With every sentence, she could let her dreams roam free. Her fantasies could become realties, if only for a little while. She could create people, create worlds. But most importantly, she could resurrect the young girl she had left behind: herself.

So, the woman closed her eyes and took a deep breath, letting the clean, air-conditioned oxygen fill her lungs. She let her thoughts transform into words and let the words dance into sentences. Her mind was fueling with ideas, with opportunities. Never before had she felt so thrilled, so alive. This was her chance to revive the child she once was, and she had never been so ready. Her eyes opened.

And she wrote.

The Ticket Stub

"Devin."

"Rich."

"I told you. Richard is my name."

"You're still just Rich to me."

"Fine. How are you doing in here?"

"Oh, real nice. You should come by later. We make friendship bracelets and sing Kumbaya."

"Well it can't be that torturous."

"You don't even know. It sucks."

"Not like you would know what that's like. You were spoiled rotten."

"Shut up. I've seen worse."

"Hardly."

"Let's forget it. There's no point fighting with you when mom, dad, and you are the only people I have visiting rights with."

"That's true."

"They won't even let me see Anna, Rich."

"Well, this isn't exactly the place to take her."

"I'd still like to see her."

"Speaking of, Dad agreed to give Anna 20% of the inheritance."

"Good. What about me?"

"He's not budging, Devin."

"Did you even try to convince him?"

"Of course, but having a hit-and-run on your record does not exactly scream Eagle Scout."

"Whatever. At least he cared enough for his grand-daughter."

"Yeah."

"How's Anna?"

"She's doing well. She says the boys in her class have cooties."

"They should. How was her birthday party?"

"Just as she wanted it."

"Good."

"Theresa made the whole Frozen theme come to life. It turned out nice."

"Theresa?"

"The new housekeeper."

"What happened to the old one?"

"According to mom, she was 'too green.'"

"What's that even mean?"

"God knows."

"Does Anna like her? The new housekeeper?"

"Yeah, but she misses you."

"Who? Theresa? That's awkward."

"Anna. She's constantly asking where her father is."

"And what did you tell her?"

"That you're off slaying dragons."

"Good."

"Yes it is."

"What? Why are you looking at me like that?"

"Nothing."

"Rich."

"Nothing."

"Stop lying to me."

"Look, they-they don't think you should have custody of Anna."

"What? Who's they?"

"Mom, dad, the lawyers."

"But they're investigating! The hit-and-run could have been anyone who looked like me with my car. It could've been you, for Christ's sake."

"Devin-"

"Just talk to those detectives. I'm sure they're still looking into people."

"Devin, they stopped investigating a while ago. They're sure you did it."

What?"

"There was a traffic camera. It caught you in your car two blocks from the scene of the crime."

"I didn't even have my car that day! I carpooled with that girl to the movies, remember? My date?"

"Yeah."

"Those detectives said they would look into it."

"They told our lawyer they couldn't see anyone else doing it?"

"And our lawyer didn't defend me? What's the point of having a lawyer with a law degree from Harvard if he can't do his job?"

"There's only so much he could do. And Sarah-"

"Wait, how do you know Sarah? We only went on that one date."

"We, uh, kind of bonded."

"Bonded?"

"It's not serious, Devin."

"Oh."

"Devin-"

"No forget it. That's not my point. My point is she was with me on the date at that time."

"Sarah said she was drunk."

"What? We only had a few drinks."

"She says she doesn't want to be liable for you when she's not 100% sure."

"Right. Of course."

"I'm so sorry, Devin."

"What about the ticket stub?"

"They looked for it everywhere and they couldn't find it."

"In my wallet?"

"No."

"Awesome, just awesome."

"The guard's giving me a look."

"I bet he is."

"I'll be back later."

"Take your time. I'm not going anywhere."

"Maybe if you weren't so irresponsible-"

"Go away, Richard."

"Forget it. Bye."

"Bye."

With that, Richard didn't feel the remorse he felt earlier. Instead, he clutched the ticket in his pocket, allowing the burden of his mistakes slip away.

Enemy Lines

Michael had enough. The enemy had crossed too many boundaries. There was a fine line between friendly hatred and full-on territory takeover. This was his land! There was no way he was going to allow this foe to win. He raised his weapon, ready to strike.

As he took aim, he grinned. "Goodbye, pesky weeds!"

Natasha Leonard

So there's not much to say about me. I don't have some inspirational quote to put here or a whole lot of words for you to read about my life. All I can really say is I'm 17 and I go Alexander W. Dreyfoos School of the Arts.

…

Ugh, I honestly wish being mysterious was a trait of mine, but it's not. The above facts are true but I also have a love for writing. Writing is to me what constipation is to you; difficult to put out but satisfying when it's finished. This program has made me such a stronger writer and for that I'm grateful.

Anyway, go ahead and check out my short-story. I think it's pretty good.

Reflection

Week 1:

Time management is a valuable skill to have. I lack time management and it was very apparent as the week ended and we rolled into week two. They said the week would go by very quickly, but how quickly could four 6 hour days go by? Too fast is the answer. By the end of the week I had one solid idea and a whole lot of work to do and soon those four days dwindled to four then three and then Friday had arrived and the week was over. Valuable lessons I learned, working while around friends is difficult. Imparted knowledge from Zelda Benjamin our guest author: do what you love, be smart about the process and the media aspect, but still have the ability to support yourself. All in all, week one of this program was one of the greatest experiences I've had this year. Oh and who could forget double trouble Adamo and Poettis, the ultimate editing tag team.

Week 2:

The end. This is the dreaded last week where works started last week come to fruition on a Wednesday and get a stamp of completion on Thursday. In other words, the week of stress. I managed to finish one piece, but hey it wasn't just any piece. The Well became a beast at ten pages long double spaced. But by far, it's my favorite piece that I've written. Probably because it's something I know I spent time on, was edited, and is completed. Oh to have something completed and not half way done.

On another note, can we just talk about the great presenters we had this week. Steve Alten, author of Meg and other novels came for a visit, as well as poet, Dwight Stewart, and magazine editor, Jennifer Tormo. Three authors, almost one for each day of the program this week. The vast amount of knowledge and experience they imparted on us was amazing. I learned so much and felt simply blessed to have gotten the chance to hear these people speak. Honestly, this program is like a two in one. You come to improve on your writing and also leave with valuable life skills and tips. Forever in love with program.

Farewell Cannon Future Authors Workshop, maybe I'll see you again next year. And bye Mrs. Adamo and Mrs. Poettis. You guys are bae.

The Well

The letter came in the mail one day in mid spring of 1918. Simple in a crisp white envelope, Miriam was the first to touch it, accidentally staining the edges of the envelope blue from the blueberries she had handled earlier. Somewhere in the depths of her mind or maybe it was the unrest she felt rooted in her soul, she recognized that this letter was different from all of the others.

Bending over and surveying his field slowly, Hanson wiped the cool sweat pooling in the creases of his forehead with a washcloth. The springtime backdrop highlighted the light brown hues in the field brilliantly; leaving a resonating brown glow that washed over him. When he had finished for the day, Hanson made his way home, ambling on the short dusty road leading to his front porch. It was then that he felt something strike his heart. The pain was quick like the sting of a bee, sharp and barely present until an underlying ache makes itself present. He stood there, halfway to his home under the hot evening sun, in a trance before he was overwhelmed by the heavy need to run home.

Miriam stood on the porch, the same berry smudged envelope now torn and on the floor surrounding her. The accompanying letter was held precariously in her thick hands. Hanson looked upon the face of his wife, noting her faraway empty expression. He had seen a crow earlier, way out in the field perched on the branch of one of his trees. He had known then, just like he knew now.

He gently pried the letter from his wife's hands, unwrapping her fingers from the stiff paper individually and slowly, as though any sudden move would break her fragile form.

"He's gone," his wife said. Her words were barely discernable. "Our baby boy's gone."

Sobs began to rack her frame and all Hanson could do was hold her, a litany of comforting words suddenly gone from his vocabulary. It was only later that night at their watering well when he got a chance to shatter the barrier holding back his fighting emotions. He found himself on his knees, staring up at the starry sky, with the tears he hid from his wife finally falling. He had last prayed after his son's birth, but now an old Bible was pulled from his back pocket and laid in front of him. Unsure of where to start he turned to a random passage and began to read aloud.

When he returned home Miriam was in the same spot he had left her hours before, on her side and under their blanket. He shuffled about the house before he found his place on an old worn rocking chair on his front porch to watch the sun rise. He wondered how Atlas was able to hold the Earth without bowing under the pressure. Hanson felt more than he saw the warm rays touch his face and it was when he blinked, waking from his daze that he caught sight of a dot on the horizon making its way to him. The dot grew larger until he was able to make out a limping figure. The figure drew slowly against the dusty road, swaying with each step. The light was still weak in its early morning stage and Hanson had to squint his eyes to make out any clear details. He sat in his rocking chair, waiting, with his bare feet firmly on the wooden floor. He saw him then when he could come no closer than the porch steps. Lanky and dirtied, the figure was no more than nineteen. His fatigues were loose on his almost emaciated frame.

The young man swayed and had to grab onto the porch railing to hold himself up. Hanson stood and walked down the steps leading to the boy and touched a finger to his cheek before flattening his hand onto his face.

"How are you here?" There was no response and fear gripped at his heart. "Answer me."

His son collapsed into his arms revealing nothing leaving Hanson to carry him inside to their couch. Standing, he chose instead to cover the boy with blankets and tend to the light wounds on his face and arms. He didn't have a fever as far as he knew, but what did he know? Some time passed before he saw hints of the young man beginning to awake. He stirred under the sheets, but was too fragile to make much of a commotion. When his eyes opened, Hanson knew he was more present than before. They looked at one another, the grandfather clock in the background ticking like a metronome.

"Pa." The words were light against the heavy air, barely audible.

Hanson stiffened nonetheless, but made no move to respond. The room remained silent with Hanson helping the boy to drink water and rest to the best of his abilities. It was after some time when Hanson decided it was time to speak.

"William, is there anything you remember?" He asked. "Anything at all?"

His voice was soft and wheezing when he spoke and Hanson had to strain his ears to hear him. "I was last in the trenches. I remember being called to the machines when a pain started in my stomach. I fell and lied there for some time before things started to get dark around me. I woke up by the well and walked home from there."

Hanson prompted him further, with more questions, but William had no other answers. However it was his last sentence that mattered most and found its place in Hanson's mind. Pressing his hand to his son's matted hair, Hanson smiled and thanked him.

Hours later when William had fallen into a deep sleep, he made his trek to the watering well with his Bible still tucked into his back pocket. The grass was crushed in places, but still otherwise undisturbed. He pulled his Bible out and went to the same spot he had knelt the night before, but came up empty in his intentions.

And it was as if God's fist of knowledge came from the clouds and punched Hanson square in the face.

"It's magical," he whispered. "It's magical."

Fingering the Bible still in his hand, he thought about all the things that had gone awry in the past month. Bertha, their milking cow, had become stricken with an illness, the eggs weren't developing right, and they were short on money. All of these thoughts ran through his mind, but he would help them get back on his feet again.

"I wish," he started, thinking of something small to test his wish on. "I wish for a new plow."

The air was still and when he looked around nothing had changed, but there was still a hope in his heart. Putting his Bible away he walked back to his home, determined to find a new plow set right in the shed out back. Instead he found, a surprised Jeffery Lee, a neighborhood boy, on his doorstep and his wife at the door eyes wet.

"Lee, now what are you doing here boy?" Hanson asked, setting a foot on the last step of his porch.

"The p-postman ran through town Mr. Friese," Jeffery said, stumbling over his words. "And you know old Ken, ever the gossip; he told me what letter he put in your box. I came to pay my respects." And then Lee bent around Miriam to gaze into the living room, "but it seems that's not at all necessary anymore."

"What do you mean, Lee?" Hanson said, eyes shifting the shed a few yards away.

"Why it seems as if Will's on your couch, Mr. Friese," Jeffery said, fumbling with is hands. "They'd know if he deserted. You wouldn't a gotten that letter saying he was dead if he had just up and left."

"You don't know anything, ya hear?" Hanson pointed stiffly at the boy. "Now get from my property."

Jeffery stepped down, eyes low as he backed away from Hanson, but there was a fire in his eyes that unsettled Hanson. When Jeffery was a silhouette in the distance, Hanson moved towards his wife who was still frozen.

"I know," he said. "But give me one second, hon."

The shed stood in all its worn and tattered beauty like the Kaaba in Saudi Arabia for Hanson in that moment. Though, it was flimsy Hanson had no other place to keep his yard tools together and safe. His stomach clenched as he stepped into the shed, letting in the light from the sun. He stepped forward and turned to his left where in the corner he kept his rusted plow. Where it was once sat pathetic and hidden by shadows, was propped a new iron one. He moved to touch it, feeling the cool metal under his fingertips. In that instance all his doubts were absolved.

...

It wasn't until weeks later that he noticed something off. Their pots were missing. Articles of clothes were disappearing. Animals were gone from their pens. Hanson, true to his words would support his family in any crisis and tried to alleviate the situation by replacing the missing items with two little words, 'I wish.'

"Handy, have you seen the new pearls you just gave me the other day?" Miriam asked, coming from the kitchen, dirty in her apron.

"You lost it already?" Hanson asked, dropping the town newspaper to eye her.

"I didn't lose it. I set it down on the side table last night and this morning it wasn't there," she said, screwing her face up.

"Well that's odd," he mumbled. "I do remember you setting it down. I didn't move it though."

William came through the door in that moment, sweat pooling around his face and causing his clothes to cling to him. Miriam handed him a dry washcloth to wipe himself with but he waved her off.

"I overheard you at the door," William breathed, the day's tiredness still weighing on him. "I think I know what's wrong."

Miriam and Hanson leaned towards him, ears wide as William began to tell his theory. The well, as good a thing it was in their life, was starting to show its other face. With everything they wished for, the well claimed something from them.

"…and now it's starting to take things we've just wished for, not things we already have," William finished.

That afternoon Hanson could be seen hammering away at the well, covering up its opening with thick plywood he had brought from home.

"We're going to have to go into town for some bricks to close it," Hanson said to William once he had returned from boarding up the well. "We'll go tomorrow."

"Why I don't think you'll be closing up anything," a voice came from their front door. Hanson moved from his position on the couch to their open front door to see a mass of people out front with a stalky young man leading them.

"Lee, what the hell is going on?" Hanson asked, crossing his arms.

"We heard about your boy," said another voice. This one Hanson recognized as the town's only shopkeeper. "I'd be mighty sorry about him if he'd actually died like the rest of ours."

Hanson felt William come to his side, but pushed him back behind him. The group of people ranged from the simplest of housewives to men he'd grown up next too and went to grade school with. Shaking his head, Hanson watched as they morphed into one form, all wearing the same expressions and all with harsh mutterings coming from their open lips. He didn't see their weapons until last.

"Go get your Ma from her room," Hanson whispered behind him to William. "And leave through the back."

"Pa, I'm not—," William protested, but Hanson's eyes left no room for argument and the rest of his sentence died in his throat.

"What do you all want?" Hanson asked, stepping fully out onto his porch.

"The well," Lee said. "I knew there was something you were hiding. I figured William had deserted and I came back the next day to let you know I wouldn't say a word. I caught you at your watering well, talking something crazy about wishes, and I hid in the bushes. But boy was I surprised when I saw a trend with things you wished for coming to life."

"Why didn't you tell us, Hanson?" a woman cried from the crowd. They pushed her forward until she was in the front next to Lee. She fell to the ground with tears streaking her face. "You know my boy Reed didn't make it. I would have loved to have him back. I would kill to have him back."

"But you're just too selfish to share, aren't ya?" came another voice.

"Yeah, we all got worries and troubles," said another. "Why do you get to solve all of yours?"

Soon the crowd was overcome with loud ramblings of terrors and qualms and Hanson felt himself become overwhelmed. Holding on to the porch column, he watched them all murmur and move as though they were one.

"Stop," he said, and then louder, "stop."

The mass came to a hush as they eyed Hanson ears, hungry for whatever words he could possibly give them.

"I've lived here for thirty-five years now and, in all those decades, I never thought I'd see the day where ya'll are grouped together like a pack of wild animals," he said. "Now I don't know what else to say except that you're not getting within one foot of my well."

Jeffery Lee backed up, his face twisted up.

"Mr. Friese," Jeffery said. "I don't think you understand. Us coming and talking to you like this is a courtesy. We will take that well by force if we have too. Now I kindly ask you to rethink your words."

"Gordon, are you going to be the one to do it?" Hanson asked, looking at a disheveled man in the crowd with his pitchfork loose in his hands. "Are you going to be the one to stab me to death and then come do the same to my family inside?"

Gordon looked away from Hanson, his pitchfork suddenly weighing a few tons in his weak hands.

"Or how about you Anna? Remember when my wife helped you deliver your baby boy? Are you gunna club her stupid with that roller?" Hanson asked, as the woman shifted in the crowd. "And you Thomas? Do you really have the heart to shoot me? Over a well?"

Murmurs ran through the crowd as Hanson addressed each individual. Their gazes by the end landed anywhere, but on Hanson's frame.

"And Lee, you too," Hanson said. "Will's your best friend and I can't fathom why you'd do such a thing to him. Now this well ain't worth your troubles. All its brought is misery into my life and I don't know why you'd invite that into yours."

The crowd remained quiet as they turned to one another and finally let their sight fall to Jeffery. Hanson could see the uncertainty that flickered through all of their eyes before they hardened with resolve.

"Handy, we're mighty sorry," said a voice, third row in the mass. "Sometimes your judgment ain't quite right when you're thinking of your family."

"I know," Hanson said standing straight. "I got a family of my own to protect."

"And protect them you do," Gordon called from the crowd. "Me and Ross will help you brick that well up alright? Tonight if you don't mind?"

Hanson nodded and he watched as Lee lost steam realizing his army of men had abandoned him. Now he was just a simple boy, lost to his own purpose. Sighing, he glanced back at Hanson before leaving with the rest of the crowd that was silently dispersing. Hanson stood there, amazed at how fast the crowd had come and gone.

"I figured that damn well could bring one good thing to our lives before we abandoned it," he heard his son say from behind him.

Hanson turned, confusion written on his scruffy face. "What do you mean?"

"That was the final wish. I wished for the crowd to have a change of heart and leave us," William said.

"Well I'll be darned," Hanson smiled, bringing his son in for a hug. "Dear God, I hope this is last we hear of this well."

Anthony Li

Tony Li started is a 12 year old Asian boy and is going to 7th grade. He attends Bak Middle school of the Arts with Keyboard as an art major. Tony likes math very much but that doesn't prevent him from writing good stories. He also enjoys reading and playing with Rubik's cubes. He is shy in nature and sometimes not that responsible as expected.

Reflection

Week 1:

During week one, I learned a lot for the first time at writing workshop. First and most important thing I learned that time passed by really fast. Occasionally, I would daydream read a bit, but then the entire first week burned up. Another thing I learned was the process of editing. Mrs. Benjamin taught us her experience with editors and what to look for.

Week 2:

During week two, I applied my learnings from week one to better my work and efficiency. Also, I learned about more types of writing, such as journalism and poetry. This is especially useful because if I were going to take writing as a job, It would be useful to have knowledge of different types of careers. The last thing I learned was that the last day for writing, things actually were crazy. Although I only got one piece in, I learned my lesson. Never to procrastinate no matter how long you think the time will last.

I Can't Bear This Anymore

The Burmese python slithered across the walkway of the zoo and the visitors screamed. They ran toward the exit. My friend and co-worker Gus and I watched as they ran nonstop to their car.

"Joe, that's another unsatisfied customer that might never come back," my Gus piped up as he threw his cigar into the elephant feed.

"You know Gus, today's my 20th anniversary at this job, I want to celebrate somehow," I said.

"Hey Joe, just go take the day off, the keeper just sleeps in all day anyways," He replied.

"Gus, you know I can't, that bear needs to be tranquilized every 3 hours, unless you would care to take over..." I said.

"Sure, anything for a friend," he said suppressing a fake grin and lighting another cigar.

I tranquilized the bear one more time and left Gus in charge, who was ruffling his grey hair and coughing wildly. Then I left to eat lunch at the new pizza place. After my meal I grew bored, so I tried out the bar across the street.

"What will it be eh?' the bartender asked me as I arrived at the counter, not looking up, afraid to look too smug.

"Uh, what is everyone asking for these days?" I asked,

"Well, lots of people bought this stuff," he said while passing a bottle to me.

Without wondering what that stuff was, I asked for a glass. When the bartender left, I lifted my head a little. There were poles on each end with women dancing on them. Furthermore, the women didn't have many clothes on them.

"Oh no, this is a strip bar, my wife is going to murder me if she finds out," I thought.

I slurped up the glass and left immediately without looking back. Walking back home I started to get extremely groggy by the second. Before long I didn't know where I was going. I ended up in the community pool without in my zoo clothes, and ruined my anniversary dollar watch. I could have drowned in that pee infested pool.

I found my way back home in my wet clothes, and took a long, hot shower. Once I get out the phone rang.

"Dude, Gus is in the hospital just want to let you know. I tried to call your cell but that didn't seem to work, he's been in there for like an hour. He said something about a bear," said the caller. I could tell it was Rob, one of Gus's good friends, he was always saying Dude. Gus was always in the hospital, for some lung treatment or something. But the thing was he said something about the bear, and I must have been a little drunk because it didn't get to me for a while.

"Bear, bear, what bear?" I said to myself head throbbing from that drink, "Oooooohh, that bear at the zoo, it needs to be tranquilized." I wasn't worried; I had about 30 minutes to tranquilize it again, plenty of time.

I walked toward the zoo, an easy 15 minute walk from my house. The only thing was that drink was still making my mind wobble. All was going fine until I saw the mob of visitors gathering around the zoo. The mob was common, but this one was probably five times as big, and they were chanting "Close the zoo!" And I, still wearing my zoo uniform, had no choice but to go to the back door, which was on the other side of the zoo. By the time I reached the back, I was out of breath. The roars and screams of the crowd started growing louder though. I grabbed a tranquilizer from the tool shelf and slowly headed to the bear habitat. Carefully I looked into the enclosure, and my stomach churned. The chains were snapped off and tufts of fur were stuck on the tall black gates that were at least 8 feet tall.

I looked outside the front gate, also not a good sight. The crowd disappeared but a couple of corpses lay on the streets. I ran to the zoo's vehicle, an old Chevy that had a sloppy "Gingham Zoo logo" painted across the rear. I worked my way inside the front seat, which reeked of coffee. After a series of troubles and trials, I worked the old automobile out of parking position. The radio begins loudly,

"Wild bear escapes deplored zoo and attacks a present mob, the bear was last seen on Sandbag Street. We advise everyone to stay indo-,"

I shut off the radio and sped toward Sandbag Street, that's where the farmers market is. As I reached the market, the entire street was vacated. The rough air conditioning in the car wasn't enough to evaporate the sweat I was breaking. Having nothing else to do I turned the radio back on.

"The death count has been raised to 7 as the bear ravaged through the farmer's market on Sandbag Street, the bear has been reported to be dangerously near Acreage Hospital. The hospital is under lockdown and residents are advised t-,"

I shut the radio back off and headed for the hospital. I rounded the corner and almost ran into the bear. I felt as if a porcupine had teleported under my butt. The bear climbed on the front of the truck. It raised its paw and landed a crack on the front windshield. Another slam… another, I started to feel the sharp shards of glass land on my wet face. Instantly I switched to reverse and stepped full on the gas. The bear lurched backward and landed into a heap of garbage bags. I didn't stop the vehicle and it slammed on the opposite wall, effectively totaling it. I got out of the car, pulling out my tranquilizer. Without making a sound I crept toward the heap of garbage bags. A growl sounded behind me and I whipped around, the bear was about 10 feet away, standing on its hind legs. It was running toward me with its paw raised.

"Agh!" I screamed. I tried to move my hands to cover my face but the tranquilizer hit me in the head.

I opened my eyes. I was back at home on the couch, my wife putting an ice pack on my head.

"I don't know what exactly happened Joe but you were found in an alleyway knocked out, oh, and you had a gun or something." She said.

"I was going after the bear," I said dazedly

For the rest of the day my wife rambled on how lucky I was to be alive and how stupid it was to go after that bear. But to tell you the truth, I went after that bear because it was my responsibility; I did technically let it out. The real thing I wondered was why the bear spared me. The only way for him not to claw me was to have his arm stop in midair. I glanced at the TV,

"Many reports on the whereabouts of the bear have been submitted, no one knows the exact position of the bear."

Then I glanced out of the window, a tuft of fur was on the fence.

Logan Lockhart

My name is Logan Lockhart. I was born May 17th, 2002. I am 12 years old. I go to Don Estridge High Tech Middle School. I am 6th grade, going into 7th. I enjoy playing baseball, basketball, and tennis. I love to read. I love using technology. I love playing sports videogames.

Reflection

Week 1:
Found my first story, got rejected, but working on fixing it.

Week 2:
Becoming confident about my story, going to finish in time.

Truth

I sat in the ice-cold chair, waiting for my interrogators. I am shivering from the low temperature. Possible or not, I know that I have to get out of this situation. The door opens, and four heavily armed soldiers come in. They separate into their own corner of the room. Another man walks in. He is dressed in a dark business suit. He is pale skinned, with gray eyes and an extremely slender body. He carries a laptop in his left hand and a small table in his right. His expression communicated his murderous capability.

The room gets colder. I'm not just fearful anymore. My fear has morphed into horror. The man's grin is malicing. Hideous. I look away, alarmed. Finally, he opens his laptop and the interrogation begins.

"Say your prayers now," the man begins. I don't answer.

He glares into my eyes. I glare back.

"I don't think you know how we operate at The Society of Truth." I look down, kicking my feet back and forth.

"Look at me!" he commands. I look up and see him smiling down at me. I look back down.

"Who is the criminal here again?" I ask.

"Keep on disrespecting me like that. You won't live for long. Tell me what you know." he says.

"I don't have to–"

"Oh? You don't? Fine then, maybe these men will change your mind."

One man quickly rushes towards me from the back, pointing a gun at my head, with his index finger on the trigger. Another man comes behind my interrogator, and aims his gun at the front of my head.

"Sup?" I say to the soldiers.

"I'll give you some time to decide on your behalf. In the meantime, my men will keep you company. Good night James," he says. He walks out of the room with pep in his step. That left me the choice of either death or telling him what I knew. I had to make it work somehow. Obviously he had won.

They escort me out, guns pointed at my back. I walk out of the room with a sour face. I look back. One of the guards had a gun waiting for me.

"Turn around," the man said.

We walk a little while, and we come across a three way passage. I scan the choices. I look down each one of them, and they are all pitch black. There were passageways that seemed almost impossible to remember. I had strained my brain, and still couldn't force my brain to take a mental picture so that I can navigate the halls for escape. *Left, right, right, left, right, left.* This leads from the interrogation room to my room.

I arrive at the room.

They open the door for me with a key, and I almost fall into the room. The first thing I notice is that the room is extremely dark. After a few minutes of struggle, I finally locate the bed, and let myself fall into it. It isn't as soft as expected.

The next day, I walked to the door and was surprised to find the same four men and the same interrogator as the day before. I took a few steps back. The soldiers followed. I looked into the slender man's eyes.

"Going somewhere?" he asked suspiciously.

"You ready to–"

"Yeah. The se–"

"Don't interrupt me." he commanded.

We arrive at the interrogation room. I get right to the point.

"Your people are surrounding you," I explain. "this exact building. They are going to ambush you." I explained.

"Who is *they*?" the man said.

"The Society of Truth's Mafia. They know." I lied.

"Know what?" He asked.

"How corrupt you are." I lied again.

"And how do they know this information?"

"I don't know. The Mafia watches. Everyone is watched by the mafia."

"What Mafia? We don't have a Mafia." he chuckled.

"Oh yes we do." I laughed, trying to hide that he was correct. The man frowned, confused.

"Men, go. Gather the soldiers. We have to find this Mafia. I'll take him to his room." The man said hate in his eyes.

I noticed a drawer that was opened a smidge. I snuck over to the drawer, and opened it. My mouth dropped. It was a map navigating the building. I closed the drawer, turned and caught up with the man. The directions from my room to the back exit were: *Left, right, right, left, right, left, left, right. The rest of the way is straight.* We turned and walked until my legs got tired. Once we finally made it to the room, I sat by the door until the hallway was empty.

I hear stomping in the hallway and slowly rise from the ground, careful not to make any noise. I opened the door just enough so I could see. It seemed nobody was in the hallway. I rush out of the door, not daring to look back.

"Hey!" someone shouted.

I turn my head, terrified.

Safety. It was all I could think about.

"Stop!" the man yelled. Gunshots.

I looked down at my body. Not even a scratch. I round the last corner.

I was almost there. I could see the door. I opened it. The sun blinded me. I still ran as fast as I could. I won't stop. I thought to myself.

I run two miles, trying to get to the city. Green grass is everywhere: To my left, and to my right. But when I look forward, I see a city.

I make it to the city. I stopped, and gazed at the beautiful buildings. I haven't gotten a chance to enjoy the city in forever.

"Hey! You again!" I heard someone shout.

Go. A voice in my head said. I dashed into the alley, pushing and shoving people out of the way. Once in the alley, I walk slowly through the darkness. I see a dumpster. I hoped it was empty. I sprinted towards it, opened it and looked inside. It was empty. I went inside and closed my eyes. Not moving, not making a sound. *I might have to stay for a while.* I said to myself.

Destiny Lumpkin

Hi!! My name is Destiny Lumpkin. I was born November 24, 1999, Destiny Simone Lumpkin-Mosley, at Palms West Hospital. I recently continued from the eighth grade to the ninth grade. I was raised in Belle Glade, Florida, most of my life. All of my hobbies are to dance, sing, draw, and write. When I graduate high school in 2018, I want to go to college and major in journalism. And, after graduation, as an adult, I want to be a full-time journalist and a part-time singer or dancer. I've had a passion for writing since I was in the fourth grade. I like comedy, romance, drama books and movies. I really appreciate this Young Authors Program, because I discovered that I not only write short stories, I also write poetry.

I appreciate my Mom, Shresee Lumpkin, Grandma Dr. Genevia Boyd, my Godparents, Apostle Devonna and Broderick Tommie, also Sierra and Daron James for believing in me.

Reflections

The first week, I kind of didn't know what to write. It was sort of like writer's block. The second day of the program, though, we went on a field trip to Don Estridge High Tech Middle School, where we met the other young authors, took pictures, and we did meet author, Mrs. Zelda Benjamin, who shared her personal experiences with publishing several different ways, and gave some techniques and outlines for writing the Romance literature she writes. We also had a tour of Canon Solutions America where we learned about the printing process of a book. My writing became a little easier toward the end of the week.

Mr. Dwight Stewart, and Mr. Steve Alten were the poet and author, whose presentations we experienced by remote telecast during the second week. I learned a lot from them also. I was amazed at what inspired them to write their poems and books. Hard times, personal loss, family matters, all things are subjects for writing. I learned a lot about what I should do when I get writer's block. Through this program, I put my talents to use for the good and not bad. I really love this Young Authors program. I had so much fun exploring through writing.

Idols and Legends

Our idols and legends mean something
Sometimes not much
They are here for a season
And only their season they can be here for
Many legends like poet Maya Angelou
Idols like Kierra Sheard and Mary Mary
That's my opinion to say
So I'll let you decide yours
It's easy as pie as I would say
Just think, decide
Take a deep breath
And tell me who are your
Idols and Legends

You Don't Know Me

You don't know me
I'm that quiet kid from the back of class
We never talk
You see me pass in the halls without a sound
I am quieter than a mouse
When bullies come around I am the first to get hit
You stand and watch as if you are afraid
I'm always by myself pleasing no one but me
No one understands me
I often feel unwanted
Do I belong here
Can anybody hear me
Why do I feel invisible
I'm very creative you know
Why can't we be creative together
We can learn from each other
Just tell me what you think
Are you afraid of me
Why don't you like me
I don't bite
We'll accept you just like you are
being yourself is more popular than anything
You Don't Know Me

The struggle.... "I Remember The Time"

Growing up in a Christian family, my life has been a struggle. The things in my life aren't as perfect as I think they should be. I've had many struggles in life 'til I loss count. I've encountered many struggles in family loss. In fact on May 28, 2003, I dreamed that my uncle Feraris "Ray" Golden had sticks growing out of his head. I was three years old; I will never forget what happened. After waking up, telling my dream, they eventually found him hanging in a tree. In our back yard across from my bedroom window. August 7, 2007, I was at my cousin's house playing hide and go seek, when her neighbor got mad because he lost the game. He then made a rude comment about my grandma and Pa-Pa on my mom's side of the family. Five minutes later as I walked back home, I saw my mom speeding back to the house. When I finally got in the house my mom calmly said, "Destiny grandma just died today after surgery". I could do nothing but cry and reflect on what that boy said. Later on, on January 31, 2009, I was told by my mom and my Pa-Pa that my uncle Anthony Jarrod Kearse was shot dead. Sad thing about it I heard that all he was doing was taking out the trash. He was shot dead in his parent's yard. April of 2011, my auntie died of cancer. For one, she told everyone last minute. But, truth be told, I had my moments when I did her wrong, and now I really regret it. I have been told by multiple people that I have to forgive myself first and try to forget. From April 2011 to February 2014, I thought it was my fault that she had passed, but it wasn't; it was just her time to go. On December 25, 2013, I received a phone call from my dad stating that my other grandmother had passed. I saved her life in the summer if 2009, so she'd say, if she were still here. Before her death she had a heart attack, went into a coma, then became brain dead. So people had already begun to give the title of being dead. Her situation was so serious to the point where I was too scared to go to the hospital to see her. I kept thinking that maybe if I would have done this or that, then she'd still be here, but I realized it was also her time to go. The struggle with me is that I let so called friends talk me into doing things I know GOD wouldn't approve of, and I bring shame to myself. Like, I recently lied to one of my god-moms, who is a pastor. When she confronted me I came clean and told her the truth. That was the first time I had ever lied to her in my life. Just because a stupid friend dared me to do it. At some point in life everyone's going to see that not every friend is a good one. I've learned to stick with the good patch of friends and not the sour patch. You never know what good and bad come within a friend, but today I tell you to start choosing them wisely.

Samantha Marshall

"And by the way, everything in life is writable about if you have the outgoing guts to do it, and the imagination to improvise. The worst enemy to creativity is self-doubt."
– Sylvia Plath

Hey, I'm Sam, born and raised in North Palm Beach Florida for (almost) fifteen years. I'll be a Communications sophomore at Dreyfoos School of the Arts this fall, and will be spending the rest of the summer making up for two lost weeks of getting ready for the school swim season- you know, the important things. Writing is for nerds.

I'd like to show my appreciation to Ms. Adamo and Poettis for making me into the flawless writer I am today. Without them, I'd still be just ok. This is my second time attending this program, and it's always amazing to meet so many great people who love to write. People always say I'm quiet- I say I make up for that with my sparkling personality and hot bod. Kidding. They're probably right, which is why writing is an important outlet for me to express myself with. So a big thank you goes to this program and the people who give their time to help improve young writers!

Reflection

Week 1:

Week one was productive; I finished a short story and helped to edit many promising pieces. That said, hands down the best part of the week was getting lost on the way to Canon. There is a bond formed between those who spend a grueling thirty minutes crammed together on a bus, stranded in some parking lot far from home. We were moments away from deciding who we would have to eat first to sustain ourselves, but such measures were rendered unnecessary when our editors lead us to our destination, where we could strengthen the bonds wrought by trauma by learning about every printer known to man.

Week 2:

This week I continued to help the writers edit their work. It's so amazing to see all the improvement in their finished pieces. I also finished a descriptive essay. We've had several great writers come in to speak with us, as well as many quality conversations about The Goonies. I think everyone has had a great time as well as become more prolific in their writing. I always leave the workshop excited to apply what I've learned to all my future endeavors and I hope all of the writers whose work I helped edit will do the same and continue to improve.

Bite The Bullet

"I already said, I'm not going to shoot you." Laurie crosses her arms and glares at the boy sitting across from her.

"Stop being boring," Jordan says, still holding his fingers out in a mock gun. He jerks them up. "You're dead!"

Laurie rolls her eyes. "Ok."

"Do you guys think we could maybe start our project?" Bradley says, wringing his hands.

The other two stare at him. He attempts a smile, his eyes shifting between the two of them. The dissonance of the classroom drills into his brain as the other fifth graders try to break the sound barrier.

"We will," Jordan says, now pointing his finger gun at Bradley.

"Oh, uh, I don't think we should waste time. My mama says guns are bad, I'm not supposed to play those games," Bradley says, holding up his hands. Jordan shoots him.

"I got you, the Russians have been defeated!" Jordan says.

"Russians?" Laurie says, drawing on her desk.

"Yeah, I don't know, I saw it on TV," Jordan says.

Bradley slides the rubric closer. "Let's choose a topic, guys."

"We should do bullying," Laurie says.

"Yeah! It'll be perfect," Jordan says. "Since we have Bradley."

"Yeah, he gets bullied all the time. We'll get a good grade for, like, helping him spread awareness," Laurie says.

"W-wait a second, I don't know if I-"

Jordan cuts Bradley off. "Remember that time Bradley's mom came to get him out of school, 'cause he peed his pants? Or when Claire watered our plant experiments with bleach so they all died, and Bradley had to go to the nurse 'cause he was crying so bad? We can do this easily!"

"You guys, I don't want-"

He's interrupted again by Laurie. "Yeah, let's get it done. Start writing about your experiences, Bradley."

"Listen! I really don't wanna do this!" Bradley says, twisting his fingers together. A ball of paper smacks into the side of his head. He flinches and picks it up, turning to the sound of laughter from the group beside them.

"Do you need this back?" He asks, holding it out.

They ignore him. He leans over to drop the paper in the recycling bin.

"Goddammit Bradley, see? You need this project," Laurie says.

Bradley hurries to cross himself, eyes widening at the slur. "Ok… if you say so." He starts to write. "You don't think that, um, writing something like this will make it worse?"

"How would it do that?" Jordan asks, flicking pieces of paper at Laurie, who just repeats in monotone for him to stop.

"I don't know, but we've gotta present it to the class, and I just think it'll make things worse, to call attention, you know…"

"Do you wanna keep getting pushed around or not? Just write the paper!" Jordan gives his next piece of paper a particularly exuberant flick. It sails over Laurie and bounces off their teacher's head like a basketball off a balding backboard. He looks up from his computer screen, eyes latching onto Bradley.

Jordan stifles a laugh as Bradley wilts in his chair.

"Bradley, you're supposed to be writing an essay, not messing around," Mr. Kramer says.

"I-I'm not, I mean I am, er, I'm working!"

"Mhm. Which is why this is on my desk." Mr. Kramer drops Jordan's paper missile on Bradley's desk.

"That's not mine, I-"

"Bradley, have you been watching too much TV? You think this is funny, hm? You like being a disruption?"

Bradley feels his palms start to sweat. He wipes them up and down his pants as his face heats up. "No, sir, my mama says TV is from the devil."

Mr. Kramer shakes his head. His eyebrows arch up, forehead creasing like a pressed shirt. "Bradley, you've interrupted class for the last time, come with me."

"I said stop shooting me, asshole!"

"Laurie!" Mr. Kramer's attention snaps from Bradley to her.

"He keeps trying to play guns and I said stop!" She flips Jordan off with both hands.

"You two, office, now," Mr. Kramer says. "What have I said about violence and language in the classroom?"

"But that time the textbook fell on your foot, you said-"

"Do you backtalk your parents like this? Where'd you learn to talk like that?"

"It's ok Mr. Kramer, my daddy calls my brother an asshole all the time, I didn't hear it on TV," Laurie says.

"Come on. Up. Get to the office; I'm having your parents called."

"Uh, sir, do I gotta present all by myself now…" Bradley trails off, wishing he'd kept the attention off himself.

"Is that going to be a problem? Are you unable to read your own paper? Maybe you got one of these two to write it for you, is that it?"

"No sir! I mean, uh, of course I can!"

As Mr. Kramer leads his partners into the hall, Bradley works on steadying his breathing and finishing his paper.

The other groups begin to present. As they speak, the dread in his stomach curdles, making him feel sick. He wrings his hands and fixes his eyes on the girl reading at the front of the class.

She holds the paper in shaky hands, while the boy beside her folds his arms behind his back and stares out at the classroom, as though daring them to doubt the authenticity of his confidence. The third girl makes faces and giggles as though she isn't facing off against an unforgiving sea of peers.

By the time his name is called, Bradley is wishing for the wail of the school fire alarm, an alien invasion, a nuclear detonation-anything but standing before the condemning gaze of a classroom full of ten-year-olds.

He's sure his legs will give way, but he makes it to the front of the class. The paper shakes in his hands like laundry hung out in a hurricane.

"Ok, Bradley, let's hurry this up, we've only got a few minutes to the bell," Mr. Kramer says. The teacher has his head propped on his hand, eyes lidded. He taps a finger on his desk.

"Um, sir, I'm really not feeling well," Bradley says, blinking under the fluorescent lights which suddenly seem unbearably garish.

"Please, Bradley, just try and get this done, class is almost over."

"Ok, well, m-my paper is on bullying. I got b-bullied into writing this paper, and um, now I'm g-getting bullied into reading it," he says, staring at said paper as though it could spare him from Mr. Kramer's narrowing eyes. He's gotten that look before, always preceding a trip to the principal, usually for taking the fall for someone else. His stomach lurches like a car going sixty slamming to a halt.

"Is he gonna puke?" One of the kids says.

"Bradley, I'm not sure where you're coming from in this essay, but I think you need to take a seat and collect yourself," Mr. Kramer says.

Bradley nearly laughs, because now that the opportunity to take a seat has presented itself, he finds himself immobilized. Self-awareness kicks his perspiration into overdrive. If he could only speak, he could salvage this- but they've already picked him apart, past skin to the squishy vulnerability of his insides, every pressure point pressed with their eyes. Every paralyzed second brings him further from being able to save face, and it's this realization that sends him dashing to the garbage can, hurling up the contents of his stomach. Orange juice and whole wheat toast taste worse in reverse.

"Jesus Christ," Mr. Kramer mutters, hurrying to Bradley's side.

"Sir?" Bradley's voice wavers. "I don't wanna get grounded, could you not call my mama about this?"

He was quick to learn that not calling wasn't an option. Mr. Kramer wasn't going to pass up the opportunity to tell his mother Bradley had been "making some wise remarks" before throwing up.

The chair outside the nurse's office is scratchy on his legs. His skin is no longer hot and flushed, but clammy and pale isn't much better.

"So. You threw up," Jordan says.

Bradley stares with watery eyes across the hall, at his former partners, seated outside the principal's office. Traitors, the both of them. He doesn't nod, still woozy and not looking for a repeat performance of the past several minutes.

Instead, he says, "Are you two in a lot of trouble?"

Jordan's eyebrows draw together. "Yeah. My mom's probably not gonna let me play Call of Duty all week."

Laurie tilts her head, staring at Bradley. "Don't cry. That's why people pick on you. You wanna come over and watch my TV this weekend?"

Bradley shrugs. "I guess I'll be in the office either way."

The following Monday, the three of them are ready for take two of their presentation.

Jordan bounces the tennis ball he brought to school while he looks over their essay. "Bradley, this is all about how we bully you, that's not what you were supposed to talk about!"

"You told me to write about my experiences with bullying, so I did!"

"We can't present this!" Jordan says.

Laurie huffs and pins both boys with her gaze. "I can't believe I let you watch my TV. And you, stop bouncing that stupid ball!" She snatches it from Jordan and tosses it away.

It flies well higher than its intended trajectory, knocking into the overhead projector.

"Aw Laurie, why'd you have to do that," Jordan hisses, watching with wide eyes as Mr. Kramer stalks up to them.

"Bradley? You want to explain why you're throwing things in class?"

Bradley holds in a whimper. "I didn't-" he looks at his partner's faces. He'd really thought they were starting to like him, especially Laurie. He sighs. "Sorry... I guess you're gonna call my mama again?"

"Wait! That wasn't Bradley, I threw it!" Laurie says. Her eyes widen and she snaps her lips shut. They open partially as though trying to take the words back, before closing in a line.

"Mhm. That's why the ball has Jordan's name on it," Mr. Kramer says, holding it up. "Right. Both of you, office, now."

"Oh goddammit, not this again," Bradley mutters. The memory of standing in front of the class all alone is enough to make the familiar queasy feeling return.

"What did you just say, Bradley? Do you want to speak up?" Mr. Kramer says.

"I said, goddammit, it was me, not them!" Bradley says. He tries not to falter on the curse, and keeps his hands clasped in his lap.

Mr. Kramer doesn't need to be told twice. Bradley casts his partners a small grin before being led out of class.

"Wow, you know, Bradley's alright," Jordan says.

Laurie's smile is faint and she's quick to push it down. "Yeah, he gave us the privilege of getting to read this paper about how we're the biggest bullies in school."

"Oh…you're right, no way! Do you…do you think we could make ourselves throw up?" Jordan says.

Laurie shakes her head. "We'll just have to hurry and rewrite it before we have to go. Or else Mr. Kramer's gonna call your mom and tell her how mean you are. You probably won't get to play Call of Duty for at least a month."

Jordan's eyes widen. He snatches the paper and begins crossing out lines, scribbling new ones in the cramped margins.

Laurie leans back in her seat and starts to doodle on her desk.

Distraction

The room appears washed out and pale under the fluorescent lights, mirroring its inhabitants. The yellow walls are nearly white, casting milky cream glow across the tiles. It reflects in the eyes of those seated in the ICU waiting room as they fixate on their shoes.

All noise is hushed and seems to buzz in the background like radio static, as though too loud a commotion could trigger some waiting tragedy down the hall. As though a raised voice would make aware to some malevolent deity the handful of existences teetering towards cessation just steps away. There are murmurs, the drone of the man on his phone just outside the door, the click of the lady at the desk's lacquered nails over her tablet as she wills away the time between calling visitors in through the door behind her, like Hade's ferryman. The black telephone beside her holds the room and its hush in orbit- its ring is a gunshot, causing every head to turn towards the noise, to see where the bullet will find its mark. A name is called and a seat vacated, leaving not a dent or a crease in the stiff green chair. The chairs are situated around a low table, on top of which sit Styrofoam cups cradling the last swallows of tepid coffee.

The waiting room slides back into stagnation. The silence left after the ring is swallowed by the hum of the vending machine in the corner and the whir of the air conditioning. The television on the wall talks to itself, vapid commercials flickering on its screen. In the absence of human noise, it is just machines, conducting an electrical conversation.

Those seated rub their shaky hands along their arms, perhaps to force warmth into the goose-bumps on their skin, perhaps in an attempt to wipe off the smell of antiseptic that seeps through the walls. The smell curls up in their nostrils, taking up permanent residence.

There are no windows, just the egg-yolk color of the walls and the brown doors. Each person has a white sticker printed with their name and photo clinging to their shirt. They peel at the edges, exposing sticky backs covered in fuzz. There is a narrow table beneath the wall-mounted television, supporting a mini-fridge and a scattered pile of magazines, their pages yellow around the edges. One of the room's two doors is adjacent to this display of attempted distraction, the second behind the telephone on the desk.

At the sound of the first door banging open, those seated give a collective jump as a gurney is pushed by steady-handed doctors in pale green scrubs. It is empty, and they pass by without eye-contact, leaving only the cluttered sound of their footsteps and the gurney's wheels running over the tiles in their wake. The second door slams shut, leaving echoes to reverberate around the room. The door clicks, throwing out another muted sound, letting the waiting room swallow it up.

Isabella Martins-Simonsen

Greetings all! My name is Isabella and I am fourteen years old. I am entering West Boca Raton High School as a ninth grader to begin the medical program. I was born and raised in Boca Raton, Florida, but my roots are more exotic—my mother is from Brazil and my father is Norwegian. I am bilingual and speak English and Brazilian Portuguese fluently. I write, obviously, but I also play the flute and draw occasionally. I want to work in the medical field and psychology especially. I am a big fan of felines and have a cat named Kaya. I live with my mom, dad, and little brother Jan Erik.

Reflection

Week 1:
When I came into the Workshop, I did not expect this AT ALL. I thought we'd just sit and talk about our writing styles before writing a full book each (although that seems quite extravagant, looking back). Not to mention, I thought it would be much easier to finish a piece.

Week 2:
I had no idea time could pass so quickly. Seriously, it's already Thursday, how did this happen? I am very glad I came here, my writing has most definitely improved (and I learned that my descriptions are "really good")

Music

A whole school's year had gone into this. Into this intricate, organized jumble of sound and emotion. Three years had gone into its foundation, into the ability to make black lines and circles on white paper air and notes and music. The song is twisting and complex, a swirling jumble of rests and beats. The fingers of the players fly, turning marks into notes and emotion as the song flows forward. There is no time for anyone to think the letters the dots-on-lines mean—only time to turn them into air and fingers over buttons.

The constants of wind instruments blend with the periodic punctuations of percussion. The flute's solo passes in moments, the sweet melody giving way to the bright brass of the trumpets. Then the song changes. Deep, ominous notes come from the tuba as the flutes chime in with high, sharp, jagged pitches. The constant thunder of the drums pound in the air.

The tempo accelerates by twenty, thirty beats. The eerie melody paints a grim picture—a tiny raft surging in a stormy sea. The music rises to its ultimate height. The music crashes to its final crescendo, the tiny raft trembling atop the massive wave before capsizing. The work of the band is not yet finished, their spell not fully woven. They bring the song to its close, three final notes completing the trap of lines and circles and sound.

They close their folders and leave the stage, murmurs of the music's sound escaping. The melody rings still, rising and falling and crashing, traces of the spell it wove lingering in the air.

Gary Merisme

I was born on October 3rd, 1998 in Brooklyn, New York. My parents, my little sister, and I moved to Bristol, Connecticut in March 2001. We moved again to Florida in September 2003. I went to Del Prado Elementary and Don Estridge Middle. I will be a sophomore this year at Atlantic High.

I really enjoy the game of basketball. I am on the basketball team at my school. I like to watch games and play NBA 2K video games. I do not see myself being a professional writer, but I do enjoying writing poetry and "rap" songs for my friends.

Reflection

Week 1:

This week was OK. It definitely was not as hard as my first week last year. I started working on my poem on the first day. The purpose of the poem remained the same, but I went through a couple different ways of presenting the poem. By Wednesday I knew how I was presenting the poem. On Thursday I helped Juan with his poem. It was kind of big to me because Juan edited my poems last year and this year. Now I was helping him. It shows how I've grown as a poet.

Week 2:

This week was good. I finished my poem on Wednesday. I am OK with having just one piece for the book. This was my first year mentoring. I think I did a pretty decent job helping people. I just made sure that I sent the people I helped to Juan so that if I made a mistake, he could correct it.

Insidious Influences

My friend, a fledgling oak, in a park, growing
Before him, life, his lack of wisdom showing
Allowing weed and vine too close in distance
Discerning not, seduced by coexistence
Soon unfirm roots are seized, leaves and limbs crippled.
A would-be broad and strong trunk is now brittle.

Depleted nutrients, decaying young tree
As leech-like plants aid in degeneracy
Impartial wind sent by blind Mother Nature
She neither punishes vile instigators
Nor pities the naivety of young oaks.
Tree toppled by gusts, parasites move to new hosts.

Elysia Ngo

"There is no greater agony than bearing an untold story inside you."
– Maya Angelou, *I Know Why the Caged Bird Sings*

My name is Elysia Ngo. I was born in Rhode Island fourteen years ago on December 18th. Living with three younger siblings is usually quite a handful, so what other way to escape the chaos than to write? To dive into another life, another world. I have been interested in writing for about as long as I can remember accompanying my love for reading. In third grade, my teacher couldn't even hand me books fast enough as I devoured them all just as quickly. It was also in third grade when I began writing my first book (that I'm now completely embarrassed of). I've started, but never finished, several books so finally finishing a piece to be published is a great accomplishment for me and will hopefully lead to more completed stories. In the future, I aspire to be either a fiction book writer or an editor. Perhaps I'll be able to do both. I like to think of being able to write as my gift. Some people are good at sports, some excel in academics. Me? I'm a writer. Writing is my way of putting my voice out into the world, my way of releasing my untold stories. From writing essays on why I should get my nose pierced to books that may one day be bestsellers, writing is my passion.

Reflection

Week 1:

After we introduced ourselves and went over the expectations, we were all hard at work beginning our first pieces. It was very productive for me, I learned a lot and finished my first bio sketch. Our first speaker was author, Mrs. Benjamin who told us about self-publishing. On Wednesday, which was also media day, we took a trip to Canon with Glades and talked a little about the publishing process and had the opportunity to view a variety of printers. The rest of the week was spent writing, in shock at how quickly the first week went by.

Week 2:

Three speakers visited us during the course of week two. Mr. Stewart shared his poetry, Ms Tormo talked about working with a magazine, and Mr. Alten spoke about his many books. We quickly finished up our work as the end of the program arrived. After several drafts, I finally completed my short story with a huge smile on my face as I got approved.

The Fangirl

I could see the anticipation dwelling in her eyes as her beloved band steps forward onto stage to play the last song, her favorite song. Her stare is fixated on the lead singer who picks up the microphone then questions crowd's satisfaction. Thousands of avowed fans respond in waves of cheering, she contributes.

Catching her gaze, I note how her eyes glisten in the midst of glow sticks and cellphones. It was like looking into the sky full of stars, the brightest one being her eyes. Her pupils dilating to the quick changes in lighting. The outer edges of her eyes crinkle when she smiles like the crisp pages of your favorite book. She breaks to glance in my direction beaming, dimples form craters perfectly indented in rosy cheeks.

As the final song begins, her arms ascend at the request of the band. There were noticeable goose bumps up and down her arms; the music rumbling beneath her skin causing mounds of excitement to arise. Suddenly not caring, she dances along with the rhythm of the music, her body moving fluidly and smoothly as if the ensemble of sounds had traveled into her nervous system and claimed dominance. She gave in to the music's persistence allowing it to take control. I watched as her hips swayed, a feather falling, influenced by the wind. Balancing on petite toes were the perfect pair of legs in agreeable proportion to the rest of the figure. When the beat picks up momentum, they decide to take action and intertwine with one another in a series of energetic motions.

The song comes to a conclusion; all the muscles in her face and body loosen. After another burst of screams and claps echoes throughout the stadium, she unbinds herself from the craziness she was so captured in for the last three minutes.

Real Gold

"I still can't believe we found all this." Christian cups a handful of gold in his hands, a few coins slipping between his fingers.

"And they told us it was just a myth! Ha!"

"Christian! Ash! You can't go out there. Everyone who ventures out there goes missing!" He snickers, mimicking our friends who had told us it was unsafe. They'll laugh once they find out how easy it was for us.

We had traveled to this island a few miles away from our home just yesterday to find the treasure that was rumored to be hidden here. It only took us a couple hours to dig up the treasure in the middle of the island, concealed only by sand and a plainly marked 'X.'

"I can't wait to show everybody," I say with a smile. And by everybody, I mean my friends. My parents died when I was only three, searching for this treasure. I fiddle with the charm bracelet that used to be too large for my wrist, a variety of charms dangling from it and a locket with a photo of me and my parents.

"Aright, the boat's just over there," he says, picking up the heavy box containing the jewels.

We make our way through the thick foliage. Something tightens around my ankle and my legs are suddenly pulled out from under me. The trees are hanging from the sky, my head about an inch above the ground.

Christian comes up behind me. "How ya hanging in there, Ash?" He smirks. "How did you possibly manage to get tied up like that?"

"Do you really think I did this to myself?" I blow a strand of hair out of my eyes.

He stepped forward. "It's a trap."

"What?"

"Someone must've set a bear trap or something."

"Pretty sure there are no bears on this island."

"Monkeys?"

"I don't really care. Just help me out."

The blood is now rushing to my head, causing me to feel

lightheaded. I swing my body upward and grab the rope.

"Well, speaking of monkeys!"

"Ugh. Christian, do you still have that pocket knife?"

"Why, yes I do." He whips it out and saws it quickly against the rope. It takes a few minutes before he even makes a tear in it.

I hum the Jeopardy theme song. "Need any help?"

"Are you questioning my skills? I was a Cub Scout for, like, five years." He stretched his torso to make himself look even taller and raised his head.

I snatch the knife from him anyway and proceed where he left off. I immediately rip the rope, releasing myself.

"You cheated!" Christian said.

"Whatever you say." I hand him back his knife, untie the excess rope that was still tied around my foot, and put the rest in my pocket.

"Why keep it?"

"There's a good five feet of rope here and besides, anything could happen."

After about two miles of traveling to the boat I'm overcome by a feeling of emptiness and realize something's missing just as we approach the shore. My bracelet.

"Um…Christian?"

"Yeah?"

"We need to go back."

"Why?"

"Well, I kind of left something."

"More rope?"

"Haha, funny. No, my bracelet."

He looked at me with wide eyes and started back toward the center. The sky was already darkening so we hike as quickly as we can manage with the 20 pound box slowing us down.

He screams. A really loud, girly scream.

"Jesus, you sound like a little girl."

"Don't. Move," he says. His eyes were popping out of their sockets.

I follow his stare to the ground in front of us. A 30 foot long, 200 pound anaconda was blocking our path only a few feet ahead, its body forming a large 'S.'

I try to speak as quietly as possible. "It won't bother you if you walk away."

He moves abruptly, pulling out the pocket knife in case he needed to defend himself squeezing the treasure box between his chest and free hand. Great, Christian, what's a tiny pocket knife going to be against an anaconda that size?

The snake jolted its head in our direction, staring at us. Christian's mouth was open, his hands were starting to quiver.

"Come," I say and try to pull him by his sleeve, away from the creature.

"We have to leave now, I really need this treasure." His voice was stern.

"But why?"

"You know exactly why."

"Is this about your brothers? Your dad?"

"Yes, you have no idea what it's like being the pathetic one. I'll never be as smart as Brandon or as athletic as Alexander."

"You don't have to prove anything."

"I do. I want to show him I can be something more than just employee of the month at that rusty old diner."

"Fine. You can wait here and I'll get my bracelet myself." I go away, hiding my tears. I don't know why I'm even crying. "You're not the only one with parents you don't want to disappoint," I say, too quietly for him to hear. When I glance back, he's trailing behind me. There were dark circles under his hallowed eyes. He catches up and I grasp the treasure chest from him, releasing a bit of weight off his body and continue on.

"Thanks," he says.

The center finally comes into view after about twenty more minutes. We must've walked around the entire island because we were entering the center from a different side. I could see where I got bear trapped on the other side and where we found the treasure chest buried yesterday.

"Do you see my bracelet?"

"Nope, I'll look over here."

I bury myself in a nearby bush with only the goal of finding my jewelry in mind.

"Found it," he calls out, five minutes later.

I would've run to retrieve my valued bracelet but I was held back by the weight of the treasure box. I was distracted by thoughts of my parents when I realized either I was getting shorter or everything else was getting taller. I feel something spongy and fluid-like consume my leg. When I looked down, I saw that I was now standing knee deep in quicksand.

"Christian! Help!" His feet pound on the ground as he runs to my rescue. The more I wiggle my body the more I sink. The treasure was only getting heavier.

"Ash! Stand still." He was frantically pacing around the quicksand, his eyes wide.

"I think you're the one that needs to stand still," I say. I keep calm for Christian's sake, taking a deep break to relax.

"Ash, your rope!"

Finally, an intelligent idea from him, I thought. I try to hold onto the treasure with just my right hand so I can grab the rope from my back pocket but it slips under the weight. I quickly catch it with my other hand.

When Christian sees me struggling, I saw his expression change; all traces of optimism drained from his face, replaced with hopelessness. The sand was up to my thighs now.

"Hand me the box."

It slips from my hand before it reaches his, falling directly into the quicksand. I try to grab it but I only find myself sinking deeper. It's too low for Christian to be able to grab it without falling in with me.

"Let's get you out first," he says, ignoring the treasure.

I take the rope out of my back pocket and throw one side to Christian. His veins pop out against his skin as he uses all the strength he has left to pull me out.

When I'm finally standing on solid ground, I turn to fetch the treasure, but it's been devoured by the island.

"I'm sorry," I said.

He embraces me in a tight hug. "The real treasure's my best friend."

"What a sap." I smile at him.

"Let's go home."

Je'Cynthia Nonor

"If you can make it through the night there's a brighter day,"
-Tupac Shakur

My name is Je'Cynthia Nonar and these are the words I live by. I'm an upcoming sophomore at Glades Central High School, and because of this, I feel as if I have to work twice as hard to be successful. Writing is a way that I can express my feelings. Through my writing, I have learned a lot about myself and how I see the world around me.

Reflections

The past two weeks were very eventful, and I really liked it because I had the experience to interact with kids from other schools. I also loved the way we received individual help from our mentors, and had the chance to improve our techniques.

Nothing Was Ever the Same

Blood was everywhere.
The lifeless body in arms seemed unreal,
But reality would soon kick in.
He was gone.

I wanted to cry, but no tears would escape.
I looked into my brother's dull eyes
That were once so luminous.
The police officer asked me to move,
But my legs wouldn't obey.
    I wanted to scream,
But my voice had vanished.

How could my brother,
The one I loved,
The one who looked after me,
Be gone?
A bullet in his chest
Knocked the wind out of him, literally.
Cold spread throughout his body like a virus,
But it was almost as if
The boy who lay in front of me,
Was a stranger.

Remember Me

I am fifteen
And I wonder why
I don't look like girls in the magazines
Or have a smile like a fashion queen
If I should die before I wake
What would you say, so that
People remember me as someone so great?

Everyone has stuff going on
While I sit in my room thinking deep thoughts
Some things in my life are going wrong
But if I'm called home at the drop of a dime
And I'm gone at the blink of an eye
What would you say, so that
People remember me as someone so great?

When I'm gone life will go on,
For you of course
Could you honestly say that we were friends?
And remain that way beyond the end
What would you say, so that
People remember me as someone so great?

Emily Pacenti

"Minority is about being an individual. It's like you have to sift through the darkness to find your place and be that individual you want to be your entire life."
– Billie Joe Armstrong

My name is Emily Pacenti and I am fourteen years old, an incoming ninth grader to Dreyfoos School of the Arts and a Don Estridge veteran. My two biggest passions are music and literature, my favorite bands consisting of Green Day, The Pretty Reckless and The Arctic Monkeys while my favorite authors are John Green, Stephen King, and (another Stephen) Stephen Chbosky. Those aren't the only ones but, they are the first ones to come to mind. I'm not too interesting of a person but, as a writer, I'm going to try and make myself sound fascinating. I play guitar, bass, and piano but am currently a guitarist in a rock band called Bad Reputation (don't laugh at the name, we love Joan Jett) We play small gigs around Boca at places like Packy's Sports Bar, or Biergarten in Mizner Park, that Ovation Studios organizes and schedules for us. We mostly do covers but, we're hoping to branch out into some originals soon.

My interest in writing mostly comes from my parents, who both work in journalism. My dad is a reporter and while he thinks I don't read his work too often, he has a shoe box full of his old writing that I love to go through. I was also inspired a lot by the books I read. Novels such as Will Grayson Will Grayson, It's Kind of a Funny Story, Perks of Being a Wallflower, and anything by Stephen King or John Green always make me want to write and I'd like to write my own book for young adults one day so we can have just a few more options outside of the vampire romance realm.

Reflection

Week 1:

The first week of the program went by in a blur. We got to meet so many amazing people that I hope to see again next year and I learned so much about the writing process in my first four days.

Week 2:

The second week was a scramble of semi-organized chaos. I finished my final piece on the very last day of the program and am currently writing this in the last four hours we have here. If there's one thing I learned this week, *it was time management.*

Musician

His hands alone captivate an entire audience. The things he can do with them are a product of years of hard work and dedication to his craft. With a single instrument, he can direct a crowd.

His fingers slide elegantly down the sleek neck of the guitar, contradicting their appearance. The tip of each finger is rough and callused. Tiny blisters and lacerations scatter them. Red skid marks are imprinted upon each digit where the rough textures of the strings have marked him. The edge of the hand that strums is a bright pink color, lightly burned from the ferocity with which he hits the strings. His knuckles are bruised and sore; a result of long periods of practice and in the webbing between his index finger and thumb was a small cut where the neck of the guitar had dug in.

The guitarist's movements are completely erratic, driven by the rhythmic thrashing of his band mates. His shoulders ache from the weight of his instrument, but his arms never cease to move. They extend from the ripped sleeves of his white t-shirt, his biceps flexing each time he strums. A prominent vein is visible in his forearm, seeming to throb each time he strikes the strings and a thin pink line occupies the other arm, a minor wound received when a string had snapped.

His feet tap on the hardwood floor of the stage with each hit of the drums, following the fluctuating rhythm without losing a beat. 1. 2. 3. 4. Over and over so that his hands knew exactly when to play each individual note. The worn and beat up black Converse barely hold together, the frayed laces threatening to fall apart as the material stretched and strained with his foots constant motion. The end of the song approaches and he positions his foot over the pedal required for the final note, a red rectangular button that will prolong the length of any note played while stepping on it. He waits for the lead singers count and slams his foot down on it, striking the final note of the song and letting it ring out until it faded and no other sound remained but feedback and the sounds of their screaming audience.

A Cemetery Conundrum

Scalpel?"

"Right here."

He took the tool from his apprentice and stared at the body on the table, considering what step they should take next. "How much formaldehyde did you use?"

"None yet, but I already injected the solution into his arteries."

"Alright good. Finish this one up for me. I'll be back down later."

Ricky nodded and took the scalpel from his father's hand, positioning it at the body's navel so that he could make the incision needed for the trocar to be inserted. "Don't worry, I got it."

"Don't kill anyone while I'm gone." He said with a smile.

"No worries, Dad." Ricky chuckled. He waited for him to leave and then put himself right to work, intent on doing a good job with this one. Ricky's family had been running a funeral home for generations and he was itching to take it over. His father was a decent embalmer at best, but a completely incompetent funeral director, always forgetting the details when it came to giving someone a proper service. Depending on how the next funeral went, he was planning on asking his father about taking over soon.

He set the scalpel aside and walked over to the end of the table, parting the legs of the body that happened to belong to a deceased seventy year old man. His nose crinkled at the smell of chemicals and decay. This was the worst part. Ricky took a small metallic pump and began an invasive process that should probably not be thoroughly described.

He was just er… inserting the pump when his phone began to buzz in the pocket of his lab coat and he reached one gloved hand into his pocket to answer. "Hello?"

"Hey what's up Ricky?" A male voice asked from the other end of the line, prompting him to roll his eyes and continue his work.

"What is it, Alex?" He asked, balancing the phone between his cheek and shoulder. "I'm kind of a foot deep in someone's ass right now."

"Jesus."

"What? I told you not to call me while I'm working."

"I'm just bored. I didn't really expect you to be taking advantage of some poor dead guy. Do you have to do that to everyone?"

"Yup."

"Gross."

"Whatever." Ricky sighed, flicking the on switch of the pump. "Hey, listen, I've been meaning to call you. I might need your help with something. I'm gonna try and talk to my dad about taking over today, but if he doesn't go for it I'm gonna have to go out on my own."

"What, like your own personal embalming business?"

"Yeah." He shrugged. "Why not?"

"I don't know. Maybe 'cause you're twenty-two and wanting to stick metal poles up old dudes' asses isn't exactly the best aspiration? What do you even call a business like that? Ricky Butts' Anal Penetration. You kill 'em, we fill 'em."

"You know there's a little more to it than draining a person's bowels."

"Still. You're not gonna have a sustainable business model with a name like Ricky Butts Jr."

"So, I won't name it after myself. I'll think of a name later, who cares? I'm going to need your assistance anyways if he says no."

"With what? Sexually abusing the dead?"

"For the last time, it's part of the job." Ricky said, quickly removing the pump and putting it back in its holster, hoping he'd remember to clean it later. "Stop being weird. I can't do it on my own if he says no."

"What do you want me to do? There's no way I'm touching a dead body."

"You won't have to… probably. Just help me, I don't know, get customers if we end up going on our own. My dad's probably gonna pitch a fit when I ask him anyways. I'm just preparing for the inevitable."

"You're such a creep. Why am I your friend?"

"Look, I'm kind of in the middle of this. Can you call later or something?"

"Fiiiiine."

"And come to the funeral tomorrow. I'm kinda proud of this one and I might need your help talking to my dad."

"Come on." Alex whined. "It's so gross. I don't even know these people."

Ricky grimaced down at the body and used his free hand to close the man's legs again, really not needing to see that at the moment. "Just show up. He didn't have a lot of friends and we need to pack the church."

"Ugh, fine. You know, I'm getting pretty tired of us only hanging out at funerals."

"But you'll be there?"

"Yes." Alex sighed. "Only because I have nothing better to do."

"Awesome." Ricky smiled, grabbing the scalpel again. "Catch you later."

* * * * *

"Did you hear what they're saying?" Ricky whispered anxiously, tugging on the hem of Alex's t-shirt. "What do they think?" He looked around the room and tried to observe exactly how everything was set up. They were still in the middle of the wake so, elderly friends and family were wandering around the chapel, mostly focused on each other as opposed to the open casket at the altar. His father was at the front door, greeting people and it made him sweat just to think about approaching him. Ricky tugged on his collar and turned back to Alex. "Does it look okay? I want them to like it."

"Dude... when people come to a funeral, they're not exactly focused on how good a job you've done draining their loved ones' bowels."

"I told you to *ask*." Ricky sighed. "And for the last time, that's not the only part!"

Alex rolled his eyes and looked around the chapel, eyeing the various grieving friends and family members. Most of them were pretty old and he didn't want to give anyone a heart attack by asking how the corpse looked.

"I think the makeup is a little off… Maybe I should go fix it."

"Ricky you are *not* going to start nitpicking this poor man's appearance at his own funeral."

"What do you know?" Ricky glanced nervously at the open casket. "I didn't put enough blush on. He looks like a ghost… I'm gonna go fix it."

"Dude."

"I'll be quick. No one's even gonna notice." He started walking towards the coffin but Alex yanked him back.

"I am *not* letting you do that in front of everybody."

"Fine." Ricky huffed. "Distract them then."

"What?"

"Distract them while I fix the body. Go over to the side, so people are looking away from the coffin, and talk. Ask people how they're doing, assure them we'll be started soon, and if I need more time, pretend to be his grandson and say a quick few words about him."

"How am I supposed to do that? I don't even know the guy!"   "His name is Stephen Vance and he's a retired mailman. Take it and run with it."

"I'm *not* doing that."

"Suit yourself." Ricky shrugged, brushing past him to walk up to the front of the chapel, the side opposite of the casket. He looked out at the small crowd of people and cleared his throat to capture everyone's attention. "Hello everyone." He smiled. "Welcome to our chapel," he gestured to Alex, "This is Alex, the beloved grandson of Mr. Stephen Vance. Before we begin our celebration of his life, he would like to say a few words." He looked over at Alex and winked. "Go ahead."

Alex's face flushed red and he shook his head desperately until everyone in the room turned to the left to face him instead of the coffin and he found himself at the center of attention. "Y-Yeah, uh… Hi, everyone." Alex blushed, waving nervously as he began racking his brain for things to say. Anything.

Ricky quickly moved away from the crowd and focused his

attention on the coffin to examine the corpse. He slipped the small make up pad out of his jacket pocket and flicked it open with his thumb. It didn't have much, just the bare essentials alone, but it did have blush and that was all he needed. He took the tiny blush and quickly applied a thin layer of pink powder to the corpse's cheeks to keep his face from looking gaunt. The last thing he wanted was for his father to see the body without proper make up. He just hoped Alex would keep him distracted. He finished touching up the blush as best he could, slipped the makeup back into his pocket, and was about to pull away when he looked a little closer and sighed. The bow tie looked a little off.

Alex watched Ricky anxiously and stared with wide eyes at the small crowd of elderly men and women. "W-We uh are gathered here today to uh… Y'know, celebrate the life of Mr. Vance."

Ricky fumbled a little bit as he tried to fix the bow tie, but he just couldn't get it right and settled on untying it and starting over again. When they dressed a body, they cut open the back of the suit, but unfortunately, this rule did not apply to neck ties.

"As Ricky told you guys, he was my uhh… grandfather, I guess." He glanced over their heads at Ricky and suppressed a sigh. *He said he was only going to fix the makeup.*

Ricky carefully lifted the head so he could properly adjust the tie and quickly wrapped it back around the neck, placing it under the collar in a much neater fashion. Ricky took a step back and admired his work, assuming it was perfect until he looked up and saw the sloppy arrangement of the flowers. The standing flower arrangements behind the coffin were all bunched together and not to mention the theme was supposed to be roses and just roses. He was positive he could count at least three daisies in the mix.

"As you guys know he was also a retired mailman and I uh… I think that says a lot about what kind of a guy he was… Rain or shine he'd always y'know, deliver packages and stuff."

Ricky squeezed his way back behind the coffin and sucked in his gut so he could fit without knocking all the flowers over, grabbing the nearest arrangement so he could pluck out the few flowers that weren't roses.

"Even if it was snowing, or hailing, or windy, or uh, well I don't know, tornado-ing. He uh…" Alex clasped his hands together and took a deep breath just for emphasis. "He always delivered those packages."

Ricky stood on his tip toes to avoid taking up too much space as he rearranged the flowers, spacing them out evenly so that they looked nice behind the coffin. It was just getting a little difficult to keep his balance…

"He was a good man. They took him away just too damn soon." Alex sighed, trying not to look over at what his friend was doing, partially out of fear for what he might see.

Ricky fiddled around a little more with the flowers, plucking out bruised petals and sticking them in his pockets. The balls of his feet were aching from balancing on them but, he was almost finished. Just a few more adjustments…

Alex looked around at the faces of the various mourners. "I think we should all come together right now and sing Amazing Grace."

Ricky grabbed onto the side of the casket for balance and tried to tip toe his way out without messing up anything he had just fixed. He hopped over one of the stands, which was on a tripod structure that only made it hard to get past, landing on one foot with his right hand still grasping the handle on the coffin. There was one stand left and all he had to do was hop over it to get out from behind the trust but as soon as he jumped, something caught him. His shoe lace was stuck on the flower stand. "Shit!" Ricky yelped as he lost his balance and began to fall back, managing to grab one of the flower wreaths out of desperation before his back hit the side of the coffin and the whole thing went down.

There was a sickening crashing sound, followed by the screams of every elderly woman in the room as the coffin fell to the floor, ejecting the body and leaving it sprawled on the floor, half-naked due to the back of the suit falling open. The expensive cherry wood cracked and splintered upon impact, Ricky splayed out on top of it with a rose wreath around his ankle and the rest of the flower stands on top..

Well, he thought, *so much for taking over the business.* This was the end for him. There was a half-naked dead guy on the floor and if that didn't constitute a failed funeral than he didn't know what did. Ricky quickly kicked off the wreath pushed himself up and adjusted his suit as he stared at the crowd of people who had gathered in front of him. Alex was hiding his face in his hands and all the women seemed to either be frozen in shock or weeping at the body on the floor while the men simply stood still and gaped.

In the midst of all this, there was his father, standing dead center. The blood rushed to his cheeks and he cleared his throat once before speaking. "U-Umm… Hi Dad."

Callista Payne

"Who are you?"
"Who? Who is but the form
following the function of what and
what I am is a man in a mask."
"Well I can see that."
"Of course you can, I'm not
questioning your powers of observation,
I'm merely remarking upon the paradox of asking a masked man
who he is."

-V for Vendetta

Reflection

Week 1:

This week was… interesting, to say the least. It basically went like this.

Mon- Writing.
Tues- No, you aren't ALLOWED to write for more than a half hour because we're doing stuff today.
Wen- Writing
Thurs- Writing/Talking/I'm officially done with waking up early.

So, I wasn't exactly bawling at the end of the week (even though the intro that I spent the majority of the work working on was thrown out), which I assume is a good thing.

Now I would like to say that I met some cool people, but in reality I taught myself to hate the cool people that I already knew less (Aalisha, Paige, etc.).

Although, this year a lot of people listened to amazing music and wore fantastic shirts.

The author and field trip this week were enriching and entertaining, and a privilege to be a part of.

Week 2:
That's fun, isn't it? To return from a three day weekend, only to go to a school? That you won't actually be attending in the fall? IN THE SUMMER??!!??!!??!!

No.
No, it is not.
So I wasn't awake on Monday.

But hey, I got my story passed on Tuesday!!!
So we had speakers on Monday, Tuesday, and Wednesday, so that was fun! We gained knowledge inside of many aspects of a professional writing career, from people who pursued different types of writing.

In The Library

Sliding into the leather first class seat, Maya Banks instantly pressed the call button. She tapped her foot against the carpeted floor of the plane as a young man took a seat in the aisle next to her, looking her up and down as she crossed her two legs over one another.

"What're you headed to Florida for?" The man couldn't have been older than 35, and was slowly situating himself in his seat.

"My dad got sick," she said, poking her head out of the aisle to look for the stewardess.

"Sorry to hear about that," the man said, turning his body towards her to engage in conversation.

"Me too. I mean I seriously don't have enough time to take an entire week off work," She started bouncing her leg.

"What kind of work do you do?"

"Lawyer, elderly affairs,"

"No," he smirked at her. "You look like you'd do something a lot different."

She stopped bouncing her leg and turned her head towards him and raised her left eyebrow.

"Yes ma'am? Sorry for the wait," the nauseatingly polite stewardess finally arrived.

"I need a dirty martini," she said.

"Will that be all?"

"Yes. Wait, no. Make it a double."

The woman's smile faded as she turned to retrieve the beverage.

"So your dad's sick?" the man proceeded.

"Alzheimer's,"

The man hissed through his teeth. "That's a bad one," The plane started its lift off. "I'm Chris, by the way,"

"Maya,"

She shook the man's hand just as the woman came back with the vodka.

"Thank you," Maya said, before taking the glass. Swallowing a burning drink of the liquid, she relaxed gently into the seat.

"So about your dad," Chris said.

"Yeah, the ass doesn't call me in over a year, and decides that when he finally gets put into intensive care, he should have someone give me a ring. The nerve, right?"

He paused before responding. "Yeah, that uh, that's rude," his eyebrows scrunched together tightly.

"What about you," Maya started, sipping her drink "Why are you going to Florida?"

"Just a little vay-cay. Getting out of the house, away from the stress of work,"

"And what kind of work do you do?"

"Anesthesiologist,"

"Interesting job,"

"Takes concentration,"

Maya hummed softly, before shutting her eyes to avoid conversation. She heard the man sigh, and then move in his seat again with a grunt.

She collected her thoughts in the newly received silence; the blow of oxygen through the plane was the only noise to distract her. She took the time on the plane to rest.

As the plane would land in the late afternoon, closer to early evening, she would wait until the next day to go to the hospital.

By the time that she had woken up, the plane was landing, and a voice was speaking, giving instructions and thanking the passengers before they were allowed to exit safely. Lugging her suitcase off of the plane, Maya found her way through and out of the airport, pausing to drop her suitcase before waving her hand above her head to hail a cab.

"Four Seasons Hotel on Palm Beach," she said, opening her purse to find some cash as the car lurched forward and out of the Palm Beach International Airport pickup lane.

Unlocking her phone to keep up with work, pressing a few buttons until she opened her emails, reading and responding to those from her most urgent clients until the taxi stopped in front of the hotel. She handed the man the fare with a decent tip before going to the trunk to get her luggage. The cab sped away as Maya entered the hotel and checked into her room. A yawn erupted from her mouth as she exited the elevator, and when she opened the door to her room. She looked at the queen-sized bed, the mattress tantalizing her with the thought of sleep.

Stepping towards the window, she opened the curtains. Taking in a breath, she gazed over the ocean, the white sand burning with heat from the sun. The sight was breathtakingly beautiful.

Maya pulled the curtains shut. It was nice, but honestly, it's just nature.

Maya sat on the edge of the bed to kick off her shoes, then stood back up as she changed into something more comfortable to sleep in.

Turning off the main-light, she clambered into bed. Pressing the power switch on the bedside lamp, darkness consumed her.

The environment was fantastic for sleep, the blanket covering her figure as she drifted into bliss.

The next day she speedily dressed, and went downstairs to grab a quick cup of coffee before hailing another taxi and directing the driver to St. Mary's hospital.

One leg at a time, she hoisted herself out of the cab, and then bent her torso back into the car to give the driver his fare.

Striding to the automatic doors, Maya put her purse over her shoulder and directed herself to a reception desk that was positioned near the entrance.

"Maya Banks, I'm here to see Richard Banks," she said, leaning gently against the counter.

The woman tapped gently against her keypad. "Room 315," she said, still gazing at the computer screen in front of her.

Pushing herself off the counter, she moved swiftly to the elevator.

She entered the room to find a barely familiar man lying down on a hospital bed. Stubble of hair coated his chin and jawline. His skin tone was closer to that of a powdered donut than the soft peach he had passed down to Maya.

As she sat in one of the two chairs next to the man, he spoke, his voice in similar condition as his physical appearance.

"Who are you? Are you a nurse?"

"No," Maya leaned forward, blinking rapidly. "No, Dad, it's Maya,"

"Maya," her father laughed gently. "My daughter's name was Maya. Did you know my daughter?"

"No- yes, wait, Dad. It's me, it's," Her voice trailed off as her the focus of her eyes darted between his faded blue ones.

"You don't remember," she muttered to herself.

Bowing her head into her hands, she took a deep breath, exhaling heavily through her nose as she looked back up at her father.

"Yeah. Yeah I know her,"

"Well, that's good,"

He went quiet as the hum of air conditioning filled the room.

"You know what I wish this hospital had?"

"What?"

"A library,"

She stared at him and all went quiet once again; the air between them thick with silence and disinfectant.

She shut her eyes for a moment, simply stuck in the Sunday's of her past.

"What day is it?" her father asked.

"Tuesday,"

When he didn't further the conversation, Maya continued.

"I have a question,"

"I'll try to answer," his lips curled upwards.

"Why do you want a library in this hospital?"

"How did you know I wanted a library?"

"You told me?"

"I did?"

"Yes,"

"Oh,"

Emptiness fell upon them again, her question remained unanswered.

"Why do you want a library?"

His eyebrows scrunched together as he looked at her, tears

fumbling over the waterline of his eyes.

"Every Sunday I used to go to the library with my daughter. It was our church,"

"You remember," she whispered, barely louder than a whisper as tears spilled over onto her cheeks.

She remembered, too. Their 'church'. Where they worshipped Steve Hockensmith, J.K. Rowling, Poe, Paulini, and so many more, rather than some invisible omnipotent God.

Richard Banks stared at the wall behind Maya, a pleasant memory bringing a soft smile to his face. Richard Banks, who could remember his daughter, but not the woman in front of him.

No Strings Attached

Clenching his neck, Sarah threw his body against the wall with all of her strength. He collided painfully with the floor, screeching in agony. His neck fractured, his dismembered being becomes useless. She glared at him with absolute loathing.

"Why can't I ever play that piece right?" Sarah grumbled, walking away from the shattered guitar.

Triton Payne

"Voilà! In view, a humble vaudevillian veteran, cast vicariously as both victim and villain by the vicissitudes of fate. This visage, no mere veneer of vanity, is a vestige of the vox populi, now vacant, vanished. However, this valorous visitation of a bygone vexation stands vivified, and has vowed to vanquish these venal and virulent vermin vanguarding vice and vouchsafing the violently vicious and voracious violation of volition. The only verdict is vengeance; a vendetta held as a votive, not in vain, for the value and veracity of such shall one day vindicate the vigilant and the virtuous. Verily, this vichyssoise of verbiage veers most verbose, so let me simply add that it's my very good honor to meet you and you may call me V." -V for Vendetta

Week 1:

This first week propelled its self startlingly quickly. I managed to have the same story approved until further thought was given, demanded a pre-story be given and then have said "pre" emphasis on "pre" story be worked into the body of the work rather than in the head of it. Extremely stressful, but ultimately worth.

Week 2:

The second week was a blur. I edited more work in the span of three hours than I thought possible. I hardly could comprehend how fast everything was moving, one minute I would sit down and then four hours would pass. It's incredible how quickly the perfunctory workings of time can pass.

Worth It

"You've got 5 minutes,"

I look at my team, "You heard the lady, move!"

Our team breaks off into two teams- one of three and one of two. I'm with Bean. I get moving; the other three can find a good place to hide. That's why they're my team.

My feet thud rhythmically against the dirt road. This feels good-the air, the burn, the chase. I pause to note where Bean is. She runs up nearly out of breath, pushing aside a stray strand of auburn hair.

"I need to run more," she puffs.

I chuckle.

"Through here," I gesture to cluster of underbrush.

I lead the way, finding a small clearing. I crouch and motion for her to do the same.

"They should start looking for us in a minute," I say peering through the undergrowth.

"Why are we doing this again?" heaves Bean.

I turn to look at her freckled face and lock eyes with her.

"It's more fun this way," I wink.

She shakes her head.

"You would do anything to get an adrenaline rush."

"What and you wouldn't?"

"I never said that." She smirks.

In all the years I've known Bean, I'd never known her to turn down an opportunity to show her superior skillset of evasion and infiltration.

Frankly it's beautiful.

"What's wrong?" she asks.

I snap back to reality; I had been staring at her.

"Sorry, spaced out." I grunt.

"It's whatever." She shrugs.

We squatted for a few minutes in silence. My mind kept finding its way back to Bean.

She's still short, but I can't rest my arm on her head anymore. That pissed her off.

I chuckle silently.

I still remember that day at the county fair. She had laughed at me for being mesmerized by the lights. I remember telling her "there's just some kind of magic about it". Or even the first time she talked to me about the guy she liked. Ironic considering he's my closest friend.

"Hello? Dude snap out of it." Bean snapped her fingers in front of my face.

I shake my head, thrown off by her reaction.

"Okay, so I space out a lot. Sue me." I exhale in annoyance.

Bean just laughs at me and looks around. Funny to think that twenty minutes ago I was talking to Chris. The thought of it is bringing the taste of bile to my mouth.

"Dude, she's incredible," he ranted over the dance music in the background.

"Yeah, so I've heard," I said to myself.

Chris had been talking about Bean for the past half hour. He had successfully said the same four "incredible things" about her in 17 different ways. I counted. The thing that Chris didn't seem to understand was how long I'd known her.

"Yeah, so I asked her out." Chris said.

My heart plummeted to my stomach.

Before Chris could continue with his "she's so gorgeous" montage (18 different ways now), Miranda calls out. Thank God.

"Okay guys, gather round. This is my party, so we are gonna play Manhunt." I let out a sigh of relief.

"I have the teams sorted already." She glares at the group of people in front of her, daring us to object. At this point she starts to list off the finders. Then the hiders.

"Dammit, Bean is with you," Chris sighs.

"Don't worry, I'll look out for her." I gave him a light shove.

Bean pushes me back into reality.

"Seriously? Again?" Bean says looking at me with less than amusement.

Even though she keeps messing with me, I can't stop looking at her lips.

"Screw it."

I lean in and put my mouth on hers.

She doesn't stop me.

After an eternal moment, I pull away.

"Well, isn't this adorable!"

I spin around to see my friend standing in disbelief with his arms crossed.

"You guys suck at Manhunt."

I feel my entire face burn.

"I was just, I mean we were…" I stammered.

"You were caught."

"It isn't what it looks like!" I protested.

"Yeah, and I'm a freaking unicorn."

"No, Chris, seriously." I got up to my feet.

"You kissed my girlfriend!"

There's only one thing running through my mind at this point.

"I'm gonna die."

I can see the vein in his temple pulsing. I am so screwed. I can already feel my jaw dislocating. Before I realize it, I'm back on the ground and now it's my face that's pulsing.

"Stay away from her" Chris grabs Bean by the hand and pulls her away.

I put my hand to my nose and feel the blood on my upper lip. I watch their figures recede as Bean turns and mouths "Sorry." But as I sit here with blood dripping out my nose, I could only think about one thing.

I'm not.

Jake Perl

Well hi there. You seem to have stumbled upon my bio. What to say about myself? I have to choose these next words carefully, because there are a lot of things to say. I grew up in Boca Raton, Florida, and I'm going into the 10th grade at Dreyfoos School of the Arts. I'd like to think I'm a humble guy, and if people disagree, I correct them.

You may be asking yourself: what's a kid like this doing inside a book about writing? That's a great question. In fact, you should actually give yourself a pat on the back for that one, reader. I'm in this book because… I've written stories. Coincidentally, these stories are… in this book. You don't have to be a mathematician to put two and two together, here. Go, read my stories, and all the other stories in this book, too. Enjoy yourself. Because, contrary to popular belief around kids my age, reading is sort of cool.

Reflection

Week 1:

"There's no such thing as writer's block. That was invented by people in California who couldn't write." -Terry Pratchett

Take that, everyone else in this book. It's not "writer's block" if ideas don't just flock to you like a herd of cattle. On that note, I got my first story done this week, and obviously met a bunch of people involved in this thing. I came to write, and writing has been done. So far, there have been minimal complaints on my end.

Week 2:

This program is eight days. I didn't realize until now what a short time that really was. I've finished both my pieces, and I'm just about out of here. I would like to thank Ms Adamo and Poettis for their valiant editing, and on more than one occasion saying collectively, "Aren't you done yet?" while sending me back to fix my piece. I hope this book is entertaining, because a plethora of people have sacrificed a lot of time to make it.

Please

I had the front-row corner seat in Ms. Mulligan's class, so I saw everyone when they walked in. Inversely, everyone saw me when they walked in, which, of course, was of larger concern to me. And so there I sat, with one hand in my grey hoodie's pocket and the other stroking my own ego. I watched different people walk in, but I paid them little heed. I needed to look like I didn't deal with peasants, and my body language implied that they were peasants. Goddamn peasants.

In walked Ms. Mulligan. This is generally where the class goes downhill. Ms. Mulligan, like many other people who deal with people for a living, claims she has no favorites. This is utterly false, if not complete bullshit.

Coincidentally, though it's actually rather uncoincidental for me, I am not one of her favorites. I wouldn't expect anything less considering how she's one of my least favorite people, but life's easier if people like you. And that class is far from easy.

The first thing she says is, "Sam, please put away your phone." Her tone was far from reasonable. I felt her say it with spite, almost as if she was spitting the words out of her mouth.

She began the lesson of the day, and I began fluttering in and out of consciousness. At one point I went from paying no attention to minimal attention. This was an unusually high level of awareness for me. At one point, I even heard a full sentence:

"Now, many people believe Hitler was the world's most evil man," she drawled, "But there were many horrible men who caused even more horrific genocides. Can someone give me an example of someone worse than Hitler?"

That was the wrong sentence for me to hear. Don't get me wrong, I'm not a huge fan of Hitler's. But I felt the need to uphold Hitler's good side. And maybe get a reaction from the peasants while I was at it, too.

I raised my hand. That really piqued her interest, because I don't think she'd ever seen my outstretched hand. She called on me, I stood, and the shitstorm began.

"First," I began, "nobody in the world is evil. Everyone has a different idea of what's good and bad, so maybe you think Hitler was bad because he killed a lot of people. But a Nazi probably has a different perspective on Hitler. Good and bad is opinion, so don't present it as fact, because your idea of 'fact' may be different from someone else's. So though you and many others may think he was evil, don't stand up in front of a class of impressionable kids imposing your beliefs on them as if they were facts like some imbecilic brute."

Silence filled the air as I sat back down. Some dumb kid from the back of the class said "Heil." The class erupted in nervous laughter.

I was lucky to find myself in detention after-class that day. This was held in none other than Ms. Mulligan's room by none other than Ms. Mulligan.

Scoping out the room, I saw a plethora of interesting things. The most apparent of which was Ms. Mulligan with these giant dull-grey headphones around her head, entranced in a computer. It's amusing to think that she might've been online dating, but she probably wasn't.

Turning in the other direction, I saw my fellow inmates, Tony Mavrogordo and Stephen Penn. Sandwiched between them was Julian Moran. This was a very unfortunate spot for Julian.

As far as idiots in detention go, there are varying levels. Julian probably got in for vandalism or something. Stephen and Tony probably got in for manslaughter.

The Neanderthals started poking Julian ten minutes in with Ms. Mulligan being none the wiser. Julian played it off as nothing, at least for the first couple of minutes after they started. They kept going, and twenty minutes in, Stephen started tapping Julian with his fist. At this point, Julian called out "Ms. Mulligan!" under his breath. I think he said it under his breath because he wanted Mulligan to hear him while his aggressors couldn't. The opposite occurred. Stephen and Tony started taunting him while they did it. "Going to be a little bitch, huh, bitch? Tell the teacher on us, bitch." Eloquent.

At this point, I couldn't stay neutral any longer. I turned my head.

"Leave him alone, guys." Maybe they didn't like the way I said it, maybe I should've said "please." Whatever the case, they lifted their lumbering bodies and started meandering towards me.

I raised my hands in a defensive motion. They hunched over in front of me, grinning. At this point I saw that Stephen had a banana in his hand. I didn't want that banana around, near, or in my body.

"Ms. MULLIGAN!" I shouted with quite a bit more urgency than Julian before me. That got her attention. She turned.

"Sam, quit making such a ruckus, or I'll have you back here tomorrow!" The imminent injury here is obvious, but to rub salt in my wounds, who uses the word "ruckus" anymore?

I turned to face my resident buffoons. But I didn't finish that turn. Mid-rotation, I felt a firm, beefy object connect itself with my face. I collapsed.

"What's wrong, Shitler?" Tony said, climbing on top of me. I'll give him credit, that line was clever. He started punching. Julian screamed. Ms. Mulligan looked up. I blacked out.

I knew I should've said please.

I woke up pretty soon after in a white room that smelled like lemony-citrus Febreeze with a bag of ice on my face. I felt that there was something wrong with my face before I saw it. I stumbled into the bathroom, looked in the mirror, and sighed.

I walked back to the nurse's office and locked eyes with Ms. Mulligan, who was sitting near the door.

"Sorry for what I said." I began. She could tell I meant it, too.

"That's a good way to begin." She replied. "Now, it's after hours and I want to leave. Where are your parents?"

"I don't know." I responded. I couldn't have been more honest.

She frowned. I looked down. I didn't want her to ask any more questions. Eventually, I looked back up at her, and she seemed sad. We both sat there in silence for a while.

She finally spoke. "Your behavior is consistently disruptive." She sighed, and then continued. "But you possess a modicum of intelligence. However, your delivery frequently conceals it. I accept your apology."

It was the nicest thing anyone had said to me in a while. I looked at her, and she looked back. This time I didn't look down.

"I'm going to kindly give you a bit of advice." She continued. "Present others with respect and perhaps they'll present you with the same."

It was good advice for a kid who just got punched.

"Thanks." I said. That line was genuine, too. I was on a roll. "So, can you help me be more bearable?"

She looked at me, amused. I might've even seen a ghost of a smile on her face. "First, ask nicely."

I let that sink in before I replied.

"Please."

Two Men Walk Out of a Bar

"Men walk into gawddamn bars all th' time," the man said, "So why're there always gawddamn jokes 'bout 'em? I say, make jokes 'bout men walking outta bars. Change the jokes!" The man let out a hearty guffaw. He belched, which only furthered his chuckling.

The bartender grinned as he polished shot glasses. He said, "How about you make a joke about it then, James?"

"A man wa'ks outta bar…" James said. His face turned bright pink, the crinkled lines in his skin visible from the other side of the bar. It sounded almost as if a whale was gasping for air.

"BARTENDER!" James jolted upwards. "I don't have no beer! Fill me up!" He belched again.

"Right away, sir." He plucked the cup out of his patron's hand, grabbed a nozzle, and suffused it before placing it back in James's outstretched hand. It was at this point that he realized his counterpart was sound asleep in the chair. He smiled.

The night continued, and about an hour later, a smaller man walked in. He acknowledged the hunched man face down on the table and took a seat next to him.

"Bartender, I'll take a beer," he said. The bartender drew a pint and handed it to him. "Thank you, sir." He sipped his beer. "The name's Robert."

There was a momentary pause. "I caught my wife in bed with another man yesterday," he said outright. He took another sip.

The bartender sighed. He'd heard this kind of story before, but he decided to humor the man.

"Classic," he said. "What did you do?"

"It's not what I did," he said. "It's what she did. She freaked out and ran me out of the room before I could get a good look at him. He was probably just some deadbeat, a guy with nothing better to do than steal other people's women. But if I could just get a good look at this bastard…"

"You'll beat the crap out of him?" the bartender said.

Robert looked flustered. "Well… Yeah. Yeah, I will. I'll beat the crap out of him!"

The bartender nodded, picked up his rag, and continued washing the bar. He'd definitely heard better stories.

"Maybe you know my wife," Robert said. "Susan Hunt."

This bartender stopped. "Your wife was Susan Hunt?"

"Is."

"You caught her in bed with another guy and you haven't quit her yet?" the bartender said.

Robert placed his empty glass on the bar and waited for a refill before responding. "You know how Susan is running for mayor?" he said. The bartender nodded.

"Turns out, people don't like seeing their possible future mayor getting divorced right before an election. Maybe these people won't vote for that person if they hear she had marriage altercations. I don't care what people think of her, though. She's got some fancy-ass friends, friends that would make me the bad guy. I don't want to be the guy who divorced the mayor just yet, alright?"

"Women," the bartender said. The man retired his story and finished his beer.

Seven beers and two hours later, both men were face down in front of the bartender. "Get up, you two. Closing time." The two men walked into the light night air, both awaiting their taxis.

"Two men walk out of a bar..." James said. At this, Robert started chuckling, which prompted the same response from James.

"You... Yer a great guy." Robert said, hunched over his new friend. He burped.

"I know," James mumbled. At this, they both broke out laughing.

A taxi appeared. "You taykit, man." James said, slouching against the bar door.

"No no no no, no no." Robert said with a smile stretching across his face. "Yew taykit."

"I want," James burped, and started laughing again. He stopped himself. "I want yew to havit."

"Thanks buddy!" Robert said. "I owe ya!" He stumbled into the taxi and sped off into the distance.

Another taxi appeared soon afterwards. James piled in. "2242 Macon Lane, ma' driver." The taxi then departed to his destination as James wobbled in the taxi.

The taxi soon pulled up in front of a large, white house. "Thanks, Buck-o." James said, lumbering out of the car. He walked up the cobblestone steps to the house, and was almost tempted to lie down and take a nap right there. But he persevered, and after much delay, rang the doorbell.

"Ey there, buddy!" Robert exclaimed, opening the door. He swaggered in the doorframe.

"Wait... You're not Susan!" James said, hiccupping.

Al'Licia Pittman

"Either write something worth reading, or do something worth writing."
– Benjamin Franklin

"Writing is an exploration. You start from nothing and learn as you go."
– E. L. Doctorow

Hello again, my name is Al'Licia Pittman, a now seventeen year old senior in high school. Once again, I have been granted the chance of becoming a published author through this program, and I am very grateful for the opportunity. With my high school experience coming to a close, I feel that this should be the year that will cause all of my previous school terms to fall into the darkest of shadows. I hope to have a great senior year, and what better way to start out than with, once again, holding a title of being a published author.

Writing isn't just a downtime hobby, it's a lifestyle, and it is a skill that I plan to make more of as my life extends. This passion that is coursing through me, is trending through my veins, and is spilling out onto paper at its own leisure. Writing is a gift; one that I cannot wait to share with the world. With a pen in one hand, and correctional fluid in the other, I am ready to walk into the world of romance, drama, and action. I am finally ready to take that leap off of that peak and dive right into more published works.

Reflection

Week one was like a meteor. It was there, souring across the sky, and then with the blink of an eye, it was gone. Honestly, although progress was made, the time went by too fast. I was able to meet new people, and quickly made a strong connection with them. Usually it's harder for me to make friends, due to my timid nature, but with these girls it was very easy to let down my walls and open up. I enjoyed the time that I spent with them, and I hope we will be able to continue this newly established friendship in the upcoming school year.

As a mentor, I was given much more responsibility than last year. My title was a mixture of Writer, Editor, Advisor, and Supporter. At times the pressure would become a bit overwhelming, as I was not only responsible for my own work, but others' as well. Still, I took on the challenge with stride.

Week two was even more rushed. We were all nervous that we wouldn't finish our pieces before the deadline, but this only pushed us to work even harder. With our totally capable guide, Mrs. Mann, we were able to work diligently and competently.

These two weeks have been great, and I am very blessed to have taken part of this experience. I can't wait to see and read the published copy of this anthology, and to see and read those of the upcoming future.

A Kiss to Remember

"I'm so happy that you asked me out, Jacob," Jessica beamed, breaking the awkward silence. Her smile was warm, a strong contrast to the frosty air that was nipping at my face and neck.

"So am I, Jess," I replied shyly, opting to use her nickname. It was true, I was happy that I had asked her out. Jessica Jones was every young man's dream. She had big blue eyes, silky blond curls that hung loosely down her back, blindingly white teeth that were only exposed when she smiled, a gorgeous face, and a banging body to match. Truthfully, the girl had legs for days, and a rack that seemed almost too heavy for her petite frame to support; yet, she carried it with a grace that ballerinas would kill for.

I was surprised when she had agreed to accompany me tonight. I have never had much experience with girls, despite people's assumptions, and was rendered to a pathetic stuttering and blubbering mess when I had finally decided to "take the bull by its horns" and ask Jessica out.

"You know," she began, sliding closer to me on the hood of my 29 year old rusted and dented Chevrolet suburban, "I never would have thought that you would've asked me out. The Jacob King, wanted to go out on a date with little old me? It's laughable really," she giggled, tossing a loose strand of hair over her shoulder and glancing up at me through her long lashes. I felt my face heat up, blushing furiously, and swallowed down the thick lump in my throat.

"Nah," I denied, "I'm nothing special. Besides, I bet you have guys lined up right outside your door just waiting to get their greedy hands on you."

"Maybe," she whispered, tentatively placing her tiny glove clad hand on my thigh, "but none of those boys could ever hold a candle to you."

The butterflies that had been fluttering around in my stomach for the last hour and a half had morphed into angry hornets that had decided to take out their aggression on the tender flesh of my abdomen.

Jessica, now zoning in on my face, removed her hand from my thigh, only to cup my frosty cheek and turn my face toward hers. My stomach was doing summersaults. I had never had my first kiss, yet here I was, sitting on the top of my old beat-up Chevy, about to lock lips with the most popular girl in school.

Once our lips met, my body began to tremble from both nerves and excitement. I placed my clammy hands on her small waist, like I had seen guys do on TV, and attempted to calm myself. I had always imagined my first kiss taking place in a much more respectable setting. Call me a hopeless romantic, but my vision never included sitting on the hood of my rundown car, right outside of a fast food place.

When she slipped her tongue into my mouth, I was taken aback by the forced entry and by the above average length attachment that was now twirling around my own. The hornets, now livid, stomped around in my stomach, the slight stings and pinches that I had once felt were now incessant dagger stabs.

The movements didn't sit well with my stomach, as I had just recently scarfed down three chili dogs, and a large order of fries and drink. I tried to quietly fight off the waves of nausea, refusing to break the kiss of a lifetime.

Jess moaned into the kiss, flinging her arms around my neck tightly and pulling her body as close as humanly possible to mine. Sparks shot throughout my body, electrifying the concoction that was bubbling in the pit of my belly. Bile rose into my throat, forcing me to gag and wrench away from Jessica's mouth.

"Are you okay, Jacob?" she asked, her lips red stained and swollen from the force that she used when kissing me, "you look a bit pale."

"Yeah," I gasped, "just needed to catch my breath."

"Poor baby," she cooed; which at any other given time I would have found seductive, but now only added to my suffering, "It looks like we're going to have to build up your endurance."

With that she forced her lips back onto mine and continued her assault. Deprived of the needed time to recover from the last waves of sickness, the offense increased tenfold. My stomach lurched once again, causing another round of gagging to take place.

Jessica, oblivious to my current state, once again shoved her tongue into my mouth, unannounced. More tongue was added than the last, so much that it reached the back of my throat and brushed against my uvula.

It was "the straw that broke the camel's back." Half chewed and processed food, along with spurts of stomach acid, shot from the depths of my stomach, out of my mouth, and into Jessica's. She dislodged herself from me choking, gagging, and shrieking; whilst I continued to brutally vomit onto her newly exposed cleavage and down her pale pink sweater.

The rest of Jessica's annoyingly high pitched squeals fell on deaf ears, as I finished painting her a rusted orange color. Once the content of my belly was finally emptied, I became freshly aware of the cruel obscenities that were being screamed at me.

God, I thought, who knew that such a pretty mouth could emit such ugly words.

Colors To A Blind Soul

Red is the color of passion.
It's an intense curling through your veins.
The heat that burns those who choose to touch it,
And tastes dangerous.
The warmth that spreads through your body when you're surrounded by those
Who share your love.
Yellow is courage.
It's the bravery of a young boy standing up to the school's biggest bully;
It's the comfort of lying in your warm bed in the early morning.
Green is nature's arms embracing the structure of your body.
It's the aroma of freshly cut grass and early morning dew.
Green is the spirit of a grandparent.
Lengthy with an eon's worth of history,
Yet still short enough to experience new beginnings.
Blue is sadness;
It's the tears that fought to fall.
Vulnerability and insecurities, molded together as one.
Blue is strength,
Because just as much power as it takes to restrict those tears of sorrow,
It takes twice as much strength to let them fall.
Purple is the wind caressing your cheeks,
It's the tugging at the edges of full lips,
It's a small child's giddy squeal.
Purple is the shape of God's hands;
It's the palms that hold a smiling infant's soul in the sincerest of security.
Color is the flavoring of foods,
It's the sound of an early morning wakeup,
It's the intensity of feelings.
Color, when described perfectly,
Can make even the darkest depths be seen in a much more diverse shading.

When I Prayed

I've never been one for praying.
Growing up in an unorthodox Christian home,
Going to church and reciting Bible verses were more considered
chores than they were redemptions.
My faith in the Lord was almost as thin as the air that he had
supposedly given us.
My mother swept her depression and feelings of inadequacy under
rugs as she cleaned,
My childhood home always smelled of bleach.
When my father came home, if he came home,
 He'd taint the sanitized air with his alcoholic stench and crass
remarks.
I've never been one for praying,
But the day that I met the one who completed me,
I sat by the phone throughout the night and awaited her call.
My small apartment sponged up her aroma.
The smells of lavender, honey, and melons stained my bed sheets.
My last name never looked so good until it had been placed next to
her first.
I've never been one for praying,
But the moment that I saw my baby girl,
Named Lillian Elizabeth after her late grandmother,
Held captive in a warm glass enclosure;
Eyes closed,
Body too weak,
Skin too colorless,
I swear, as the Lord is my savior, that I would sprint the mile and a
half to the nearest Baptist church.
Spill my heart out to the Holy Spirit, himself,
Ask that my sins be forgiven,
Sing the hymns that my mother had once hummed,
And pray to the God above, that my second love would live to see
another day.

Julian Pollifrone

I was born on August 15, 1997. I am a student at South Tech Academy and a martial artist of 10 years. I am the son of Nick Pollifrone, a Lawn Maintenance Business Owner and Lisa Pollifrone, a stay at home mom (a great one at that). I also have a beautiful boxer named Mango. I am a Florida native, growing up in both Lantana and Boynton Beach.

This was my second year attending the Future Authors Project, which was a great honor for me. I actually got to be a mentor which was both difficult and rewarding. Difficult in the sense that I am partially responsible for the work that I looked at but rewarding in the sense that I got to help others hone in on their potential and create amazing pieces.

My ambitions in life include becoming a bestselling author and a screenwriter-director for film. Thanks to the Future Authors Project, my skills have improved substantially and I am on a well paved path.

Reflection

Week 1:

As I walked into the media center of Don Estridge High Tech Middle School, I was warmly welcomed by friends that I have made last year in the program. I also made many new friends like Lauren and Natasha. They are really cool. I am a mentor now as well, meaning that I get to help the new writers with their work. It has been a great experience but I also feel a little pressured because I am now partly responsible for the work of others. As far as my work is concerned, I have not made a lot of progress. My original short story was severely disjointed and way too supernatural. Honestly, I agree with the editors. I regret wasting so much of my valuable time on a discombobulated story but it also gave me inspiration to write my new short story, *The Fight*.

Week 2:

This week proved to be a lot more productive than week 1. I finished my short story, *The Fight*, about an MMA fighter in the fight of his life, not only against his opponent in the Octagon but against the painful memories of negligent father. The piece was approved on Tuesday. Thursday, the final day of the project, I got my poem, *The Enigma*, approved. I received a lot of help from my fellow mentors Triton, Gary, and Juan. Without their encouragement and expertise, I probably would not have finished in time. I have had an amazing time this year and I hope to come back again next year.

The Fight

It is a packed, sold-out crowd in the American Airlines Arena. MMA fans of all ages are circled around the Octagon in anticipation for the fight between Daniel Davidson and Rick Reyes. The cacophony created from their screams is loud enough to break the sound barrier. A middle aged woman is bouncing up and down in her chair in the middle section of the stands. She is sporting a newly purchased fur coat, obnoxious pearl earrings, and clenching a leopard printed purse that would make any ordinary kid embarrassed. Jodie's son, Daniel, however, is anything but ordinary.

In the backstage area, Daniel sits in his locker room, resting his head in his tape wrapped hands. Suddenly, the door swings open. Manuel, Daniel's trainer, emerges into the room and leans against Daniel's locker.

"What the hell is the matter with you boy!?"Manuel shouts. "You are supposed to be preparing for the fight, not watering your eyes for the theater." Daniel takes his hands away from his face and glances at his trainer with his face scrunched up and his eyes watery and beet red.

"What? Did you tire yourself out cryin'?" Manuel asks. Daniel stares at his locker. "Okay, what's the matter? You're usually chattier than this."

"It's my dad. I can't seem to get him out of my head," Daniel replies.

"Your dad? You mean that good for nothing, Corona chugging, red faced, potbellied loser that felt that it was a good idea to walk away from you and your lovely mother to become a dumb sucka on the street?"

"That's the one."

"Daniel, my mean karate kid, don't you worry about that man. If anything, imagine that he is Rick Reyes and pound his brains out. Speaking of brains…"

"Yeah, I know the story," Daniel rolls his eyes. "Those Vietnamese suckas almost blew my damn brains out in the war."

"Ha, okay David Letterman, save that comedy stuff for the press after you wipe the floor with Reyes tonight." Daniel rises up from the locker room bench and bangs his fist against the locker.

"Yeah, that's the cat I like to see!" Manuel laughs. They exit the locker room and stand in the backstage tunnel. Daniel clasps his hands around his neck.

"You got this man!" Manuel reassures him. Daniel nods as they rush out of the backstage tunnel. The crowd goes into frenzy. Fans from all sections are flailing their arms and waving their "Daniel is #1" signs.

"We love you Daniel!" a few girls screech from the front of the crowd. Jodie is standing up and waving her arms in the air.

"That's my baby!" she cheers. "That's my son!" Daniel and Manuel approach the Octagon's steps, face each other, and nod. Daniel turns to the ring and climbs up the steps. A ring judge opens the steel door for him. Daniel walks into the ring and stares down his opponent. Rick Reyes is everything his reputation entails. He is stocky, fierce, and has an acquired taste for blood. Daniel, in contrast, is lean and reserved in manner. The announcer and referee sprint into the Octagon. The announcer holds up a gold microphone with his left hand and waves to get the crowd's attention with his right. The crowd dies down.

"Ladies and gentlemen!" the announcer booms. "Tonight's bout will determine the winner of a six figure UFC contract. In the blue and white trunks, from Mexico City, Mexico, weighing in at 150 pounds, Rick Reeeeyeeesss!" Rick pumps his fist in the air. The crowd gives out a brief cheer.

"And his challenger," the announcer continues. "In the black and green trunks, from Miami, Florida, weighing in at 145 pounds, Danieeeeellll Daaaaaviiiiddsooon!" Daniel waves to the crowd. The crowd goes into an uproar. The announcer exits the octagon and locks the cage door. The men face each other as the referee stands in between them.

"Okay guys; let's give these people a good, clean fight." The referee steps back. Ding! Ding! Ding! The two fighters touch gloves and inch back into their fighting stances. They shuffle around the ring, exchanging jabs that strike nothing but air. Rick closes in on Daniel and knocks him back with a right elbow. Daniel counters with a powerful roundhouse kick to the left side of Rick's ribs. Rick puckers his face and grabs his ribs. The crowd applauds. Daniel moves in to follow up on Rick. Suddenly, a gravely, southern voice pops into his head.

"Daniel, you can't do anything right." Daniel freezes. He recognizes the voice. Rick catches Daniel off guard with a swift jab. One after another, the jabs keep coming to Daniel's face. Daniel backs up and counters with a few jabs of his own but to no effect. The ending round horn sounds off. The referee steps in between the two fighters.

"Good job guys. Go to your corners." Daniel walks to his corner with his head down. The trainers enter the Octagon. Manuel rushes to Daniel's side with a stool. He sets down the stool for Daniel.

"What the hell is the matter with you!? You could have finished that sucka up in a few punches." Daniel stares out into the front of the crowd. He sees a chubby, middle aged, red faced man drinking a beer. The man is looking right at Daniel. Daniel closes his eyes and opens them back up. The red faced man is gone.

"Hello? Earth to sucka!? I want you to get out there and give these people a worthwhile fight!" Daniel gets up from his stool. On the other side of the ring, Rick takes a long swig of water. The two men make their way to the center of the ring. The referee stands in front of the two fighters.

"Okay guys, round two!" Ding! Ding! Ding! The crowd cheers. The referee backs up. Rick rushes right into the fight, completely ignoring Daniel's fist bump offer. He rains down punches upon punches to Daniel's face. Rick rears back his right arm and delivers a nasty hook punch to Daniel's left cheek, knocking him down to the canvas mat. Blood pours out of Daniel's nose.

In the stands, Jodie is firmly clenching the arm of a man sitting adjacent to her left and is fanning herself off with a fight program.

Back in the Octagon, Rick towers over Daniel, who is still lying on the ground. Daniel notices that Rick's lips are moving, but that the words coming out do not sound like his voice.

"I always knew that you were a loser, Daniel. I can't believe that you were dumb enough to think that you and your mom could live on your own. It's time to finish you off." Daniel stares into Rick's eyes. Inside, a red faced man throws a beer bottle at the wall of a miniscule apartment. He walks out of the door and slams it behind him.

Back inside the ring, Daniel clenches his teeth. A massive vein bulges out of his forehead. Rick lunges in for Daniel's face with a right vertical punch. Daniel swiftly adjusts his body to the left at a forty five degree angle, avoiding Rick's punch. Daniel places his left leg across the back of Rick's neck and lifts his right leg over his own left ankle, securing Rick in a triangle submission hold. Daniel raises his hips off of the ground and squeezes his legs together around Rick's neck. Rick rocks his body side to side, making minimum progress of escape. His face becomes redder than a clown's nose. Rick's struggle ceases. He taps the right thigh of Daniel. The final horn blows. The crowd goes into an uproar as the referee breaks up the submission hold.

"Daniel! Daniel! Daniel!" the fans chant. Daniel runs around the interior of the Octagon, pumping his fist in the air. His showboating ceases when he spots Rick sitting up with his head down. Daniel offers Rick his hand. Rick accepts and allows Daniel to pull him off of the mat. The audience's cheers intensify.

Back in the stands, Jodie is sobbing uncontrollably. She is nearly choking on her tears. Manuel charges into the Octagon. He embraces Daniel, smacking his back as if he is attempting to rid a couch cushion of dust.

"You did it man! You did it!" Daniel unfolds a large, radiant grin and releases a crazed battle cry. This is what he lives for. To prove doubters wrong. He lives for the fight.

The Enigma

The other side of the door
Contains a lackluster world.
With a hint of light
Gleaming at its core.

The other side of the door
Holds walls stark and spare.
Strangers lurking the corners
Stalking your shadow on the ground.

The other side of the door
Booms with beautiful blossoms
On the sides of a vast road
Paved out of abundant riches.

The other side of the door
Is a puzzle with scattered pieces.
One you must open
To create the grand picture.

Juan Puerto

I entered this world on the 28th of December, 1996, in Bogota, Colombia. However, about a year later the decision to move to Florida was quickly made, and my father, mother, and I began our American dream. The rest of our immediate family followed suit and now the majority of the Puerto/Garcia clan is residing here, in the sunshine state. However, my plans for the future include moving far away from here, maybe returning to the urban sprawl from whence I came.

In the meantime, I will continue to write, more specifically, poetry. My aspiration, for the near future, is to become a spoken word artist and enter the slam scene. On top of that, I hope to attend Carnegie Mellon or Georgia Tech to study computers in order to become a computer engineer. Of course this will come after graduating from Suncoast Community High School this year.

The past five years at this writing workshop have taught me a myriad of valuable things. Show, don't tell. Each word on the page has a reason for being there. The list could go on and on, and although I hated those sentences when they were being spoken at me, they have helped me to become a more mature, and in turn, better writer. Although this may be the last year I have the pleasure of having Ms Adamo and Ms Poettis destroy my writing, they'll always be there on my shoulders, repeating their phrases of wisdom, whenever I write about coal paste or plantains. It has been a great five years writing and mentoring for this writing workshop and I will miss it dearly.

Reflection

Week 1:

This week, as always, has been difficult. The writing process is a process which requires time and effort to get back in to, especially after a year of avoiding it. However, it is nice to finally get my ideas out on paper again, albeit with lots of struggle.

My first piece, Grass-chins and Pebble-faces, was inspired by a beard. Working at Taco Bell, I must keep my face clean shaven, although I do try to bypass that rule, which lead me to thinking about beards and what they really represent. As always, my editors were wary of the idea, but let me work on it knowing that a majority of my poetry relies on random objects. Although it is not one of my favorite poems, I did enjoy writing it and will enjoy reading it in the future when I get forced by my manager to shave.

Week 2:

The writing this week was much easier. The words seemed to flow out smoother and without that much of a struggle, probably due to the full week of dedication to the craft.

My second piece, Garage Sale, was inspired by my friend, Nate, when I read the words "Garage Sale" in her story. It inspired me to write about a garage sale and I thoroughly enjoyed writing the piece. It is actually one of my favorite pieces and I can't wait to show it to my friends.

Tin Can is a story that was written in this same workshop two years ago. However, in the book, only the first page of the story was published. Hopefully the full story will be published this time around.

Grass-chins and Pebble-faces

Grass-chins are those
with jaw-lines that cut down mountains
and arms that swim seas.
Tar-black forest commences at side-burns
covering cheek bones,
meeting right between the nostrils.

Pebble-faces are those
with glistening eyes,
hands guarding ears from answers,
fearful heart will crumble.
Smooth cloth coats their facial structures,
until a grass-chin comes along
planting seeds upon un-sown fields.

Dark stems shoot forth,
triggering
a sudden metamorphosis in the pebble-face,
a sick cycle of early maturity,
where pebble-faces' eyes are dulled,
hands tied down,
flooding heart with answers.

Soft lips, shadowed by newly formed stalks,
speak pebble-face words.
Distorted by grass-chin roots,
they no longer reflect the soul's intent.

When the masquerade ends,
sudden deforestation occurs.
Cloth comes back to surface,
jungle unnecessary to shroud personal fears.

Garage Sale

Saturday morning dew settles
Enveloping everything in a humid
Cocoon.
Beach towels stretch across the unkempt lawn,
a rainbow of tattered clothing mounds.
Baby onesies concealed by an extravagant fuchsia prom dress.

Un-even tables tetris-ed across faded pavement.
A typewriter is placed dead-center.
Father's intellect memorialized by
rustic keys coated in his
oily fingerprints.
Imprints of desperate late night clicks
lie locked in manila folders,
accompanied by red-stamped bank letters.

Mother's medley of cooking utensils,
quasi-disciplinary tools,
strewn about cluttered table.
Rice-cooker,
once filled with pale grains,
now occupied by Sunday night memories.
Memories of fiery stove top
flicker,
extinguished
As gas bills pile atop.

Stained pearl-white pointe shoes
next to rusted baseball bat.
Daughter's tu-tu slightly
ripped,
reminder of playful summers when
prince and princess strolled through

jungle-like backyard
until prince grew ill
and princess' soul
ripped.

Photo frame flat.
Chipped gold adorns rotting mahogany.
Broken family glued together by
picturesque moment.
Falls apart
when shell is sold.

Tin Can

"Ring ring," Jared said into the tin can. Attached to the soup can was a string exiting through the window and entering the window of the house attached to his. It glistened, like spider silk illuminated by the moonlight.

"Ring ring," he repeated, pulling the string more taut and transitioning the cup from his mouth to his ear, hoping for a response.

"Hello, it's Bella, I can't come to the phone right now, leave a message after the beep. Beep!"

A snicker could be heard emanating from the window. Jared smirked, after about 30 seconds of quietly contemplating snarky responses, he simply responded, "Just answer you loser."

"Hey Jared," Bella responded in between chuckles.

"Whatsup?"

"Nothing much, just relaxing. Listening to some music. You know, the usual." The gentle guitar strum of Jack Johnson could be heard over Bella's soft voice. Jared couldn't help but smile at the sound of her sweet voice. She had been out of town for about two weeks and he had missed their late night conversations. Now that he thought about it, she'd been gone a lot recently.

"That's cool. Where ya been?"

The wind blew through Jared's open window, carrying the awkwardness from Bella's room with it. The cold gust struck Jared in the lower back, causing a chill to rise slowly, working his way through his spinal cord, eventually reaching his skull.

"We've been traveling…uhm just visiting family…" The grand pauses between her sentences alerted Jared that she was lying.

"Whatever, I'll see you tomorrow," he responded, aggravated that she didn't trust him with a simple secret after a life of friendship. He tossed the tin can aside and turned to fall asleep.
     ✶✶✶✶

The Mickey Mouse alarm clock on Bella's mahogany night table lit up. The bright red numbers flashed 10:47 on her ceiling, revealing that she had woken up late for her morning jog with Jared.

"Ah, crap," she muttered, still half asleep.

She quickly changed into her workout clothes and dashed towards the front door, nearly knocking over the collection of boxes stacked along the walkways. She hoped Jared hadn't left already. Her mother was already up; face still covered by a drowsy haze.

"Good morni…"

"Hi mom, bye mom," she responded, throwing the door open. The combination of a column of humid air hitting her, and the sun blinding her, caused her to backtrack, nearly tripping over the door frame.

Once her vision returned to her, she turned to see Jared stretching on the sidewalk.

"Hey Jared!" He was in his normal attire; a school gym t-shirt cut up in a manner to show off his so-called "guns" and black shorts, matching his gray and black Nike's.

"Hi." He made his frustration with last night's conversation blatantly obvious.

"Someone's in a bad mood today," she mocked. He rolled his eyes, ignoring the comment.

"You ready to go?" He asked, quickly bouncing on his heels. Bella didn't respond running off without him.

"I guess she is," Jared mumbled to himself as he started after Bella. She jogged far ahead of Jared, avoiding the same conversation that had made her stay up last night. The Florida climate made it feel more like swimming then jogging, slowing her down and allowing him to eventually catch up.

"So… about… last… night…" Jared said between breaths.

"What?"

"Are you going to… answer my question?"

"I'd rather not," she tried to focus on the task at hand.

"Why won't you just tell me? It's not a big deal Bella!" Jared reached for her shoulder, trying to stop her. Bella swatted his hand away, swerving to face him.

"Can we just finish this jog?"

"You can finish it by yourself." He turned and began his stride back home.

"Don't be stupid Jared!" Bella shouted after Jared. The words just seemed to pass over him. "Stop!" She began to follow Jared, hoping the truck wasn't there yet.

****

The moist air wrapped around Jared like a watery cocoon, limiting his movement heavily, not really helping his temperament. It's not a big deal. I just want to know where she's fucking been, he thought to himself.

"Jared!"

Just ignore her, if she won't tell you, then don't talk to her. She'll have to tell you eventually.

"Jared!"

God I'm bad at being a douche. As Jared approached his olive green house, he was cut off by a large U-HAUL.

Bella's front lawn was adorned by large cardboard boxes. He looked over at the front door and saw Bella's mom waving at him, mouthing words that he couldn't comprehend. His hands trembled from an overflow of emotions.

Bella finally caught up to Jared, "I was gonna tell you after our jog but you sorta ran off on me."

He sat down on the sidewalk placing his head on his hands. He could feel his heart beat pulsing in his head. Stupid. Stupid. Stupid. Jared got up, walking towards his house. "You should've just told me yesterday Bella." he said.

"I'm sorry," she called after him.

****

Bella fell into her bed, the only furniture in her room, after a long day of packing. Outside the sky was jet black, the moon looking like a hole in the dark veil, exposing the brightness of day, the soft rain shower outside providing nature's melodic song. She picked up the metal can.

"Ring ring," she whispered into it.

"Hey," Jared said back.

"We were in Georgia looking at houses."

"Cool."

"I'll be back to visit though! We can hang out then."

"Alright. Sounds good."

"I'm sorry Jared; I didn't know how to tell you…"

"It's fine, I'm glad you're coming back though." The annoyance that occupied Jared's voice was replaced by hopefulness.

"You better keep in touch, loser."

"I will." The words Jared had been wishing to tell her since last night were muddled by the rain droplets hitting the string. "Goodnight Bella."

"Goodbye Jared," Bella said, feeling the string go slack.

Lillian Riso

"The goal, I suppose, any fiction writer has, no matter what your subject, is to hit the human heart and the tear ducts and the nape of the neck and to make a person feel something about what the characters are going through and to experience the moral paradoxes and struggles of being human."
–Tim O'Brien

Hullo, there! My name is Lilli Riso, and I'm a writer. Not professional yet, of course, but getting into this book is a pretty good start. And, before we get into the actual autobiography part, I'd like to welcome you, reader, to this book, and congratulate you on picking it up. It's a very good book, and I really hope you enjoy every single story, poem, or other form of writing in it.

I'm fifteen years old, born on March 26, 1999 in Sacramento, California, though I came to Florida soon after and have lived here ever since. I'm the third daughter in a family of six, with three sisters, two parents, and a puppy in a pear tree. In August, I'll be a sophomore at Suncoast High School, and hopefully I'll find time in between homework to keep writing. In the future, I hope to be an author, as well as a book translator to support myself in between book sales.

I've always loved reading, usually only fiction and fantasy, but I only really got into writing seriously in fourth grade. Since then, my dream job has been to become an author. I hope to keep improving my writing to make my dream a reality, and this workshop has been an enormous help with that. In my life, my biggest author inspirations have been J.K. Rowling, Rick Riordan, Lemony Snicket, and Jodi Lynn Anderson, because their books are those that I can pick up and read over and over without tiring, and that's what I hope to achieve with my stories.

Reflection

Week 1:

This week was my first ever in this program, and I've been pleasantly surprised by how much it's helped my writing. Normally, ideas just float around my head doing whatever they please, but having a deadline forced me to actually put them on paper. I've learned a lot about what really goes into writing professionally (especially all the editing), met published authors, and even made some friends. It's been a great experience so far, and I can't wait for more next week!

Week 2:

As this week ends, I find that it's been even better than the first. Although the pressure was on for everyone to get their pieces finished and approved, it was still great fun and a good learning experience. I had to go through more rigorous editing and scrambled to get my final piece approved, but it was worth it. All the authors who came in during this final week helped me learn more about the mechanics of getting a book edited and published, which I feel will better prepare me for a future in writing. Overall, this program has been a great experience for me. In fact, I'd say these two weeks have been a definite *turnip point* in my life, don't you agree, Monica?

Nothing Special

Taylor nervously twisted her hair around her pencil, wincing when it got caught. Untangling it granted her a few seconds of distraction, but then the butterflies returned to rioting in her stomach. Despite the obvious consequences, she continued twirling the pencil while the bald man in front of her read over the sheet of hand-drawn musical notes. He squinted, making him seem even more critical than usual, then sighed. He put down the papers and looked up at Taylor. She braced herself for the worst while praying for the best.

"Well…I think it needs more work," Mr. Carol droned. Oh, come on! Taylor wanted to scream. She'd been in Mr. Carol's class long enough to know that "it needs more work" really meant "you need to rewrite the whole thing".

She took a deep, calming breath, then asked, "What's wrong with it this time?" This was the fourth time Taylor had submitted the stupid piece, and she was absolutely done with it.

"The same as your earlier pieces, Miss King. There's just no… passion, no emotion. How can you expect people to listen if there's nothing special to hear?"

Taylor's cheeks flushed bright red. She'd spent hours writing that last score and Mr. Carol had just gone and called it "nothing special". She made herself feel better by thinking about what a hypocrite he was, talking about passion in such a boring, monotone voice.

"I don't know, Mr. Carol. How am I supposed to make it better?" Taylor was getting so exhausted of asking him that after every failed submission. She practically could've answered for him at this point.

"Well, without an emotional base, this piece is rather flat…And it's very difficult to add passion to a flat piece. You'll have to redo it." Again, Taylor added mentally, noting how he didn't seem a bit sorry for casually tossing hours of her time into the bin. "Please keep in mind, Miss King, that the concert is in only three days. You must have your piece written by then, or I won't be able to allow you to play."

Taylor's heart stopped. Her concert piece was a quarter of her final grade; an F would drag her down to a C for the semester. Her dad would kill her.

"I'll get it done," she mumbled, not bothering to pick up her old score before leaving.

*****

"Really? The exact same thing?"

"Word for word!" Taylor groaned. "So now I have to rewrite it, again."

Isaac laughed. "Man, that's like the fourth time now, isn't it?"

"Fifth," Taylor grumbled.

"Wow, you must really suck at writing music," he chuckled. Taylor crumpled her piece of sheet music and hurled it at his head. He raised his hands in surrender, "Kidding, kidding."

"Has anyone ever told you what a supportive big brother you are?"

"Nope."

"Good." She leaned forward, letting her head hit the desk with a dull thud. "You're a junior, how did you get your music piece past Mr. Carol?"

"Easy. I'm a drama major, not a band major."

Taylor smacked her palm to her forehead. "I knew that."

"Sure," Isaac snickered. "But my friend was a band major. She had to deal with Mr. Carol, too."

"And?"

"She wrote her music about her boyfriend."

Taylor stared at him. "Wow, really? Using love, the very epitome of emotions and feelings, as the emotional base of the song! I never would've thought of that. In fact, I'll write my piece about my boyfriend, too! Oh, wait, fresh out of boyfriends."

Isaac smirked. "Well, you could always write your piece about your girlfriend…"

Taylor shot up, sending her chair clattering to the floor. She pointed at the door, clenching her jaw. "Get out of my room."

He rolled his eyes. "Tay, come on-"

"No, I'm serious! Out, right now!"

He frowned, actually looking serious for once, leaning forward and searching Taylor's brown eyes with his green. "Tay, I know you're scared of what Mom and Dad would think, but you can't just ignore that you want Lizzy to be more than just a friend. It's kind of obvious."

"Isaac, we're not talking about it. Not now, not ever. So shut up and get out."

There was a short pause, then Isaac sighed, standing and walking out the door, shaking his head like Taylor had disappointed him. She glared at the door for a while, then sat on the edge of her bed, contemplating her brother's words. She didn't care what Isaac or anybody else thought; Lizzy was her best friend, nothing more, and that was how it was supposed to be. That was all it would ever be.

It's kind of obvious, Isaac had said. Taylor frowned. What did that mean? Did lots of people think she liked Lizzy? She thought back to any past conversations she'd had with her. She was sure she'd never done anything a best friend wouldn't do. How did he think it was "obvious"?

As if her thoughts had summoned it, Taylor's phone started ringing, playing Lizzy's favorite song. She smiled automatically, but froze when she realized her heart had started pounding. Probably just because the call surprised me, she told herself as she answered the phone.

Yeah, right.

"Hello?"

"Hey, Tay!" Taylor ignored the way her heart skipped at the sound of Lizzy's voice. Just a friend, just a friend, just a friend.

"Hi, Lizzy, what's up?"

"I missed school today. What was the French homework?"

Taylor thought back to French class. She'd definitely missed Lizzy's presence. But best friends missed each other, right? That didn't mean anything. "There wasn't any, just study for the exam next week."

"Awesome, I'm all about no homework!" Lizzy's bubbliness was contagious, even over the phone. Taylor bit her lip to keep her own smile from growing. "So, did I miss anything else?"

"No, everyone just wants us to study." Taylor found herself fighting to keep her voice casual. Doesn't mean anything. I just like talking to my friend. But she wasn't a good enough liar to make herself believe that.

"Cool! So, bye then-"

"Wait!" The word slipped from Taylor before she could stop it, desperate to keep listening to Lizzy's voice. She winced. Not only had that sounded clingy, it was also a pretty drastic response to keep talking to just a friend.

"Yeah?"

"Umm…" Taylor swallowed. "Well, I just…wanted to talk. Like, if you're not busy…"

"Ah, don't worry. I'm not doing anything, and I'm always open for talking to you." Okay, that made Taylor happy. She felt her cheeks flush, and her heart started pounding harder. Just a friend, just a friend…

Then Taylor realized something. Yeah, Lizzy was just a friend, but Taylor already knew that. Telling herself that did nothing, because the important thing wasn't what Lizzy was, it was what Taylor wanted Lizzy to be. She wanted Lizzy to be more than just a friend.

Oh my God, I've got a crush on Lizzy.

"Tay?" Lizzy asked. Taylor's heart skipped again and she almost told herself again, just a friend, but then she smiled and just let it skip and dance and pound as it pleased. It felt so free, she realized, to not keep lying and hiding her feelings from herself.

Wait a second; she wasn't hiding her feelings anymore. She grinned and grabbed another piece of sheet paper. Let's see how much passion Mr. Carol finds in this!

"Yeah, Lizzy?"

"What do you want to talk about?"

"Anything."

*****

Déjà vu, Taylor thought as she gently tugged her pencil out of her hair again. She glanced toward the stage from her current position behind the side curtain. Justin Kane was currently playing his piece; that meant she was next. Trying to ignore her clammy, sweaty hands, she reread her finished piece. Beautiful! She remembered Mr. Carol's uncharacteristically cheerful voice when she had turned in the latest copy. Marvelous! Bursting with passion! Much better, Miss King, much better!

However, despite his once-in-a-blue-moon praise, Taylor felt like she was about to be sick. Writing the score had felt great, and she was happy she'd been able to let her feelings loose on the page, but the thought of playing it in front of a live audience felt like she'd be ripping out of a shell, leaving herself raw and exposed in front of the crowd. She'd poured her heart and soul into that piece, and even though not everyone would be able to read the emotion in it, Lizzy definitely would.

Lizzy loved listening to all kinds of music, even Taylor's oboe practice. She had been blind her whole life, but that only made her hearing better, and she was fantastic at interpreting music. Taylor just knew Lizzy would be able to read her song like a book, and then she'd know all about Taylor's feelings. Yes, Taylor had accepted that she liked Lizzy, but she wasn't sure she was ready to tell her friend about it. She had no idea how her best friend would react, and playing this piece at the concert was a risk that Taylor was starting to rethink. She quickly went over the plan in her head: Play the piece, talk to Lizzy. Play the piece, talk to Lizzy. That's all; piece of cake. You can do this.

Applause broke out on the other side of the curtain, and Justin walked across the stage. Taylor closed her eyes. Crap, he played fast. She took a deep breath, grabbed her music and her oboe, and stood up. She forced herself to walk into the bright stage lights, praying the audience couldn't see her hands shaking. She kept her gaze locked on the music stand as she approached it, sure that she'd pass out or get sick if she saw all the eyes on her. Once she reached it, she put the music down and semi-gracefully collapsed into the seat. She paused for only a second, and then raised the oboe to her lips.

And Taylor began playing, telling her heart's story.

In the low, shaky beginning, she heard her shyness. Her denial cried out in wavering trills, only to be soothed by the loud, clear notes of her freedom slicing through the air. The low, flat melody of her parents' intolerance was shattered by the energetic joy of her own acceptance. And, at the end, she closed her eyes, knowing this movement by heart. The slow, passionate song of her feelings for Lizzy. She had written this part while talking on the phone with Lizzy, matching the notes to the cadence of her voice. Lizzy would be able to crack this song wide open and read it like an audiobook, and suddenly, Taylor found that she didn't mind. The song gave her the courage not to worry about the consequences, because she needed to tell Lizzy how she felt. She'd been harboring and being ashamed of her feelings for too long. It was time to let them go, and rather than anxiety, Taylor found herself looking forward to Lizzy's reaction with excitement.

The piece ended quietly, carrying Taylor's unspoken hope, her wordless question, of whether Lizzy felt the same. The meaning was obvious, even to her. She knew Lizzy would understand.

The audience exploded into applause.

A grin spread over Taylor's face. Her cheeks felt hot, but in a good, exhilarated sort of way. She felt like the weight of all the world's secrets had been lifted off her shoulders, especially the weight of her own. Everything was out in the open now, and she only needed to see Lizzy's response. She turned, looking right in the middle of the front row, seat A-15, the seat number she'd memorized after seeing it on Lizzy's ticket, the only seat that mattered to Taylor in the whole auditorium.

It was empty.

*****

"Good morning, Tay!" Lizzy sang Monday morning when Taylor sat next to her in study hall. Taylor clenched her teeth. She'd had all weekend to think about what she'd do today, but seeing Lizzy was still harder than she'd predicted. Can't you at least sound like you're sorry?

"Hi," she mumbled back, wincing at her gruff tone. Lizzy frowned.

"Well, aren't you grumpy? What ruined your life today?"

Taylor swallowed. She'd planned this conversation in advance, thought exactly how to make it sound not too accusing, not too dependent on Lizzy's responses, not too forgiving. Seeing Lizzy, all that flew out the window.

"Why weren't you there?" Taylor winced at the desperate tone of her voice.

Lizzy's brows furrowed. "'There'?"

"My concert." Taylor clenched her jaw. Maybe Lizzy had forgotten. Still rude, but not horrible. They could deal with a simple memory slip. "On Friday? I bought you a ticket, remember?"

"Oh, right. Well, that's kind of a long story." Taylor wanted to scream at Lizzy's lighthearted voice, wanted to shout at her that this was important and it meant so much and why wasn't she taking this seriously.

"Tell me anyway."

"Okay!" Lizzy grinned, suddenly glowing with happiness. Taylor was glad she couldn't see her scowl. "Well, you know that kid, John, right? From English class?"

"Yeah. What about him?"

"Well, we'd been hanging out for a few weeks, and then on Friday, totally random, he just shows up at my house, right? So we go up to my room and just kind of hang out and talk for a bit, and then, out of the blue, he freaking kisses me!"

Lizzy's final words were almost shouted, leading to several shushes from other students in the classroom. But Taylor hardly noticed, because oh-my-God-she-just-said-that-CRAP. This kid, John, had only known Lizzy for a few weeks, compared to her and Lizzy being friends since before they could crawl, and then he just goes and kisses her and Lizzy misses Taylor's most important concert EVER.

"...Oh."

Lizzy frowned. "Well, you sure sound excited. What's wrong with you? Aren't you happy for me?"

No. "Well, I just...Th-That's kind of soon, isn't it? After just a few weeks?"

Lizzy raised an eyebrow. "No. I don't think so. I mean, he actually became my friend first. That's more than a lot of the idiots at our school would do."

Taylor swallowed and mumbled, "I just…don't want to see you hurt."

Lizzy blinked, then smiled. "You overprotective dork. Look, don't worry about me, okay? I know how to take care of myself. Besides, he's not after me like, 'Oh, let's take advantage of the blind chick'. He sees me…for me. He doesn't care that I'm blind." She sighed, smiling and resting a cheek on her fist. "He's the first person to look right past all that, you know, and just like me for who I am."

Taylor jerked back in her seat as if Lizzy had just smacked her. Okay, that stung. Taylor had always been there for Lizzy, had always helped her out, and she had definitely never treated her different for being blind. How could Lizzy just forget all that because of this John kid?

"Anyway," Lizzy continued, "we just spent the rest of the day together after that. And we decided that it'd really be too much trouble to go and buy John a ticket, and then get my mom to drive us to the school, and we wouldn't even be sitting together…It just wasn't worth it." She shrugged. "Sorry, I guess. But I've been to, like, every other concert ever, so no big deal, right?"

Taylor didn't move. She focused on taking deep breaths, calming breaths. Yes, Lizzy had consciously missed the concert; yes, Lizzy had just majorly downplayed their friendship; and yes, Lizzy had just unknowingly stabbed Taylor in the back. Trying to move past all that, she focused. What would she do if she weren't furious with Lizzy right now? How could she be just Lizzy's friend in this situation?

"…He really makes you happy, then?"

Lizzy rolled her eyes. "Duh."

"…Congratulations, then."

"Thanks!" Lizzy smiled. "So, the concert. Did I miss much?"

Taylor's jaw clenched, and she stared at her hands. "…No. Nothing special."

Soldier

The soldier was facing an undefeatable enemy. His eyes darted around, searching for an escape, but his opponent had cornered him. Giving up all hope for survival, he braced himself for what was coming. A shadow of death loomed over him.

The shoe slammed down on the ant, and the tiny soldier was no more.

Carlos Rivera

Week 1:

If there's anything I learned during my first week at the Canon Future Author's Project, it's that it is not that easy to get published. I went through one short story, and when I showed it off to one of the editors there, she immediately though it was too long when I asked for twenty pages. Of course that was an estimate, as I didn't even finish it yet. They said no to it and I trashed it. However, it is something I would like to revisit one day as a possible short story in my own published omnibus of stories. So after that was trashed, I wrote an ode to quenepas, a cultural fruit found in tropical and subtropical areas that I honestly couldn't live without. That got trashed, too, when the proctors thought it was too similar to an ode found in a previous book. And so that day, after we agreed on trashing the ode, they asked me a simple question:

What is important to me?

At first, I answered with an incredibly shortsighted answer: Movies. Classics, to be particular. I mentioned *Casablanca, Alien, The Exorcist, Star Wars*, and others of the likes. Only, if I used that idea of movies, I really wouldn't know what to have written other than a story about some guy that went to the movies all the time and watched all those movies in digitally restored versions. That story would have gotten nowhere. Then I asked myself the question.

What is important to me?

I responded with baseball.

Week 2:

There it was. The idea literally and figuratively hit me. A baseball story would be intriguing (if I managed to pull it off), and at the same time I could add characters that would mean something to the story, since I had previous experience with other topics other than sports, and so I could try and develop those characters as well as the story.

So I came up with the first line:

"The kid's dreaming."

But I quickly stopped myself, realizing I was writing about a dream and nearly wrote an entire story about a dream. "Aww crap," I said out loud, ruffling my hair with my hand. "I almost started writing about a dream."

Mrs Adamo, one of the editors here nearly threw a pen in my direction, because of the fact that one of the first things she told us not to do was to write about dreams. So I quickly adjusted it:

"The ninety-mile-per-hour fastball captivates him." And so started the story of Logan Klein battling memories of his father before he left him, as well as the pretentious pitcher on the Orlando Blue Jays, Mickey Dugdale. But the thing was that, I had only started getting intrigued by baseball. I mean, I knew about the sport and all, but not enough to write a story about it.

Monday night, I rang up my great friend, Nick Lipinski, and asked him every question I had about baseball, him being an avid player himself and being the reason why I ever picked up MLB 14 The Show on my PlayStation 3.

"Nick! Hey, how's it going? Listen, I had a question or two about baseball, if you're willing to mind my not knowing all too much about baseball." And he responded each question with an answer that made sense, from what an RBI was to a walk off to how innings ten thru one-thousand worked. I didn't necessarily use all that knowledge in the story, but it was a key moment to the development of the story.

Then came the editors. I prepared myself by putting on some thick skin when I awoke Tuesday morning and confronted Aalisha, who would be the death of me through editing. While I did know that the story was far from perfect, I didn't expect for her to return it to me all bloodied up with red pen marks. She absolutely hated my story. And then, NINETEEN drafts later, here I am, at the end of the process, done with writing and editing and all that jazz.

So I hope you enjoyed my story. I hope you enjoy the brief tale of rivalry between Logan Klein and Mickey Dugdale, Logan's father, and the Bottom of the Ninth.

The Bottom of the Ninth

The ninety-mile-per-hour fastball captivates him. From his seat in the dugout, he glances at the roaring crowd, almost every person with a hotdog in one hand and a drink in the other. The blinding white lights shine on the clay diamond, illuminating the field.

There's a player on each base, ready to run at the hit of a ball. On the scoreboard, Logan notices it's the bottom of the ninth, and that the Miami Stealers are down 3-0 to the Orlando Blue Jays. The kid's up to bat.

"Ladies and gentlemen, Logan Klein, number 9, third baseman," One of the announcers says over the intercom as he makes his way to home plate.

His father throws him the ball. He swings, and manages to get it between second and first base.

"Good, kiddo." A second ball is tossed to him, and Logan swings again, but sends the ball straight back to his father's glove.

Logan firmly plants his feet behind the marker, checking his distance with the Louisville Slugger. His stance is perfect. He takes a practice swing just to reassure himself, adjusting his position.

The pitcher gloves the ball. He and Logan stare each other down. On the back of the pitcher's teal and white shirt, the name Dugdale is inscribed in withered patches of letters, with the number 32 below. He's got a ripe pimple on his face the size of a walnut, probably the reason why he manages to strike out four out of five of the batters he pitches. It's a distraction, really; having a pimple like that should be illegal.

Logan's ready for the pitch. He stands a foot away from home plate and keeps his eyes on the ball, his gaze neglecting to waver from the red stitches holding the leather together.

His father smiles. The wrinkles that surround his eyes show his age as they crowd together. His eyes shone with hope and pride. And although he had caught the ball, Logan's father couldn't have been more proud.

"Logan! Run the bases with this one," His father said. Logan nodded.

He pitched the ball, Logan swung, hit the ball parallel to the first baseline, and runs the bases. His father counts the time. Eight seconds from home to first. He grins.

The ball flies out of Dugdale's hand, but Logan holds himself back from swinging.

"Ball!" the umpire yells.

The catcher throws the ball back towards pitcher's mound, where number 32 catches it gracefully with a backhand. Logan breathes in a sigh of relief. The signs in the crowd remind him of the stakes at hand, GAME 3 CHAMPS! GO BLUE JAYS! and FINAL GAME! TEAR 'EM APART! But the thing was that despite the series being tied 1-1, there was talk statewide about how the Miami Stealers deserved the win after a hard-fought season. They couldn't let the Blue Jays tear down their reputation. Logan wouldn't let that happen.

The second pitch hurtles towards Logan through the air. Dugdale's given him the perfect one, but he misses.

"Strike!" the ump yells, and the word echoes through Logan's mind. As the catcher throws the ball back to the pitcher, the sinking emotion of dread overwhelms Logan. It feels as though instead of landing in the catcher's glove, the ball hit him square in the chest.

Logan stares at him – Mickey Dugdale and the strangely pink, bulbous zit covering half of his face. The two had never liked each other. Because Logan had a tendency to badger on about Dugdale's crusty acne or his egocentric schemes to sabotage Logan.

The teams were warming up in their locker rooms, playing a short game of catch and taking practice swings while Logan was at the vending machine buying a Gatorade. Mickey showed up at his side.

"Hey fat boy!" Mickey called, "How about trying some water?"

"Why don't you tell that to your friend over there on your cheek?" Logan said, avoiding eye contact by watching the blue Gatorade bottle that's dropped to the hatch. He reached in and pulled it out.

"The hell's that supposed to mean?"

"It means I'm not in the mood right now," Logan said. He began to make his way back down to the locker room where the rest of the Stealers were still warming up. Mickey grabbed him by the shoulder and stopped him.

"God, you can be so stupid sometimes. I really hate you."

"I know. You don't need to remind me."

"I mean, seriously. You used to be a hell of a hitter, and now you play like Helen Keller. It's probably the same reason your dad left." Mickey shrugged. Logan drops the Gatorade and grabbed Mickey by his arms. He shoved him into the vending machine with a loud clunk.

"Don't talk about my dad, alright? I don't need your crap." Logan warned him. "Got it?"

The catcher on the Blue Jays heard the commotion and saw them. "Hey Logan, get off him!"

Logan considered his options. "Give me a good reason why I should."

"Go ahead, hit me. You won't," Mickey tempted him. "C'mon."

Logan formed a fist, but just as he did, he lowered it. "No, you're not worth a game." Instead, he shoved him into the vending machine one more time for good measure.

Mickey grabbed Logan's arm. "Hey Logan – "

"Get your hand off me, you freaking perv." He said, swiping his hand off of his shoulder.

"I'll see you on the field, Logan," Mickey said.

Bases are still loaded.

Logan is still up to bat, one ball, one strike, and two outs.

The ball sails from Dugdale to home plate once more. Logan doesn't swing, thinking it's out of the strike zone. But it was a bad call. "Strike!"

When he slides back home, Logan's father approaches him, and helps him back up onto his feet. He then kneels down, and Logan knows he's going to tell him something.

"Damn!" Logan says under his breath. That's two.

The catcher tosses the ball to Dugdale once more. Mickey and Logan make eye contact. Mickey clutches the ball, attracting the attention of the crowd. Logan repositions himself to batting stance, making the players glare in anticipation.

His father's voice rang through his head:

"Learn not to miss."

The crowd watches, enraptured, screaming at the players, shouting basic cheers and failing several attempts at a wave. For the last time, the ball is thrown to home plate. It's headed straight down the middle, and Logan knows this is the perfect pitch. He takes one last look at the ball. With everything he has, he pulls the bat from behind his shoulder, swings, and strikes the ball.

He drops the bat and runs.

Logan ignores the soaring ball as he barrels toward first base, where the baseman is looking awestruck. Logan then dashes to second, third, and finally home.

Home plate stands clean. The catcher's not in a rush to push a play, nor is there anyone else standing there with one foot on the marker and the ball in their glove, waiting for Logan. Just an empty home plate, waiting for him. Logan slides in and the ump calls it safe. The crowd upheaves in a roar, everyone cheering for their win. Logan turns to check the scoreboard.

Stealers lead 4-3. The team rushes to Logan, picks him up from his feet. They cheer, scream and high-five.

The bases were now empty.

He hit the grand slam.

He didn't miss.

Jac'Quanda Robinson

"I don't think of myself as a poor, deprived ghetto girl who made good. I think of myself as somebody who from an early age knew I was responsible for myself, and I had to make good."
– Oprah Winfrey

My name is Jac'Quanda Robinson, and I a fourteen-year-old African American young lady. In the fall, I will be advancing as a sophomore at Glades Central Community High School. I was born and raised in my hometown, Belle Glade, Florida. I am more than just a girl with a hobby that just happens to be writing. I am a writer. Additionally, I am a great believer in receiving upright justice. I am a craver of adventure. I am a girl that sets goals and achieves them. I am a mermaid. I am a fan of the arts. I am in search of beauty. I am me. Food is my kryptonite. Although you don't know me very well, let alone know anything thing about my character, I am hoping that subsequent to divulging in my masterpieces, you will. After all, I have shared a piece of my soul with you.

Reflection

Exhilarating, magnificent, and splendid are only a few of the words that I can use to describe my time spent in the *Canon Solutions America Future Authors Project*. The eight days that I spent in the program have been exceedingly beneficial towards my writing. I can honestly say that I see improvements in my writing. During the course of the first week I met my first author and that was exciting. We traveled to Don Estridge High Tech Middle School, and I had the chance to receive creative insight from a real author. I also enjoyed spending time with other aspiring young authors. The icing on the cake was both of the presentations by Canon Solutions of America. The second week we did more rigorous writing and a lot of peer and self-editing. All in all, I was proud of what I had to accomplish, and I can't wait for everyone to see.

The Person Behind the Person

Beauty goes beyond the surface of the human eye and its visibility. It is not about appearance, but undoubtedly about heart. Beauty cannot be attained by altering one's physical features. To the poet Khalil Gibran, "Beauty is not in the face; beauty is a light in the heart." I find that to be very true; because no amount of plastic surgery or designer items of clothing can make you truly beautiful. When you are beautiful on the inside, your light will shine through, and others will see it on the outside. There aren't a set of criteria or legal standards that someone has to meet in order to be deemed beautiful. Beauty is defined by any and everything you do and say. Beauty is unveiled by the heart's true intentions. Sacrificing yourself will not allow you to experience being truly beautiful. To be beautiful is to be true to yourself. Beauty is present in many different shapes, forms, sizes, and ages. A person's beauty is unique. It is pure. It is raw.

Culture

It ignited at a young age
It was a snake in the grass

The feeling is fire
The experience is divine

It permeates my being
It engulfs and molds me

Your attire,
Your distinguished appetite

Your choices of art,
Your beliefs and values

Your morals and ethics
Your perceptions of life

Have pride in it
It is beautiful

Showcase it to the world
Grasp your roots

Embrace your being
Remember your upcoming

The wondrous fever of the world
Present in every boy and girl

So many different colors
And wonderful traditions

Hoping to replenish new beings
It is your one and only culture

Diary of Naj Patel

Dear diary,   October 12, 2013
It seems like everything happened just yesterday. But, from what I have been told, I have been deprived of a third of a year. I just don't understand. They tell me that it's not my fault, but I continue to blame myself because I could have done more.

Dear diary,   January 1, 2014
My life is completely in shambles. It's New Years, I should be celebrating, right? Wrong! I am depressed, I am sad, I am angry, and I am mad at the world. I need answers. I deserve answers. Anthony B. Cartwright, he should be in prison, not walking around as a free man.

Dear diary,   June 11, 2014
Tomorrow is my best friend's seventeenth birthday, and I have no clue on how I am going to get through the day. I had it all planned out. I knew what I was going to wear, how I was going to style my hair, what gifts I was going to give her, and even her reaction to the surprise Bollywood themed sixteenth birthday party that we threw for her. The only thing that I didn't have planned was her not being there to enjoy it. It was my duty to get her there safely and on time. Mrs. Huffington trusted me with that responsibility, but I failed. Tremendously.

Dear diary,   June 12, 2014
I brought her a dozen of beautifully fluorescent red roses and we had a much-needed conversation. Well, I talked; she listened. Even though I was unable to see her physical being, I could feel her presence. "I'm sorry, I'm so sorry, please forgive me," I pleaded with her over and over and over again. I needed her to know about all the guilt, remorse, and anger afflicting me. That night I did everything right.

Francisca Rodriguez

Hello, my name is Francisca Rodriguez. I was born on November 20, 1999. I have many names like Franny, and French fry, but I'm mainly known as Francis and Tweety. I have a passion for sports, yet my passion for writing is even stronger. My goal in life is to get into a good college with a Basketball scholarship, so I can make it into the Women's National Basketball Association (WNBA). I realized that I loved writing when I was in 4th grade. I was the only girl in class who would write two or three page length stories; to everyone else's one full page. I appreciate my whole family for believing in me, for believing that I would get into this program, as they all are aware I love writing. I am grateful for this opportunity of becoming a published author as well as the opportunity to make my family proud. So, I am very grateful for this program.

Reflections

On the first week of the program we reviewed and learned some new genres of writing, different writing skills, and some common elements to look for in our drafts to tighten up our writing. We also got to read each other's poems, short stories, essays, and more. We learned some different ways to conquer writer's block. Suggestions were given by the first author we met, Mrs. Zelda Benjamin, who presented to us on our field trip to Don Estridge High Tech Middle School on the second day of the program.

The second week, we learned how magazines, books, and the things around us can inspire our writing, and how they influence what we write. This was advice given by author Mr. Steve Alten, who presented to us by interactive TV. Poet Mr. Dwight Stewart shared personal experiences and spoke his dynamic poetry with musical backgrounds. We learned from all of the authors that it's best to write about what we like, things that we are familiar with, or be prepared to research in order to present credible information in our writing. Research on the subject we're writing about also will help us to avoid writer's block.

Our Protectors

Hey! Let me ask, has your parent ever started to have a conversation with you about something you did that put you in great danger; then, it turns into arguing? After a short period of time, you get into trouble or you get grounded, then you yell out to them the most hateful words ever, "I Hate you!" But, you never know why they are trying to protect you; you never know whether the same thing had happened to them.

Our parents are like dream catchers. They take those bad dreams away from you, as if the bad things in life are the bad dreams. It's like my Mom and Dad, they are my protectors, but my Dad is especially protective of me because I'm his only Daughter. Unlike my Mom, she is protective of me when it comes to school and how some schools are like somewhat kind of dangerous. She wants to make sure I don't get into any trouble, and can be quiet when in class.

When it comes to being outside of school, it's different when we go to church. Because we are Christian, we don't go to parties a lot. This always creates a problem as I get invited to my friends' Quinceaneras; yet, I can't go. I always tell them my parents won't let me, so when I go home, I tell my mom about it and she says, " We can go, but you can't dance." I always get mad, and I always tell my friends the next day that I can't go to their Quinceanera. My parents always tell me, " Okay," but I know that they're trying to protect me, because it's dangerous at some parties.

At home when it's just my parents and me, it's always a lazy day. When it comes to these types of days, it's when all problems are behind us and we just sit there on the couch or on one of the beds; we eat, and watch television with each other, and they know that they are raising me right, and that's why I love them with all my heart. And that's why you should too!

"A child looks up at the stars and wonders. Great fathers put a child on his shoulders and helps them to grab a star."
– Reed Markham

"For all my love little monsters I am your Mom you are my child in my hand I protect you like my eyes but don't worry I'll catch you if you fall."
– Lady Gaga

The New Girl and Her New Best Friend

"Taylor! Taylor, sweetie you're going to be late for your first day at your new school!" Taylor's mom yelled upstairs to get Taylor to hurry. No sound of footsteps, no running water, no noise that suggested someone was preparing to scoot off to school in a few minutes. "Taylor! C'mon now, so you can be on time."

"Okay I'll be down in a minute," Taylor yelled back, walking down the stairs with no intention of going to her new school.

"Aren't you excited for your first day at your new school?" Taylor's Mom asked.

"No. Why do I even have to go to this school? I liked the old one better, I have friends there, and at this school I doubt that I'll make any friends," Taylor responded.

"Just try to get along with everyone, and I'm sure you will make some good friends here too, sweetie," her mother assured, always the optimist. Taylor looked at her with annoyed eyes.

As Taylor drove to her new school and pulled up in the parking lot, the appearance of the school caught her attention.

"This school looks a little messy, but it can't get any worse," Taylor noted as she walked inside, and was met with a large hallway, full of people she didn't know. She ambled around the unfamiliar faces, randomly asking them where her new classes were, but to no avail. Upset and ignored, she just continued to walk until she noticed a girl standing alone beside a locker.

"Excuse me; do you know where this class is?" Taylor asked, flashing her new schedule.

"Upstairs, go straight until you're at the end of the hallway, and then make a right and the class will be right there," responded the girl.

"Thanks. What's your name?" Taylor asked, curiously.

"My name is Jessica, and your name is…?"

"My name is Taylor," Taylor responded.

"Nice to meet you, Taylor, and welcome to Westwood High School! Let me show you around," Jessica beamed.

Coincidentally, the girls had most of their classes together. They made steady conversation, and quickly took a liking to each other. After a few months into the school year, Taylor and Jessica were closer than ever. They went to class together, and they would hang out with each other in and out of school. More months passed.

"So Taylor, how do you like Westwood High now? " Jessica asked sarcastically, knowing of Taylor's former reluctance.

"It's great, especially since I have a new best friend!"

"Who?" Jessica asked, looking uncertain.

"You!" Taylor exclaimed, locking arms with her new best friend.

Brittany Segura

"Funny how when your life is mostly bullshit, you turn off feeling. Sometimes it's hard to turn it back on again."
– Ellen Hopkins, Identical

I am a teenage girl who has set more expectations for herself than her family has set for her. My achievements never satisfy me, because I constantly try to outdo myself. I am fifteen years old, from a tremendous Dominican family, and currently living in Belle Glade, Florida. When I get older, I want to become a Forensic Odontologist (fancy phrase for forensic dentist) and hope to attend New York University for Dental School. I'm Brittany Segura, and I'm more than just a writer.

Reflection

These last eight days in the Future Authors Project have taught me an abundance of things. I genuinely believe I have grown as a writer thanks to the support I've received from the other members and Ms. Mann. One thing I really enjoyed about the program was being able to receive educated critique from other outstanding writers, rather than just family and friends (who always seem to love your work either way). This summer, I became friends with people who I would see every day around campus, but never spoke to; now we have something distinct in common. It's been amazing to be in such a positive and productive environment, and I've really treasured my time here with the other Future Authors.

24 hours.

It's dawn,
She beams
She giggles
She parties
She jokes
She LIVES.
It's dusk,
She sobs
She hides
She cuts
She screams
She DIES.

Hanging Fire

I am young
And my expectations haven't yet been met
My hair resembles that of Medusa
And my nationality
Is constantly questioned

What if I fail?
And let myself down
They would all notice
They would all speak
But will that make mom and dad speak again?

I have three brothers
All different compared to me
All younger than me
All sons of my stepfather
Who's been a tremendous part of my life
He keeps my mom sane
Although she seems to become more lost
As the days pass her by
I stick around
Mostly out of guilt and criticism

But what if I fail
And let myself down
Will that make mom and dad speak again?

"People come and go," they say
But in my life
I bounce around from home to home
So they never get the chance to go
They stay around while I grow
I am as independent as possible

For a fifteen year old
I am self-motivated
But honestly afraid of my every move

Because what if I fail
Will that make mom and dad speak again?

The Ward

I awoke in a blur, an unfamiliar and barren room surrounding me. I couldn't bring myself to stand; my legs felt numb and my head, heavy. I sat on the bare bed in absolute confusion until I heard locks turning. I looked toward the door to see a man in scrubs enter.

"Breakfast is in ten minutes, put on your uniform. The other patients are anxious to meet you."

"Patients?"

"What? Did you think you were the only person in the psych ward?" he probed.

I sat in silence trying to absorb what this stranger was telling me. I was in a psychiatric hospital…as a patient. He snickered once and was turning to leave before I stopped him.

"Wait, wait! Who are you? Why am I here?"

"I told you all of this valuable information when you were admitted earlier this morning, but anyways, my name is Steven. I'm the ward caretaker," he stated in a lifeless tone.

"So why am I here?"

"Amanda, you were found miles from your foster home. We've determined you were in a fugue state, but we aren't sure of how you got so far from Belmont. You were discovered trying to jump off of the Bailey Island Bridge."

"I blacked out?"

"Sortof. During a fugue state you do things that you aren't aware of."

"I'm not a f__king psycho!"

"Whoa, we don't use that term here. We prefer to say mentally disabled. And, word of advice, that type of hostility isn't going to get you anywhere. Now, hurry up and put on your uniform," Steven instructed, before he shut the door, making sure to lock me in again.

I dressed quickly, stripping off my torn jeans and slipping into the scratchy beige uniform. Steven came back and guided me to the cafeteria, disregarding all my questions and responding with exasperated sighs. The whole hospital was like one immense contradiction. The cafeteria had bleached marble floors and blinding lights, but the somber aura was one that might be found at graveyard. The other patients would appear sane to outsiders, but slight actions – a constant twitch, a fluttering of the eyes, an incessant tapping- revealed their true nature. I requested to meet with the psychiatrist; the man who would get me out of here.

"Hello Amanda, I am Dr. Roth. Welcome to your new home here at the Maine Central Psychiatric Hospital."

"New home? Are you sure I'm the mental one here?"

"Listen Ms. Richardson, you're here because we want to help you. Do you remember anything that occurred the last few days?"

"No. Enlighten me."

"You were found miles away from your adoptive home, high on methamphetamine, and attempting to commit suicide. We're not here to judge you or call you insane; we're here to help you recover."

"The crystal helps me stay happy."

"That's what you think Amanda, but in reality that's one of the many side effects of methamphetamine. It gives you a false sense of pleasure and security."

I stood up and strolled back to my room, the **warden** rushing after me. He observed me as I laid down, pretending to go to sleep. When I was certain that he was gone, I took the pillow case off the tattered cushion, placed it over my head, and tied it snugly around my neck. I couldn't breathe. Slowly I began to suffocate. Finally, I was happy again.

Rose Sintulaire

"I can do all things through Christ who strengthens me."
—   Phillipians 4:13

"Love what you do and do what you love. Don't listen to anyone else who tells you not to do it. You do what you want, what you love. Imagination should be the center of your life."
—Ray Bradbury

Rose Sintulaire [rohz-sent-ul-air] is an aspiring young lady who has been trying to unravel the world since she was born into it on August 17, 1997; who's infatuated with reading a little more than writing, adores helping others, and is impatiently waiting to graduate from high school in 2015, who values her relationship with God, learning, and meeting new people, who enthusiastically takes on new challenges while eyeing the glass as if it were half full, who admires her family- blood related or not, and could not see life without them.

Reflections

I had an awesome two weeks in this program. Not only did I meet new faces who share a love for writing like I do, but I also had the opportunity to work with one of my favorite writing instructors, Mrs. Mann. Additionally, I don't think I could have done without the help of both of the mentors.

During the first week, I learned about the writing process itself. How the work goes from the brain, word processors, to editing, and books. I also learned about the editing process, and how it is the most challenging part of the writing process. I met a great author, who writes romances that gave awesome tips for beginning writers. The first week is also the week that I started writing. I must admit, I was not overflowing with ideas of where to go with my first piece, but inspiration hit me, literally, in the right moment.

The second week was the hardest week, because by then I was pulling my hair out of my scalp, thinking to myself: what in the world am I going to do next? Once I was done with my first piece I thought something else was going to hit me, but the sad thing was it didn't. Thankfully, Mrs. Mann started talking about world events (I love when she does that) and it got me thinking about things that are currently happening at this moment. Out of hundreds, I came across the one that hit me the hardest, and hopefully I did it justice. My last piece was a work in progress. It started before I did, so when I started thinking about it, I was not quite sure about it, but in the end it all worked out. I am glad I was on the other side of the publishing process even though it was tough work.

Bring Back Our Girls Alive

You want Me to hide behind you?
Float in you muddy shadows?
Bury my entity because of your idiocrasy?
Cover my mouth to cage my voice?
No opinion no choice?
But I have Nations behind Me.
You have guns.

You can snatch Me from my circle.
Parrot the sobs of my sisters.
Ignore the wails of my mother.
Guffaw at the pleas of my father and brothers.
Still, I have Nations behind Me.
You have guns.

Are you mad that I am educated?
No longer submitting to your brainwash?
Speaking a tongue that hardens your heart.
When you stand, I don't fall apart.
Again, I have Nations behind Me.
You have guns.

Give Me my Freedom!
You had enslaved Me once before, and I was freed.
I want my freedom back!
I demand to march next to you!
To show my exquisiteness, to subordinate your stupidity!
To challenge my mind, to rule in the world!
You don't want this.
You don't want women's empowerment.
Once more, I have Nations behind Me.
You have guns.

Doorboxed

I am stuck.

Perched in a corner of a box; hugging my knees to my chest.

On each side of the box there is a locked white door.

On each door there is a golden doorknob, the keyhole side facing me.

In my hands are a set of Keys, but these Keys, they don't unlock any of these doors.

I pound and wail desperately for someone's help while charging at the door, but there is no answer.

I wonder about what's on the other side of each of the doors, and about the world I could possibly walk into...

I have visions, and pray of being freed from this box, of someone opening one of these doors.

What will I do if all the doors open together?

Will I be indecisive?

What if I don't leave, what if I do?

Will I take the Keys along, or will I leave them behind?

I decide I'll take the Keys, for I don't know if there will be another door for me to unlock,

Or if I will be locked in a box again.

But until then, I stare at the whiteness of the doors, and wait...

The Wrong Way

I remember the day I saw it. It felt like the image was tattooed in my head just yesterday. *Don't go down there*, the voice in my head knowingly cautioned. *Turn around, go the other way!* It commanded again, but my stubbornness won over. It did not foreshadow the impending traumatic scene that was to happen. It was a total smack to the face.

I was walking through the shortcut I discovered when I was younger. Although woodsy, it was a nice contrast to the hard cement of the city sidewalk. Along the way, sun rays stung my puffy cheeks, my back soaked from the perspiration of the humidity of the day. My freshly painted blue toenails burned in my froggy flip-flops, as I traipsed on the wet grass. Birds flew above me from tree to tree, laughter in their songs, and crickets in their mouths. Sea blue skies illuminated the green leaves of trees and bushes. The break of day gave birth to an earthy steamy smell. The sight was captivating. After passing by my favorite oak tree, I suddenly stopped, something did not seem right. I stood there - frozen, my feet sensed the horror before me, my bones, stiffening into painful poles.

"Huuuh!" I gasped, inhaling into chest pain. "Ahhhhhhhhhhhhh!" an abrupt ear-piercing sound came out of nowhere. Looking around to determine the guilty brute, I shamefully covered my mouth with a balling fist.

My senses sharpened at the sight. My skin prickled, felt like millions of ants parading on my epidermis in lockstep, as I stared at the lifeless creature laying on the dirty ground coiled around itself. Its mouth was covered in bits and pieces of feather, stunned. I held its glare, as I stared into its yellow eyes. Its scaly, orange- yellow, blubbery body swam in its own coopery pool, as gnats danced on the open wound. Its breakfast, I guessed, a chirpy bird half digested, gave a swollen golden bulge around its midsection. I stood four inches from where it was sliced in half, so close to the pool of blood. I was one step away from gliding over the bloody pond.

As I stood there examining the dead serpent, I could feel my heart in my throat. I took a couple of rickety steps back, and every step felt like I was squashing the dead creature. I was quivering all over. I wanted to run, but my body stiffened even more.

Finally gathering enough courage, I turned around and dashed away. I ached for a redo. The previous vision was now engraved behind my eyelids, making me shiver again. I want to go back to the greenness, birds, and sunshine. I paranoidly toppled over a bulky tree root, scraping my knee and elbow in the process.

Trying to clear my thoughts, I walked down the road I should've gone down from the start, and tried to obliterate the horrifying images from my skull.

Kiara Smith

My name is Kiara Smith, I am sixteen years old, and I'm becoming a junior at Glades Central High School. I was born on the 5th of March, 1998. Belle Glade, Florida is my hometown, where I was raised by my mother, Lucille Travetta Harris-Carney, and my father, Anthony Smith. I began writing in the 5th grade, when I attended Gove Elementary School. I never truly took writing seriously, until the 7th grade. That year I attended Roosevelt Middle School in West Palm Beach. There, I wrote short stories that I gave to my friends to read. I also became aware of the website called Wattpad, where other amateur and skilled writers posted short stories to be read and critiqued by the public. I used Wattpad and my peers to grow and enhance my writing skills, which helped me when I reached my 9th and 10th grades at Glades Central Community High School. My Creative Writing and English classes both helped me to expand my knowledge of writing and exercise the different ways in which to write. In the 10th grade, I was given an AICE General Papers class that further broadened my skills at writing. Currently, I am still writing short stories, better and more detailed, for the public.

Reflection

My first week of the program was actually very eventful. I had an idea for a short story and plotted it almost instantly. Within the last few hours of the first day, I already had about two pages written. The second day, we took a trip to Don Estridge High Tech Middle School, where we met the author, Mrs. Zelda Benjamin, and went over the processes of publishing and self-publishing. We also took our pictures for the book. Afterwards, we went over to Canon Solutions America, where we toured the building and saw all of the different methods for printing different types of projects, such as comics, poster boards, standees, and even tables. It was pretty cool and a nice way to find out how books are made.

My second week was totally and completely hectic. Not only was I working to finish my short story (not to mention two possible poems), I was also dealing with Driver's Ed classes that were also on campus. So with only half of four days to finish, I was on edge trying to finish three creative pieces, a biography, this reflection, and a thank you letter. Yes, I was quite busy, working at home and at the school, but I made it through.

Excerpt from "Clash"

Jordan groaned as she woke up, a light sleepy moan escaping her lips while she stretched herself awake. The sunlight beamed dimly through her sheer curtains, a silent reminder that she was about to be late for school. Springing up into a seated position, she snatched her alarm clock from the bedside table and checked the time -- 6:47 AM. She had missed the bus. Again.

"Damn," Jordan exclaimed, silently. She climbed out of bed, tearing the comforter from her body, and darting into her closet, grabbing the first things she saw to wear. Once dressed, she sprinted to her bathroom to brush her teeth and apply quick make-up. She shook her slept-on locks to bring volume to her naturally curly hair, grabbed her bag, slung her guitar case over her shoulder, and slipped on a pair of flats. She had rushed all the way down the stairs before she realized she had forgotten her phone. Throwing her bags by the door, she ran up the stairs and bumped into her sleep-dazed dad, and stumbled a bit.

"Whoa, babygirl, where's the fire?" He chuckled groggily.

"Sorry, daddy. I'm late." She replied, already rushing past him and into her room.

"Do you want me to call Charles to drive you?" Her dad called to her.

Charles was the chauffer; although, he was more like a family member. Paid a weekly salary, he only came once or twice during a week to actually drive someone; though, he was always invited for dinner and family outings.

"Yes, please. I need a ride," She called back from the room. Almost instantly Thomas was on the phone with Charles.

"Thanks, daddy." Jordan skittered out of the room and quickly tiptoed to kiss his check, then ran downstairs to meet Charles at the door.

"Good morning, Miss Brown." Charles greeted, as Jordan opened the back door to put her stuff in the shiny white BMW. After shutting the door, she hopped into the passenger seat with a sigh.

"I thought I asked you to call me Jordan, Charles?" She smiled, buckling her seatbelt.

"Sorry, Miss, er, Jordan," He chuckled, scratching the back of his head. Jordan laughed a little also, as Charles started the car's ignition.

~ ~

Charles slowed to a stop in the Student Drop-off loop. Putting the car in park, the young man turned to face Jordan.

"Do you need me to come sign you in? You are rather late." He asked, concerned.

"Nah, I should be fine. My first period teacher loves me," she lied. Charles gave her a questioning smirk. "Trust me. It's good."

"Very well, then," He nodded. "I'll see you around,"

"Thanks, Charles,"

"No problem, Jordan. Enjoy your day."

'Ill try...' Jordan thought.

Jordan got out and grabbed her things from the car, waving Charles off as she turned to walk into the office.

"You're late, Jordan." The woman at the front desk said sternly.

"I overslept, Ms. Fox." Jordan groaned.

"Oversleeping is not an excuse. Learn to set your alarm."

"It was set. When I get home, I actually take out my books and study, unlike other kids. You'd know from my grades." Jordan smirked cockily at Ms. Fox's defeated scowl.

"You've got detention, Jordan. Since you think being ten minutes late to school is okay." Ms. Fox smirked back at her, regaining the upper hand.

"For?" Jordan raised a brow. "School doesn't start until the bell rings, which was five minutes ago. I wasn't on campus, ten minutes ago. I know my schedule. And, you're not penalizing me for anything." She placed a hand on her hip as she challenged Ms. Fox.

"I'll let you off with a warning," Ms. Fox complied reluctantly.

"Thank you," Jordan gave her fake smile and took the pass Ms. Fox quickly scribbled out.

"Next time I won't let you off so easy," Ms. Fox called after her.

"Yeah, yeah." Jordan pushed the door open and headed to class.

~ ~

On the other side of the school, Amber sat at her desk in Geometry class, struggling with the day's assignment.

"Do you understand the lesson, Amber?" Mr. Jones asked as he walked up to her desk.

"Uh. Not really, sir." She smiled sheepishly.

"It's okay," he chuckled. "Come on to my desk and I'll reteach it for you."

Amber followed the jovial, middle-aged blonde back to his desk and pulled up a chair. As he explained the lesson again; this time, slower than when he taught the class, Amber began to understand better and even started to finish his examples before he was done explaining them.

"See, now you've got it," Mr. Jones smiled proudly.

"Yeah, it's not so hard now," Amber laughed as she began to complete the day's assignment.

"So, do you think you've got the assignment now?" He asked about the class work, overlapping his hands on his desk.

"Yes, sir. Thank you." Amber smiled, thankfully rising to return to her desk. As she sat, she thought about her grades. They were starting to get better the more her teachers gave extra help with her work. But, she knew she still had to work really hard to make good grades.

Amber had asked her parents several times to give her the freedom her friends had. She wanted to go out, to hang out with them, a car to drive herself places. But, her parents were strict; they didn't agree. Because they consistently struggled to make ends meet, they wanted good grades out of Amber, before they'd give her permission to do such things. They wanted to assure that she was on the path to becoming successful – a college-ready, self-sufficient, scholar, someone who could move on to metropolitan cities with big business, arts and entertainment districts, interesting places to work and move up corporate ladders, places like New York City, or even big diverse states like California. Anywhere, but this run-down hellhole, where they lived. They only wanted the best for their little girl.

So, Amber strove to get her grades right. Lately, she was doing great, making progress, and had all A's except for two classes. She was finally going to be able to accept her friends' invitations to outings and parties.

~ ~

"Mr. Jones, I need to talk to you about my grades," Amber was snapped from her thoughts by a girl who abruptly burst into the class.

"Jordan, you're interrupting my class," Mr. Jones groaned.

"I wouldn't have to interrupt if you hadn't screwed up my grades." She marched up to his desk and placed her hands on her hips. She seems like one of those spoiled girls, Amber thought. She looked Jordan up and down, as the girl argued with the teacher. Jordan's delicate, natural beauty was obscured by her funky attitude and her attempt at a funky style: curly black hair that would be long if she got it straightened, a layered bang dyed purple at the tips. She was very pretty, beautiful, in Amber's opinion. She was tall and had a nice body shape; not too fat, not too skinny. She had a nice complexion, as well, with a chocolate skin tone.

"Uh, problem?" Jordan snapped. Amber jumped a little, snatched, once again, from her thoughts, by the girl.

"N-no," Amber stuttered, dropping her head and beginning to fiddle with her pencil. The classroom was quiet now, only whispers being heard about "that girl."

"Jordan, I'm going to have to ask you to leave. You're disrupting my class. You're free to come after school." Mr. Jones gestured to the door calmly, but he spoke sternly.

"Thank you." Jordan gave a fake smile and strutted out. Once gone, the whole class went into a gossiping frenzy about the situation.

"Quiet! Everybody hush, now!" Mr. Jones yelled over the fuss.

Amber was quiet. She'd never met anyone so mean. Even the gangsters and thugs on the streets weren't so rude. Then again, she was mad about something serious. It's easy to lash out at others if you're facing a tough issue. Maybe that's what it was, she thought.

~ ~

Amber walked in the cafeteria with a mission, determined to find that "Jordan" girl and see why she was upset. She was going to befriend her and to apologize for staring. Mother always preached that staring is wrong.

Amber speed-walked through the cafeteria, maneuvered around people and through tables. Standing on her tiptoes, she looked over heads for that curly black and purple hair. Finally, she spotted her, sitting on a table top, strumming a guitar, near the back of the cafeteria. Quickly, Amber rushed to the back, stopping a few feet away from Jordan's table, to calm down a bit. She took a few deep breaths before speaking.

"Um. Hi." Amber inched around into Jordan's view and gave a shy wave.

"Hey." Jordan looked up briefly from her guitar to acknowledge the girl's presence.

"I, uh, don't know if you remember me, but I'm the girl from Mr. Jones's class." Amber explained. Jordan looked up, confused, before realization dawned upon her.

"Oh, um, sorry about that. I was in a bad mood, as you probably figured out." Jordan scratched the back of her head, now ashamed of her behavior.

"It's okay," Amber smiled, tucking her long almond locks behind her ear. "I shouldn't have been staring. Mother always told me that was rude, so I kind of deserved it." She smiled. "My name's Amber."

"Jordan." She returned the smile.

"I, uh, apologize again for judging you." Amber looked down, fidgeting with her bag's strap.

"Huh?" Jordan cocked her head to the side.

"When you stormed in the class earlier, I automatically thought that you were one of those stuck up, rich girls. I mean, you just walked in and yelled at the teacher. The teacher!" She laughed, unbelievingly. "Not only did you chew out a teacher, your clothes -- they look like they're really expensive. I mean, mauve cashmere sweater, crisp white cotton blouse, jeans with top stitching, embroidered foreign label.

"So, I just instantly judged you. That is totally out of character for me, so I apologize." Amber was shocked to hear laughter coming from Jordan.

"Girl, everyone thinks that. No need to be sorry," Jordan laughed. "I have a hot temper and am prouder than anything. Everyone's first impression is 'stuck-up'. I just learned to get used to it." She explained.

Amber joined in with Jordan's laughter. Such a turn-around encourages laughter. Here, Amber thought Jordan would jump down her throat for judging her, but she was totally understanding about it.

"Aye. You seem cool. Wanna hang out at my place?" Jordan offered.

"But...I just met you," Amber's eyes went wide with such an abrupt invite.

"Eh. It's fine. My people are cool with it. Maybe..." Jordan trailed off.

Jordan's parents were uber-nice people, but they were judgmental. In front of Jordan's friends, they were cordial and accommodating, the best hosts. However, when guests left, all Jordan heard were their criticisms and what they thought was wrong with the person's outfit, or their hair, or their social status. They were like gossipy senior citizens, if they learned someone's family lineage and their "dirty laundry". Jordan hated that, but what could she do?

"Well. Uh, I'd have to ask my parents," Amber ran a hand through her hair in thought. "They should let me since my grades are coming up."

"Grades?" Jordan asked.

"Yeah. I'm a C student..." Amber blushed.

"Tch." Jordan sucked her teeth at the girl. "Girl, give me your number." Amber, confused, looked at Jordan. So Jordan repeated herself. "Give me. Your number." Amber rambled off the digits to Jordan as Jordan typed it into her phone.

"Talk to your people. Be at my house, after school, on Friday."

"O-okay." Amber stuttered again. Her shyness was starting to kick in again. "But w-why?"

"I'm going to tutor you. No offense, but if you're going to hang with me, you've gotta have grades like me." Jordan scanned over Amber, head to toe. "Fashion, however, is for another day." She was referring to Amber's grey tank top, black jacket, tapered jeans, and sneakers.

"Uh. Okay." Amber looked down at her clothes. She thought she looked good.

"Then it's settled. Amber...?" Jordan trailed off.

"Lee. Amber Lee." Amber finished.

"Amber Lee, you're now my friend," Jordan smiled with a quick, confirming nod.

"Cool." Amber smiled. "Can I sit here?"

"Sure." Jordan scooted over a bit to make room for the petite Amber. There, until the end of lunch, they chatted as if they'd been friends for years.

~ ~

Amber checked the time and decided to take a shower and relax in the house. Coming out the shower in a towel, she heard her phone vibrating, as soon as she got into the living room. When she picked it up, she saw it was from an unknown number. Jordan... Amber thought. So much for relaxing at home. Amber secured the towel around her and sat on the couch to return the call.

"Hello?" After three rings, Jordan picked up the phone.

"You called?" Amber replied.

"Did you talk to your parents?" Jordan got straight to the point.

"I'll call and ask," Amber trailed off in thought.

"Cool. What subjects do you need help in?" Jordan asked.

"Uh, Science and Spanish II." Amber sighed after some thought.

"That's easy!" Jordan scoffed. "Go ahead and call your folks and get back to me on that." Jordan concluded.

"Okay then." Amber agreed. With that, Amber hung up to call her mother.

~ ~

"Hey, Mommy," Amber cheerily greeted when the call was answered.

"Hey, baby," Her mom replied lovingly.

"Is it okay if I go to a friend's house?"

"Umm… How are your grades looking?" Instantly, her mother's voice morphed from bubbly sweet to hardline strict. Her brief pause showed Amber that her agreement was not guaranteed.

"They've gotten better, Ma," Amber smiled though she knew her mom couldn't see it.

"Meaning?" Her mom asked, for clarification.

"I've got all A's, except for two classes, which is why I'm going to my friend's house." Amber explained.

"Oh, that's great, baby!" Her mother cheered gleefully.

"Thanks, Mommy," Amber smiled bashfully.

"Hmm. Well. You can go to her house…it is a 'her', isn't it?" Her mom suddenly asked skeptically.

"Yes, Mom, it's a girl." Amber groaned.

"Good. It better be. But, it's okay if you go. Be home by 11 o'clock, though." Her mom said.

"Yes, Mommy. Thank you." Amber silently cheered for her small feat.

"You're welcome, baby. Have fun. Behave. Study hard with your friend." Her mom concluded.

"Okay, I will. Bye, Mommy. Love you." Amber said.

"Love you too." With that, Amber ended the call and skipped into her room to prepare for a milestone achievement in her life – going to a friend's house for the very first time.

The Artist

Watch as the pencil glides across the page
Curly Q's and long waves
She's lost, she's gone
In her own world, only distraction is the music on her phone
The world is cruel, deceitful, conniving
But she just draws a new way of living
She ignores the pain, hides the shame
Avoids the questions screaming "WHY?!"
Drawing instantly, on the fly
People don't understand
How she copes with what others can't withstand
But it's all within the pen
The paper, the pen, the insight within
Is all she needs
To hold back
The End.

Moyra Stewart

I came into this world in March of 2000, I was birthed in the very unspectacular town of Boca Raton. For the first thirteen years of my life I was homeschooled with my two older brothers, until I started attending Boca Raton Middle School in September of 2013. I graduated from Boca Middle in June of 2014, and by August this year, I will be a freshman at Boca High. Returning back to my early life, I moved with my family to Scotland in 2004 where we lived for five years. Thanks to the fact that my brothers and I were homeschooled, we had the flexibility to move and traverse around the cities, visiting museums and more castles than you would wish for. I have many fond memories of my time in Scotland, and some very good friends that still keep in touch after all these years.

Getting to the point though, I can trace my love of writing all the way back to my first memories, of course like any writer, I was first an avid reader. I recall being read The Chronicles of Narnia (The Lion, The Witch, And The Wardrobe), which stands to this day as my favorite book. When I was old enough to read by myself, I read everything I could get my hands on. There were nights that I couldn't go to sleep without reading a book, so I would plow through three or four paperbacks in one sitting until my eyelids would no longer stay open. At first, all of the stories that I wrote were my own little fantasies that disgraced the pages of the composition journals that they were written on. My main protagonist was always a young girl (Surprisingly like myself), who looked like me (Weird right?), and liked all the same things that I did (I wasn't even trying to be discrete), and every story was the same basic idea: A ordinary suburban girl who has destiny literally fall into her lap as she finds some magical person or world that whisks her away like Peter Pan. I can honestly say that I would cringe and go running for the hills if I ever encountered those works again, and I thank everyone who

I cajoled into reading them for putting up with my childish antics. But there is a reason that I always wrote a superior version of myself, and made a world with magic, and destiny, and true love. It's because the fantastical is so much better than the real world, where anything and everything is possible, where you can escape for a little while to a world where the characters worst fear is that they won't find their true love, instead of facing debt and death. But I think most of all I write things that I would want to read, in the words of the famous Stephen King: "If you want to be a writer, you must do two things above all others: read a lot and write a lot."

Reflection

Week 1:

Like any new environment, it was all very strange and unfamiliar when I first came to the workshop. I didn't know a single person, which made it all the more uncomfortable. But by the second day, I had made a few acquaintances, and Ms. Adamo and Ms. Poettis seemed a little less intimidating. When I first got here I had absolutely no idea what Biosketches, or Nanofictions, or other such things were. I realized though that many of the other kids around me were just as clueless as I was, but we are all writers, so we already had two things in common. By the end of the first week I had settled in, and was avidly working on my first piece, I spent my days printing out copy after copy to be snipped and chopped down to perfection. Others may despise the editing process, but I'm thankful to have Ms. Adamo and Ms. Poettis who edited my work without any bias.

Week 2:

As promised, the first week went by very quickly. I doubted that I would be able to get both pieces finished by Thursday. But with help, and a thesaurus, I managed to make two works that I can say I'm proud of. I very much enjoyed my time at the workshop, I learned so much about writing, and editing, and the publishing process, and I met some pretty cool people. I hope I will be able to return next year!

The Mountain

A rustle, a movement in a bush, a whispering among the trees, a rock shifts, then another, until it blossoms into a thunderous dance. Jagged bits of stone and dirt bid farewell to their dwelling and pursue one another with no common route. Clouds of grey dust permeate the air, forming a syrupy concoction: thick and heavy, nearly impossible to breathe. The towering peak stands firm as a part of itself is detached, and joins in the downward dance towards earth. The mountain seems to rise higher the longer you look, as if its love is in the stars, and it's longing to go home. The scene is a beautiful tragedy, an eruption of deadly proportions, yet the grandeur of it all seems ethereal, like that beauty doesn't belong in this world.

Still further above the peak stretches a cloudless, baby blue canvas that seems as if it would crumble at the lightest touch. Strokes of white can be seen far off in the distance, groups of cotton balls scattered here and there, soft and inviting like a bed. But they lazily drift off on their merry way, not threatening to compromise a perfect day. Hung like a lantern in the sky, the sun blazes with an unquenchable intensity. Its rays find the Earth, shattering the sky, and basking the entirety in heavenly, white light. Warmth creeps in like a thief in the night, and snatches away the cold, leaving only a tingling sense of balmy comfort. It is a hot day, but an enjoyable one, a clean, crisp, bright heat, a heat that comes after an icy glass of lemonade on a sultry summer day.

Spread out beneath the mountain, is a vast carpet of the greenest grass. The mass of green resembles that of a hedgehog's back, prickly and uneven, sharp to the touch. Trees grow in dense patches of foliage that border the mountain, a welcoming embrace branching out to either side. Yet from afar, the full beauty cannot be appreciated. Outstretched branches from which new needles are sprouting an innocent shade of green. Sounds of a mighty symphony commencing at the mere prompt of the wind. The rough feeling of the bark beneath your fingertips, the scaly, patchy, hard skin that withstands the test of time, the armor never wavering. And the aroma of the pines, like taking a plunge into a chilly stream: fresh, clean, sweet, a sharp sensation that would wake up the drowsiest soul.

The same hands that hung the sun in the sky slowly drew it back down, promising a fair share of tomorrows. As day evolves into night, so begins the symphony of twilight, the music never ending. Stars litter the night sky, crystals twinkling with a beautiful ferocity, scattered throughout the vast expanse. Night is short, and love is fleeting, but the mountain cannot help but feel, for however short a time, that it is home.

Rotten Love

Scarlet, polished skin, hanging from a stem
Crisp, crackling, divine nectar to the ears.
Forbidden fruit, gives way to sweetest gem
Soft, tender, innocent for its short years.

Fierce love bursts forth into passionate dance.
Lover, sluggish, foul, vermin of Eden.
Obsession's prowling claws ensnare romance
Purity taken, leaving them beaten.

Paramour suddenly crippled by strife
The worm, utterly consumed by hunger.
How can one battle the love of her life?
Lest she too be dragged along down under.

Moreover, torment remains his alone
Move past it with joy, and let that be known.

Monica Tam

Born on June 24, 1999; this little baby came out a little bit late. Ever since then, it seems that everything she does, she does *late.*

Other than that, she herself feels as if she's really grown as a writer, and even if she never publishes in hard copy, that's okay. She's got the internet to tell her she's better than that. No matter how discreditable online opinions can be.

Reflection

Week 1:

The first week is always a struggle, albeit not as bad as the second, but when you miss two days out of four because of a sinus infection there's bound to be trouble. Luckily, I didn't miss any visiting authors or, ahem, free food. Ah…moving on! In retrospect, my total of 8 days had been cut short to 6, but I was still able to come up with at least one approved idea out of my current two.

Week 2:

If the first week was a struggle, the second was complete agony. The first day was spent in depression (that's what happens when you get something rejected), the second with renewed hope after a really well-timed presentation from a visiting magazine editor, and the third was spent on caffeine after a very dedicated all-nighter. However, because of said all-nighter I was able to have two approved ideas and in the end, I honestly had a lot of fun *and* grew as a writer. So, Lilli, I agree. This experience has been a definite *turnip point* in my life.

Dropping Like Flies

Caroline's friends were vanishing before her by the second. Their faces, which had glowed so brightly, now diminished to gray. Her hands shook as she pressed them down into the bed, unable to accept that soon, there would be no one left.

Devastated by the barren chat room, Caroline decided it was time for bed.

The Sole Ascension

She watched the child as he made his way across the street. There he was, plump, happy, and utterly delicious. She could just imagine the way he would taste in her mouth, the way she would crunch on his bones. Yes, it was him. It would be him. This child, scrumptious and fat. Tonight she wouldn't starve anymore, she'd be full.

There were times when she thought of the wrong she was doing. How if she were young, if she were still alive, she would be horrified at her deeds. But no, she wasn't young anymore, and she wasn't alive. She'd spent 30 years living, and a thousand watching others live and thrive while she shriveled up and walked the road of the dead and broken. She was condemned, left to spend the rest of her existence walking earth's plane, thirsting for the breath of air, craving the taste of food. Forever wishing for the life she'd lost. But now it was time for her meal, and she couldn't afford thinking, lest she decide she should let the poor young soul live. No, she shook her head; take what you can, while you can. That was the rule she lived by now.

She followed the child, shaking her head slightly at how easy it would be to devour his little body. He was naive, innocent, and inexplicably curious. He wandered around the street, scanning drains and small sinkholes. He jumped over dusty ledges, walking back around only to try jumping straight onto them, coughing as clouds of dust would rise up. Then as he walked away, she saw her chance. Just up ahead, where his destination was located, was an alleyway. Small, dim, and desolate, it was the most perfect place for her to strike. She followed the child, smiling through dry cracked lips.

As he stepped in, she followed. Each and every step, he looked around curiously, studying the moldy walls and slippery pavement. Just up ahead, there seemed to be some kind of a crevice in the wall. She peered at it, curious herself, and felt something nag at her memory. What was it about that dark shadow? That empty, seemingly endless hole? Just as she remembered what that emptiness meant, it was too late. Something moved in the darkness, a shadow in a shadow, and dark clothed arms sprang out. They captured the small boy, caged him in their horrible embrace. The child, frightened and skittish, opened his mouth to scream, but it didn't quite matter. A hand had covered his mouth, leaving the boy mute.

As the owner of those covered hands and arms stepped out of the shadows, she felt a moment of nostalgia, but not the good kind.

In that moment, the man's face appeared and although the structures were different, the expression was frighteningly similar to another face that she had been unable to forget.

Suddenly brought back to the day of her death, her vision seemed to swim in confusion. That day, or was it night? She couldn't seem to remember anymore, but it didn't matter. What mattered was that on that date, she died. By the same kind of man, with the same sort of smile and eyes that glinted with a red light, crazed and craving blood. She felt, actually felt, in that moment a sense of dread and desperation. She was at least thirty years old when she was murdered, slit at the throat and robbed. But this boy, this small and beautifully curious boy was only, what? Six? Seven at most, and he was going to die.

She glared at the man. Her soulless black eyes shriveled in dark fury. No. No one was going to die anymore, not like this, not like him. Not so young and so full of possibilities. He had a future, a life to live. He wasn't like her, already spent and simply waiting to get to the finish line. He hadn't even started, and that was what set her resolve.

As she watched, the man seemed to draw out something from his pocket. It was long, sharp, and glinting in the dim lighting, much as his eyes were. She stepped forward and grabbed ahold of his wrist, her flimsy transparent hands keeping a firm hold. The man seemed to shriek, spooked by his sudden lack of control over his limbs, but after a while, he became mute. She watched her connection to him, her hold on his flesh, and saw the skin burning through and turning into an almost gas like substance, floating its way to her. Without another wasted moment, she shoved the child aside and jumped on the man, pushing him to the ground as her hands both wrapped around his neck. After that, she waited for his essence, the dark gas like substance, to rise from his body and drift into her mouth in a steady current. When the man was gone, and there was nothing left but empty burned through clothes, she got up and turned around. The child was still there, watching her with startling interest.

She knew she was visible now, as she always was for a short time after devouring another soul. She could even imagine how ghastly she looked. Pale and sunken face, lips stretched and cracked as her hair hung dull, stuck to her pale white gown with a tar that seemed to manifest from the roots.

The child, mouth wide, ran away quickly. She watched him run, faster than anyone would think possible, almost in desperation. She followed, no longer finding him appetizing, and knew that she was once again transparent.

She found him tumbling into the arms of a dark-haired woman. He was panting; panting so hard he had trouble speaking. Finally, however, he seemed to find enough breath for words. He opened his mouth, and she cringed. She could already see what he would say, how the mother would react, and what would happen after that. He would tell her that he saw a monster, a terrible monster. The woman would shush the child and tell him there was no such thing, that monsters didn't exist. Then he would start crying and hug her tightly, weeping that he did see such a monster, a horrifying thing that devoured another living person.

"A monster helped me, mommy! A monster helped me!" the child cried.

The woman smiled and brushed back the child's hair. "Are you sure it was a monster?"

The child's face scrunched up in consideration. "Well, she looked like one."

"But she helped you, didn't she? She didn't hurt you?"

"No," the child shook his head. "She saved me."

"Then she couldn't have been a monster," the mother smiled, hugging the little boy tight. "She must have been some kind of superhero that rescued you from the real monsters."

"Do you think she was an angel?"

"I'm not sure; I didn't see her for myself. What do you think?"

"I think she's amazing."

The woman laughed. "Then should we go now? Then you can tell me more about what happened today."

The child nodded, and they left. Not moving as she watched their retreat, she continued staring at the place where they had been. Then, as if the world was blurring, lightening, and glazing over, her vision changed. She closed her eyes briefly, and felt herself falling, or was she flying? She couldn't tell anymore, not after so long.

When the world stopped, and she opened her eyes, there was a distinct point of light moving closer and closer. It shot towards her, aiming for her chest. Unable to move, her eyes squeezed shut as the heat enveloped her, but there was no pain. Cool caresses soothed away any irritation and as her eyes opened, feathers fluttered this way and that. They were endless in count, too beautiful to bear. She felt tears sliding down her cheeks and dripping onto her chest as she stared in wonder at her hands. From where she started, all the way to where she ended, was no longer flimsy transparency, but whole tangibility. And behind her was not the heavy darkness of her past, dragging her down. Behind her were the wings that would lift her up and send her soaring.

Lauren Villanueva

"When I look at my room, I see a girl who loves books."- Looking for Alaska

My mom used to take me to the library at least twice a week when I was younger. I developed my love of books and even now, 17 years later, I always have a book in my hand, so, thanks Mom for that.

I'm a senior at Spanish River High, meaning this time next year I'll be away at college; hopefully Ohio State for Criminology. I take my writing from things I've either experienced firsthand or if someone close to me has gone through it. When I'm not writing or reading, my time is divided between Criminal Minds reruns, Twitter, and obsessing over clothes I can't afford.

Reflection

This is my second year at Oce and first as a mentor. My experience here has been incredible, as always. These 8 days have flashed by, leaving me shocked to know it's already our last day. I've met new people and hung out with people I met in the previous year.

I would like to extend a massive thank you to Mrs. Adamo and Mrs. Poettis who have provided me with criticism I needed to improve my work. For 2 years they have helped me develop and master my writing style and for that I am extremely thankful.

Night of the Beast

It blended in with the night sky around it, practically invisible if it weren't for the line of people queued outside. Garbled rock music blared from its many cracks, and it seemed to rock on the weak foundation. Teenage boys hugged their girlfriends, as if that would protect them. Attendants ushered unknowing guests inside before they could change their minds. The line shuffled forward as more prey entered the crumbling edifice.

Its surroundings were almost as gruesome as the house itself. The pungent smell of cheap metal and sweat blanketed the fairgrounds as chainsaws ripped through the air evoking fearful screams. Mini carnies ran through with malicious grins. A buttery aroma floated close to the food trucks, belonging to the deep fried Oreos. From a nearby trash can, the vile scent of vomit assaulted passerby's nostrils. Unstable rides groan out as they start up. The merry go round's music was slowed and increased to a piercing decibel. Sobs rang out, identifying the weaklings.

Deep in the belly of the beast, entertainers run through with makeup swallowing their faces, deforming what's underneath. Performers scramble on all four limbs invading customers' personal space. A thick fog covered guests' ankles as they tried to maneuver through. Strobe lights momentarily disoriented vision, providing a sense of helplessness. The inflatable walls expanded to envelope the house inhabitants. Man-made monsters hung off cages, trying to crawl their way out. A neon exit sign was in stark contrast with the pitch black hallways, and provided an escape for those who couldn't handle it. Performers ran after the quitters, shouting profanities in their direction. Those left to continue their journey encountered the black and white pinwheel on the wall, churning, contorting their version of reality. A flickering candle in the distance stole their attention away from the hypnotizing wall. People cling to the flame, the only source of light, and travel down the endless stairs in pursuit of the candle. The torch dies, leaving them in complete darkness. A scarred, burned face appears with the scream of a tortured soul.

Her dim flashlight trains on the small creature approaching the group- a devilish entity. He pins the group to the wall, as someone releases a blood curdling scream. Two wimps run back up the stairs, to that illuminated exit. The devil cackles, lights going out, creating paranoia. Fog dissipates, leading to a hidden door. Participants crawl through, into a fluorescent room filled with carnival music. The group cowers as six foot creatures pop from the floor, balloons surrounding them. Their faces plastered in white, with blood red smirks and faded, torn polka dot jumpsuits. The balloons pop, tiny insects flowing out, shrouding the floor. Running, aimlessly, the victims push past the final obstacles, only a few pedestrians made it through to the exit unharmed.

Back by the pulsing music, the jittery teenagers, and the roaring chainsaws, attendants reopened the rope, allowing the house to swallow its next victim.

Regret

It reeked of disinfectant. The cluttered surroundings made the walls tighten, allowing claustrophobia to set in. Screams and groans pierced through the hallway from adjacent rooms. I heard the snap of rubber gloves as he came at me with the sharp object poised. "Stop," I protested, bolting upright. "Never mind, I don't want the tattoo!"

Welcome Home, Spencer

Jane stretched across the four poster bed and buried her nose in the pillow. She always slept on his side when he was gone. Her nose picked up on the pinewood scent immediately and inhaled deeply. A picture of John was on their nightstand, his signature smirk was in juxtaposition with his stern, army green beret. A prayer escaped her lips, as it did every morning when she locked eyes with John's portrait. Jane swung her legs over the mattress and ambled over to the television set. She had the channel preset to play the morning news; her ear was already fine-tuned to any mention of Afghanistan.

"We're starting this morning with news of an oil spill in the Gulf. BP offers no comment at this time."

Jane ignored the perky blonde news anchor and walked over to her vanity. In the oval mirror, she lifted her camisole and rubbed her 9 month belly.

"Good morning baby Sarah, how are you today?"

Jane turned to the side, imagining the human inside her. Her doctor had said Sarah was scheduled to arrive around Christmas. "A present," Jane had said, beaming. Even now her smile was bright as she pictured John setting up their Christmas tree as she held their baby girl.

"Breaking news from Afghanistan."

Jane moved for the remote, clicking the volume up a few notches. She was standing in front of the TV, hoping the news would be of their homecoming.

"Earlier this morning an American fighter plane was shot down by the armed rebels."

Jane's legs betrayed her as her knees buckled and her legs fell beneath her. She was rocking back and forth, completely engrossed with the TV.

"Three were killed instantly, while a search and rescue team is recovering the other soldiers. No names have been released."

An inaudible whimper escaped Jane, followed by a flow of unstoppable tears. John was a pilot.

***

"Hold on baby Sarah, hold on." Jane had turned off the TV and was pacing the length of her bedroom clutching her stomach. "Things will be okay. Your daddy will be okay. He probably wasn't even flying. He's smart, he would have survived. He will be okay. He is okay." Jane was mesmerized by her stomach. This little girl could come home at any moment and her dad might not be here for it. Jane heard the phone ringing but couldn't make a move to answer it. The ringing continued until Jane made a move to answer it.

"I'm guessing you've seen the broadcast by now. I'm already on my way over, we'll figure this out." Nell was already taking action and Jane was perfectly fine with that.

"Nell we need to call someone, I need to know about John-"

"Jane, breathe. You getting worked up isn't getting us anywhere. When I get there we'll find out whose desk we need to tap dance on to get answers."

Jane was grateful for Nell. Her brother had been deployed around the same as John and they met in one of those support groups for family members of soldiers. When Jane had opened up to the group about her pregnancy, Nell had been right there smoothing down Jane's hair. Nell had even accompanied Jane to her first ultrasound appointment.

"Why are you on the floor?" Nell broke into Jane's thoughts from her bedroom doorway.

"Oh." Jane realized the phone was still against her ear. She hung up the phone and walked over to Nell who standing in the kitchen.

Nell pushed Jane into the kitchen. "Did you eat anything yet? You're still in your pajamas. Sit. I'm making coffee." She steered Jane into a chair and grabbed at the coffee pot. "Decaf? Never mind, I'll look in the pantry. How's the little one?"

"She was kicking a whole lot last night. Maybe she sensed something was wrong with John, oh Nell what if she knew and that was her warning-" Jane was trying to get off the stool and grab for the phone.

"That's ridiculous," Nell was pushing Jane back into the chair.

"The baby couldn't have told you anything because she didn't know anything. Your baby is not psychic, she was just active."

The coffee pot came to a boil as Nell gathered cups and the creamer from the fridge.

"Drink this. I'm calling the office at the base. If anyone knows anything, it's them." Nell reached for the landline and sipped at her coffee. After entering all personal information, they patched Nell to the offices at the base. "Oh Janie-"

"What did you hear any news? Is it John?"

"Oh no, I'm still on hold. Your tree is crooked though." Nell placed her coffee cup on the granite countertop and moved towards the tree. "Oh here, hold this." She tossed the phone at Jane, who clutched it as if it were a lifeline. Jane pressed the phone to her ear only to hear the elevator music.

"Son of a-" Nell was leaning over the tree, all the ornaments rattling. "You will be straight damn it."

"Nell, it's fine really." The music was giving Jane anxiety and clearly getting them nowhere. "I don't think I want to hear this. I need to talk to someone, maybe. I don't know."

"You're right, I'm going to start the car." Nell grabbed her purse off the couch. "Oh and sorry about your ornaments, I'll replace those."
***

"Okay so we clear on the mission?" Nell turned to Jane as they entered the army base. The glass building was a hub of all army activities within the city. "We are charging up to those offices and demanding answers."

"I just need to find out if he's safe." Jane hobbled on her swollen feet to keep up with Nell's forceful strides. She was already inside in the elevator when Jane came panting through the doors.

"Floor 8 is where all the pretentious jerks are, so that's our destination," Nell slammed the button as the elevator ascended.

"What if we don't get answers?" Jane said her voice wobbling.

"Oh Janie, we'll demand answers and won't leave until we get them." The doors opened and Nell grabbed Jane's hand. "The captain's office is right through there."

The girls pushed open the door to a frantic scene. Men were bustling back and forth, shoving papers in and out of drawers.

"I'm sorry ma'am. I can't release any information." A balding men was speaking into a phone, while staring at the TV on the wall. They were showing video footage of the plane explosion.

"Oh Nell, look." Jane pointed at the screen, her eyes widening. "How could anyone survive that?"

"John could have. Come on, we've got an appointment with the captain." Nell pulled Jane into the madness and weaved them through the activity until they were in front of the captain's desk.

"Oh Ms. Warren go home. I can't tell you anything right now." The captain tried dismissing the girls, but to no avail.

"That's not good enough, captain. We both have someone in that war, and need answers." Nell slammed her fist on the desk and Jane swore she saw the Captain jump.

"I have 37 men on that flight. I only have 22 accounted for. I have bigger issues right now."

"Who are the three dead?" Jane spoke up from behind Nell, not sure if they could hear her over the commotion.

"She is pregnant Captain, 9 months pregnant."

Jane felt woozy. The captain clearly wasn't telling them. She rubbed her belly, trying to calm her down. John can't be dead, she kept thinking, he has to be alive.

"WHAT AREN'T YOU TELLING US, CAPTAIN?" Nell was leaning over the Captain's desk, fully invading his personal space. Her voice made Jane jump and tears swelled from her eyes. This wasn't supposed to get to this level, everything was getting out of hand. Jane felt a pressure deep in her stomach. Her head began to pound and her legs wobbled. The floor splashed with liquid, soaking Jane's dress and legs.

"Oh my God," Jane clutched her stomach as a pain made her scream out.

"Your brother died Penelope. I'm sorry." The Captain stood up and shouted to no one in particular. "Why is no one calling this woman an ambulance? Come on men."

Nell slid into the chair with a vacant look on her face. Jane had never heard anyone call her by her full name. Spencer was dead. Nell had lost her brother. The pain shot through Jane, and she could no longer hold it in.

"Oh my god Jane," Nell rushed from the chair and grabbed Jane's hand. She took in the pain and liquid that covered the floor. "The baby is coming now."

***

"Push Jane push," Jane was gripping Nell's hand so hard it was turning a shade of purple. "Jane she's going to be here any moment."

Jane's hair was matted flat against her forehead with dried sweat. Her back hurt from being crumpled up and she wanted the baby to just be here already.

"You're doing so good Jane. One more push," the doctor perked his head up from between her legs.

Nell held her iPhone up and positioned it down Jane's body.

"I want to get this on film," she smiled and rubbed circles on Jane's hand. "She's going to be so beautiful."

Jane looked at her friend and pushed with every fiber of her being. She pushed until she felt the veins in her forehead throbbing. She pushed until she heard that sweet cry fill the room. Her head fell back onto the hospital pillow as she let her breathing catch up to her.

"Nell I want you to cut the cord," she looked up at her friend who had been her rock this whole time. Her friend's eyes widened at what had just been asked of her.

"Jane I can barely cut paper in a straight line," the doctor ushered Nell over and showed her where to cut.

"Oh Jane she's beautiful." Nell had tears in her eyes when the nurses whisked the baby away for cleaning. She returned to Jane's side and hugged her friend from the side. A vibration broke up the moment as Nell reached for her cell phone. "This looks important, sorry Jane."

Jane nodded, understanding the importance.

"Congratulations on your baby boy Jane," the doctor handed Jane her baby, wrapped in a blue blanket.

"Wait, a boy?"

"Yes, that is most certainly a boy. A healthy boy at that," the doctor smiled at Jane. "The nurse will take the name down for the birth certificate." The doctor exited the room, leaving Jane alone with the nurse and baby boy.

"Oh I hadn't planned for a boy. Her name was going to be Sarah," Jane held the bundle in her arms, taking in his features. He had a little pug nose and a full mouth, just like his daddy. Jane looked up to tell the nurse she would name him after her husband when she saw Nell through the glass window. She was pacing the hallway, tears filled in her eyes. Nell was strong, a fighter, and took charge when she needed. Jane would never be like Penelope Warren, but she hoped her baby could be. "Spencer," Jane said looking at the nurse. "I would like to name him Spencer."

The nurse jotted the name down and left Jane with Spencer.

"Nell I just got a phone call from the captain," Nell came back into the room swiping at her eyes. "Why is that baby in a blue blanket? Did they run out of pink ones?"

"This is Spencer," Jane looked at Nell's face as recognition crossed her eyes. Nell's tears came faster, releasing everything she had been holding in from the army office. "Spencer, meet your godmother Nell."

"Jane he's beautiful," Nell said when Jane passed her baby boy. Nell cradled the baby under her bosom, and rocked him back and forth. "Oh, completely forgot, the captain is on the phone for you." Nell passed the phone to Jane.

She was so caught up in Spencer's birth she had pushed John to the back of her mind. Now that the baby was here and it was a reality, Jane needed John a lot more than before.

"Captain please," she pressed the phone against her ear and already wiped the tears that were forming.

"Jane, John is alright," relief washed over Jane as her tears came faster. "He was not scheduled to fly that plane. He's okay." Jane expressed her gratitude before hanging up the phone.

Nell crossed back over the room with Spencer. She handed him back over and pushed Jane's hair away from her face. Nell leaned down so her face was level to Jane's as she stroked Spencer's head.

"Merry Christmas Jane."

Noelle Wamsley

I feel like writing is a way to escape from the real world and create your own. A place to express the people in your world and their stories that are somewhat your own stories. For me, I was born December 1st, 1999 in West Palm Beach, Florida and I'll be a freshman at Dreyfoos School of the Arts next year. Writing is a passion for me as well as reading. I enjoy writing fiction stories and reading ones like the Harry Potter and Mortal Instruments series. One day I would like to make a career out of writing in Journalism and maybe even publish a book, fiction of course. I get most of my inspiration from people I have met and my family. I hope to continue writing as I get older and work my way up the ladder.

Reflection

Week 1:

My first week in the program allowed me to have new experiences in writing and the process. At first I had a hard time thinking of a story. Writer's block tried to get me, but eventually the words started to flow. The first week went by a lot quicker than I thought it would, but I still met people who helped me through the process. The field trip to the Canon Offices was really interesting and I liked hearing about how they are involved with the book and publishing industry. The entire program was a learning experience for me about the time and commitment it takes to publish a story.

Week 2:

The second week went by even quicker. I was on serious time crunch, working every minute I could. At the same time the authors were very interesting to listen to and inspiring. All of them were very helpful in giving tips and notes about writing and the process of publishing. My story was also finally starting to come together and be a piece of writing so I was very happy. On the last day we were treated with Panera Bread so that also made me happy. I enjoyed the whole experience and definitely learned a lot about writing as I move forward.

A Dark World

As blackness fades away, streams of light and blurred images fill my anxious mind as I feel the edges of my eyelids barring a way for consciousness. I live in a dark world. I give no love and get no love in return. I have lived in it my whole life, but this year has been different. *The first day of school I decided to go get high in my friend's garage instead of collecting supply lists and making new friends and I was fine with missing out, but when I finally showed up to my history class a week later, I was greeted in a way I wasn't expecting. As I was sitting in my desk our new teacher was explaining our first assignment for the nine weeks, which was to write about our summer vacation. "Would anyone like to talk about what they did this summer?" No one raised their hands, smart kids.*

She looks at me. "What about you Rachel? Did you do anything entertaining last week while you were out?" The way she looked at me was playful and good natured but there was something in her eyes that told me she knew something I didn't.

"Um, I just watched T.V and stuff..." She just smiles at me.

Her name was Ms. Mallemo. There was something interesting about her in that she would always call on me or challenge me with questions during class. It was like she thought I was secretly a genius or something and I was just hiding it. I could never figure out why she looked at me until I ran into her while walking my dog, around my own neighborhood.

She knew when I left my home or if I was up to no good, but all she would do was nod and smile. After class, the next day, she'd always let me sit and talk to her about the stuff going on in my life, eventually it became a routine. Most of our chats included my parents, but she always listened to me and looked me in the eyes. She seemed like the only person who really cared.

I glance around me now to see our substitute droning on about the current events happening around the world. " In the Middle East, U.S. soldiers are still fighting in Iraq..."

We've had a substitute for about a week. Last week, Ms. Mallemo was in a head-on collision with a truck on her way home from school one night. She survived, but the doctors aren't sure if she'll stay alive for long. It hurts me of course, but whenever I think about her accident, I feel nervous and almost paranoid, like there's a piece missing.

"Japan has had another earthquake off the coast of Morioka…"

I listen to all the devastating news about tsunamis and war, but I don't think about the destruction, I think about the people. How it feels to live in a world of chaos and fear. Do they cry over their loved ones that won't return or do they crumble under a memory of their life that was once normal?"

Suddenly I feel my chest tighten and I see the red and blue lights from flashing cars. Branches are scraping my body and people are coming out of their homes with flashlights, screaming.

"I'm so sorry!" It's harder to breath and I feel like I'm suffocating. It's dark around me. I see wreckage in the street. My fingers clench to hold on to something, to keep me from falling into oblivion or being sucked away. Breathing hard I raise my head and see everyone is staring at me in nervous silence, watching me with curious faces, but I feel like I'm going to implode.

"Rachel, what's wrong?"

I stand myself up, ready to vomit, racing out of the classroom, racing out of the school, racing all the way home.

That night I lay awake, staring up at my ceiling, fighting the temptation to light the glass pipe tucked away in the sock under my dresser.

I hear a knock at my window and see my friend Julia. Unlocking the latch, she slips in and lies next to me on the bed. I can see worry in her face. "Hey, I snuck out while my parents were watching re-runs of Top Chef." Her smile appears forced.

"How are you doing, people told me you freaked out during the sub's lesson today?"

Sighing, I roll over to face her. "Ms. Mallemo's accident is just putting me on edge that's all."

"Oh, are you thinking about what happened that night?'

"Yeah, I mean... I'm just going crazy. I feel like there's a part of this that has to do with me. I keep seeing pictures and stuff in my head, but when I see them I feel like I'm going to die."

Julia was silent for a minute and stared away into the room. "Listen, after you left school today the principal came on the speaker and gave an announcement that the hospital called." Pausing, she fumbled with the covers on the bed. "They don't think Ms. Mallemo will last much longer, like maybe a day or two at most." My hands hurt and I realize I'm digging into them with my fingers.

"We all visited her after school. I know she cared about you, so maybe you should go see her before she goes."

I can't stop myself as I pull at my hair with my shaking hands. "Why?" I start bawling. Rolling off the bed, I stick one leg out through the window.

"Rachel! Where are you going?" I didn't give her an answer.

Two streets down from my street is Lilac Avenue. Caution tape is still posted a week later. As I see skid marks and dried blood on the asphalt, I drop to my knees, feeling the tears pour from my eyes, rolling over my cheeks

The fast scraping of the wheels create sparks against the pavement as the fresh night air engulfs my face. I kick and swipe at the rigid ground with my foot as hard as I can, making my board accelerate to a dangerous speed. I had been out all night since school ended, not remembering what time it is. I know I'm not supposed to be out this late but I don't care. My parents probably aren't even home, this early into the night.

I start to see lights up ahead getting brighter and brighter like an angel coming out of the darkness. But suddenly the light is too bright. A deafening blare comes off from it, sending me swerving toward the sidewalk into the bushes as enormous crash sounds behind me. A collision.

The wind blows soft and quiet, but all I hear are loud sobbing voices in my head. I did this. I caused the accident and let her pay for it. I don't even remember everything that happened. I know I have to go see her.

I stare up at the glowing sign with the words, "Belleview Hospital" and I still see shadows around me, even in the dark. I make my way inside and head down the hallway, my body cold. I turn a corner and see her room. I slow my steps as I walk through the doorway, not sure what I'll see. Will she be awake or will she be drifting in and out?

Stepping to the middle of the room I see her there. Her eyes are closed like she's asleep. She doesn't look like the steady, caring teacher I remember, she looks pale and cold lying there. The heart monitor's beeping is the only thing reminding me she's still breathing.

I walk over to her and stare down at my feet. "Hi, Ms. Mallemo. So…I kind of pissed off the tag lady when I came in, and she chased me…." I can feel tears start to form around my eyes.

Silence creeps between us for what seems like forever when she starts to move. Breathing out, her eyes open and come to rest on me.

"Rachel."

I don't respond. Here I am, staring at her, what I did to her and somehow it's a lot harder to think of something to say.

She peers at me looking at her I.V tubes and sighs. "Don't let this consume your life, Rachel."

She places her hand on my cheek and looks at me for a minute. "I have to go where God takes me. I believe in you more than you give yourself credit, remember our talks, but move on."

I looked at her, ready to start sobbing. "How can you say that? I basically killed you!"

"We make mistakes, but you're like a daughter to me." I stare at her, wanting her to hug me.

"I want you to know, Rachel, that I forgive you."

Then her hands drift down and her eyes turn grey, with a tiny smile on her lips. I just sit there and stare, my mouth dry and silent. Yet somewhere I can see myself, tears rolling down my face, walking into the light.

About the Teachers

About the Teachers
About the Teachers
About the Teachers
About the Teachers
About the Teachers

(l to r) Diana Fedderman, Nicole Adamo, Katrina Sapp Holder, Cartheda Mann, and author Zelda Benjamin

Nicole Adamo

Nicole Adamo has been an English teacher for more than ten years, including the past seven years as a Don Estridge High Tech Middle School seventh grade language arts teacher. She is the proud mother of a one-year-old son, and always encourages her students to never settle for mediocrity in their writing.

Diana Fedderman

Diana Fedderman has worked as an English teacher and curriculum administrator for the School District of Palm Beach County for twenty years. As a former student in the Palm Beach County school system, she developed a love of writing in our classrooms. She is committed to fostering an appreciation of writing among the district's students and is thrilled to be a part of the Canon Future Authors Program.

Poettis - Katrina Sapp Holder

In 1997 this University of Miami alum went from writing to reciting poetry. Pooling together her experience as a playwright and short story author, this spoken word artist is able to create enthralling presentations in the art form of performance poetry. Revered for her free styling aptitude, Poettis has graced the stage with some of the brightest and best from various entertainment genres; ranging from gospel to neo soul. Having a genuine love of composition and the creative process, Poettis enthusiastically shares her academic knowledge, professional creative advice and god-given talent for writing prose or poetry with the future authors of this generation.

Cartheda T. Mann

Mrs. Cartheda T. Mann, English Department Chair and Writing Coach at Glades Central Community High School, is a Belle Glade native and resident, and has taught language arts at Glades Central for 16 years. She has a BA in English from Fisk University, Nashville, TN, an MA in African American Studies (Major concentration in African and African-American Literature) from Boston University, and has twice been selected as a finalist for the William T. Dwyer Award for Excellence in Education, among other awards. Mrs. Mann began her professional career as a staff writer for the Palm Beach Post, and is currently a freelance writer for area newspapers, while working on personal projects that include historical fiction and children's literature. She has travelled extensively throughout the African continent, completed a graduate assistantship at the University of Monrovia in Liberia, West Africa, and uses her wealth of knowledge and experience to engage students in African cultural exploration and writing.

About the Authors

About the Authors

About the Authors

About the Authors

About the Authors

About the Authors

Steve Alten

Steve Alten grew up in Philadelphia, earning his bachelor's degree in physical education at Penn State University, a master's degree in sports medicine from the University of Delaware, and a doctorate of education at Temple University. Struggling to support his family of five, he decided to pen a novel he had been thinking about for years. Working late nights and on weekends, he eventually finished *MEG; A Novel of Deep Terror*. Steve sold his car to pay for editing fees. On September (Friday) the 13th, 1996, Steve lost his general manager's job at a wholesale meat plant. Four days later his agent had a two-book, seven-figure deal with Bantam Doubleday.

MEG would go on to become the book of the 1996 Frankfurt book fair, where it eventually sold to more than 20 countries. MEG hit every major best-seller list, and became a popular radio series in Japan.

Steve's second release, *The TRENCH* (Meg sequel) was published by Kensington/Pinnacle in 1999, where it also hit best-seller status. His next novel, *DOMAIN* and its sequel, *RESURRECTION* were published by St. Martin's Press/Tor Books and were runaway best-sellers in Spain, Mexico, Germany, and Italy, with the rights selling to more than a dozen countries.

Steve's fourth novel, *GOLIATH*, received rave reviews and was a big hit in Germany. *MEG: Primal Waters* was published in the summer of 2004. A year later, his seventh novel, *The LOCH*, hit stores -- a modern-day thriller about the Loch Ness Monster. Steve's eighth novel, The *SHELL GAME*, is about the end of oil and the next 9/11 event. The book was another NY Times best-seller, but the stress of penning this real-life story affected Steve's health, and three months after he finished the manuscript he was diagnosed with Parkinson's Disease. Steve's ninth novel, *MEG: Hell's Aquarium*, is considered to be the best of the best-selling MEG series. Steve says his best novel is *GRIM REAPER: End of Days*.

For more information, contact the author at Meg82159@aol.com

Zelda Benjamin

A pediatric ER nurse with a passion for story telling, traveling, and everything chocolate.

I write happily ever after stories. The heroes in my stories are sexy men who you can't help falling in love with. My heroines are sweet and sassy, independent women who know what they want out of life. Like everyone, they sometimes hit a bumpy road to get there.

I grew up in Brooklyn, NY. I like to think of each Brooklyn neighborhood as a small town with its own stroy to tell. The books in my Love By Chocolate series are set in Brooklyn, where the characters are connected like any small town.

To learn more about me follow my blogwww.lovebychocolate. blogspot.com www.lovebychocolate.blogspot.com.

Sign up for my newsletter for info about new releases. http://mad.ly/signups/87977/join

Dwight Seon Stewart "Spirited"

Dwight Seon Stewart "Spirited" began writing poetry at the age of seven with a poem titled Spring. Today, he still uses his great gift to encourage spiritual renewal in ways that celebrate humanity. He is a poet, songwriter, educator, lyricist and scholar.

He has published two thought provoking and inspirational books of poetry titled *I Know How People Die* (2002) and *Words to Heal* (2009), which was self published using Océ digital printing technology.

He has also written lyrics for singer and music producer Julian Owns on his soul inspiration album, "Here's Life Vol. 1." "Spirited" has shared the stage with the hip-hop group, De La Soul, and spoken word artist and film maker, Tehut-Nine. In addition, he shared Black History Month at renowned Vermont Law School with civil rights activist and professor, Kathleen Cleaver. Students in the elite Phillips Exeter Academy and Oakwood Friends prep schools, as well as public schools throughout New York City and Florida have enjoyed his poetry performances.

He graduated from Wesleyan University, with bachelor's degrees in philosophy and government. He also earned joint degrees in the arts of teaching and history from the University of Vermont. Most recently, he earned an Ed.S degree in educational leadership from Nova Southeastern University.

Jennifer Tormo

Jennifer Tormo is the managing editor of Gulfstream Media Group, which produces six lifestyle and four interior design magazines in South Florida. She is a journalism graduate of the University of Florida, a South Florida native and a storyteller at heart. She is passionate about profile and travel writing, and has written and edited numerous award-winning profiles and features. Jennifer teaches photography for Cameras for Kids Foundation, a non-profit organization dedicated to providing art therapy to foster children. She wholeheartedly believes breakfast is the best meal of the day, and loves home décor, window-shopping at Anthropologie and reading endless magazines on her iPad.

About the Program

Canon Solutions America
FutureAuthorsProject
A partnership with the School District of Palm Beach County

Canon Solutions America Receives Business Partner Award

The School District of Palm Beach County Recognizes Future Authors Project

Melville, N.Y., July 1, 2014 – Canon Solutions America, Inc., a subsidiary of Canon U.S.A., Inc., was honored recently for their Future Authors Project by The School District of Palm Beach County, Florida, with a Bronze Business Partner Award in the large business category. In its ninth year, the private-public partnership with the school district helps students learn about the processes of writing, editing, and digitally publishing books.

Middle and high school students are nominated by their language arts teachers to participate in a free eight-day summer writing workshop, where they spend time with teachers, authors, and previous participants to practice creating written pieces in various genres. Their writings are then compiled, professionally published, and digitally printed in final book form by Canon Solutions America's Production Print Solutions division. Nearly 400 Palm Beach County students have participated in the program since its inception.

"What an honor it is to be counted among such major companies in South Florida as Publix and PGA National Resort and Spa to be recognized for our Future Authors program," said director of marketing, Production Print Solutions Eric Hawkinson, who is based in Canon Solutions America's Boca Raton offices.

"We've seen first hand how this program has helped to ignite a passion for writing in the young people who participate, and look forward to working with the District to help more students achieve their dreams of becoming published authors."

For more information about how to support the Future Authors Project, contact the Executive Director of the Education Foundation of Palm Beach County, Mary Kay Murray, at murraymk@palmbeach.k12.fl.us

Canon Solutions America's Future Authors Project Launches 2014 Session
More than 40 Palm Beach County Students Join Ninth Annual Workshop

MELVILLE, N.Y., July 8, 2014 – Canon Solutions America, Inc., a subsidiary of Canon U.S.A., Inc., announced today the launch of its ninth annual Future Authors Project, a private-public partnership with the School District of Palm Beach County, Florida. Nearly 400 students have benefited from this unique program, which was created to help students learn about the processes of writing, editing, and digitally publishing books.

More than 40 middle and high school students have been chosen from nearly 100 applicants to participate in a free eight-day summer writing workshop held at both Don Estridge Middle School in Boca Raton and Glades Central High School in Belle Glade, where students participate via distant learning technology. Throughout the workshop, students spend time with teachers, authors, and previous participants to practice creating pieces in various genres. Their writings are then compiled, professionally published, and digitally printed in final book form by Canon Solutions America.

Published authors and writers donate their time to share experiences and writing tips. The 2014 writers include poet Dwight Stewart; Jennifer Tormo, the editor of Gulfstream Media Group's seven magazines; Zelda Benjamin, a pediatric emergency room nurse and romance author; and Steve Alten, the author of 12 novels and advocate for teen reading.

According to director of marketing, Production Print Solutions division of Canon Solutions America, Eric Hawkinson, the Future Authors Project has been a source of great pride and inspiration for the company and the community. "We are honored to be able to offer students who have a passion for writing a fun and educational experience that culminates with the real-life opportunity to be published," he said.

He added that the printed book remains a popular medium, especially with digital printing technologies revolutionizing the book publishing business. "Publishers can now cost-effectively print books in run lengths anywhere from one to 10,000, creating exciting opportunities for anyone who dreams of becoming an author, especially our own future authors," said Hawkinson.

Director of Secondary Education for the School District of Palm Beach County Diana Fedderman, who manages this public-private partnership for the District, says that programs like this are essential for the enrichment of students who love to write. "Our teachers don't have as much time as they would like to work with the students on creative writing projects," she said. "This program, which is open to students of all backgrounds and academic levels, offers students the chance to hone their skills and explore their love of writing."

The Lawrence Sanders Foundation provides the funding to support the certified language arts teachers who lead the workshop. This year, the teachers are Nicole Adamo and Katrina Sapp Holder of Don Estridge Middle School, and Cartheda Mann of Glades Community Central High School.

An official book signing to unveil the 2014 book will be held in the autumn at the City of Boca Raton Spanish River Library. For more information about how to support the Canon Solutions America Future Authors Project, contact the Executive Director of the Education Foundation of Palm Beach County, Mary Kay Murray, at murraymk@palmbeach.k12.fl.us

Canon Solutions America
FutureAuthorsProject
A partnership with the School District of Palm Beach County

About Canon Solutions America, Inc.

Combining the strengths of the former Canon Business Solutions, Inc. and Océ North America, Inc., Canon Solutions America provides industry leading enterprise services, advanced production print technology and large format solutions supported by exceptional professional service offerings. Canon Solutions America helps companies of all sizes to improve their business by increasing efficiency, controlling costs and becoming more environmentally conscious. A wholly owned subsidiary of Canon U.S.A, Inc., Canon Solutions America is headquartered in Melville, NY and has more than 6,500 employees in over 150 offices across the country. For more information on Canon Solutions America, please visit www.csa.canon.com.

###

Canon is a registered trademark of Canon Inc. in the United States. All other referenced product names and marks are trademarks of their respective owners.

is made possible in part thanks to a grant from the

LAWRENCE SANDERS FOUNDATION

In his time, Lawrence Sanders was as popular as Stephen King and Danielle Steel. He didn't write his first novel until he was 50 in 1970. Yet, the very next year, Sanders received the prestigious Edgar Award from the Mystery Writers of America for The Anderson Tapes. The book became a hit movie, as did his 1973 book, The First Deadly Sin, with Frank Sinatra playing the lead character.

Lawrence Sanders was born in Brooklyn, NY in 1920 and earned a bachelor's degree from Wabash College in Indiana. Upon graduation, he worked at Macy's Department Stores before joining the U.S. Marine Corps. He was discharged in 1946 and went on to work as a journalist for more than 20 years. He wrote for such publications as Mechanics Illustrated and Science and Mechanics. Before his death in 1998, he had published more than 30 books, many of which were bestsellers.

Despite his celebrity status, Sanders lived a quiet life in Pompano Beach, Fla. Frugal in his lifestyle, yet shrewd in his investments, the author amassed a large estate that today provides hundreds of thousands of dollars each year to communities throughout Palm Beach and Martin Counties through the Lawrence Sanders Foundation. Managed by long-time friend and Boca Raton attorney, Daniel Brede, the Foundation has supported the Future Authors Project since 2008.

Sanders would have enjoyed knowing that his investments helped to provide the opportunity for young writers to pursue their own passions for becoming authors and to experience the thrill of having their works published.

Among the many other local organizations benefiting from Lawrence Sanders Foundation gifts are the Martin County Council for the Arts, the Community Foundation for Palm Beach and Martin Counties, Palm Beach Drama Works, Boys & Girls Clubs, Habitat for Humanity, ARC and the Salvation Army.

SCHOOL DISTRICT OF PALM BEACH COUNTY

The School District of Palm Beach County is the 11th largest in the nation with 185 schools serving over 181,000 students. Eleven thousand five hundred students graduated this year and earned nearly $110 million in scholarships. The majority are going on to some of the best colleges and universities in Florida, throughout the nation and abroad. Others are entering directly into the workforce armed with career academy "industry certifications." This is a tremendous accomplishment and comprehensive credit is given to our focused students, the diligence of our teachers, the leadership of our school-based administrators and the support of the community and staff. There are 21,449 employees which include 12,898 teachers. Over 41,000 community volunteers work with our students and schools through the Volunteers In Public Schools program and 1300 business partners support our students and schools through the Partners In Education program.

EDUCATION FOUNDATION OF PALM BEACH COUNTY

Now in its 30th year the Education Foundation of Palm Beach County continues to serve as the designated 501 c (3) support organization for the School District of Palm Beach County. Its mission is *"Advancing excellence in public education by increasing public awareness and sustaining community support for programs focused on Learning, Literacy and Leadership."*

In carrying out its role the Foundation currently provides programs and services directed at several areas of focus to include improving literacy, increasing graduation rates, supporting career academies in both middle and high schools, improving academic performance through arts integration and classroom grants, providing teacher training/recognition and advancing leadership skills. To learn more visit the website at **www.educationfoundationpbc.org**.

The Spanish River Library

The City of Boca Raton's Spanish River Library is a beautiful and convenient community space for learning, recreation, and special events. The library is located on Spanish River Blvd., halfway between Military Trail and the I-95 overpass, on the Blue Lake. The two-story, 40,900 square foot facility provides adult, teen, and children's areas as well as indoor and outdoor public space for meetings, gatherings, and events.

Inside the stunning Mizner inspired building, visitors will find outstanding youth services areas including a story time room, teen room, kids' computer room, and a spacious area for play and reading activities, as well as children's books, movies and other materials. A large meeting room is available for more popular youth programs. The building also features an adult computer lab, wireless network services, study rooms, a Café, Instructional Services, and a significant collection of popular books and audio-visual materials for patrons of all ages.

The first floor of the library is the focal point of the building, with restful lake views. The Lakeside Patio provides a 10,000 square foot open air plaza regularly used for special events including weddings. The second floor Rooftop Terrace, Catering Prep Kitchen, and the 4,500 square foot Mezzanine support a wide range of activities, parties, and cultural events.

The Boca Raton Public Library provides outstanding library services, resources, and programs that meet the educational, recreational, cultural, and informational needs of library users. For more information about the Boca Raton Public Library please visit http://www.bocalibrary.org/.

Spanish River Library
1501 NW Spanish River Blvd.
Boca Raton, FL 33431
(561) 393-7852

expand your horizons
@ Boca Raton Public Library

City of Boca Raton

201 WEST PALMETTO PARK ROAD • BOCA RATON, FLORIDA 33432-3795 • (561) 393-7708 • FAX (561) 367-7014
INTERNET: www.ci.boca-raton.fl.us

MAYOR
SUSAN HAYNIE

DEPUTY MAYOR
CONSTANCE J. SCOTT

COUNCIL MEMBERS

MICHAEL MULLAUGH
SCOTT SINGER
ROBERT S. WEINROTH

Dear Future Authors:

As the Mayor of the City of Boca Raton, I am thrilled to be congratulating another class of Future Authors. This is the seventh year the City has been a partner in this incredible program.

We are proud to be involved in a program that exemplifies the power of collaboration between the public sector and private companies and proves that we can bring enriching experiences to our students no matter what challenges we face.

Once again, we are pleased to be able to offer our beautiful Spanish River Library as the venue for the book signing and the backdrop for a life-changing experience for participants in the _Canon Solutions America Future Authors Project_.

I applaud all of you who took time out of your summer vacation to become stronger writers. I wish you the best of luck in the pursuit of your writing dreams and look forward to see many of your books on our shelves here at the Library.

Sincerely,

Susan Haynie

Mayor